Sarah

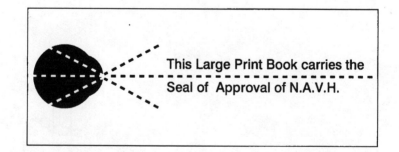

This Large Print Book carries the
Seal of Approval of N.A.V.H.

Sarah

Book One of the Canaan Trilogy

Marek Halter

Thorndike Press • Waterville, Maine

L.T.E.
H1972 sa

Published in 2004 by arrangement with Crown Publishers,
a division of Random House, Inc.

Thorndike Press® Large Print Basic.

The tree indicium is a trademark of Thorndike Press.

The text of this Large Print edition is unabridged.
Other aspects of the book may vary from the original edition.

Set in 16 pt. Plantin by Al Chase.

Printed in the United States on permanent paper.

Library of Congress Cataloging-in-Publication Data

Halter, Marek.
  [Sarah. English]
  Sarah : a novel / Marek Halter.
    p. (large print) cm. — (Book one of the Canaan trilogy)
  ISBN 0-7862-6624-4 (lg. print : hc : alk. paper)
    1. Sarah (Biblical matriarch) — Fiction. 2. Large type
books. I. Title.
PQ2668.A434S2713 2004
843′.914—dc22   2004047923

Sarah

As the Founder/CEO of NAVH, the only national health agency solely devoted to those who, although not totally blind, have an eye disease which could lead to serious visual impairment, I am pleased to recognize Thorndike Press★ as one of the leading publishers in the large print field.

Founded in 1954 in San Francisco to prepare large print textbooks for partially seeing children, NAVH became the pioneer and standard setting agency in the preparation of large type.

Today, those publishers who meet our standards carry the prestigious "Seal of Approval" indicating high quality large print. We are delighted that Thorndike Press is one of the publishers whose titles meet these standards. We are also pleased to recognize the significant contribution Thorndike Press is making in this important and growing field.

Lorraine H. Marchi, L.H.D.
Founder/CEO
NAVH

★ Thorndike Press encompasses the following imprints: Thorndike, Wheeler, Walker and Large Pr int Press.

Therefore a man leaves his father and his mother and cleaves to his wife, and they become one flesh.
— GENESIS, 2:24

If a man is a river, a woman is the bridge.
— ARAB PROVERB

Frailty, thy name is woman!
— WILLIAM SHAKESPEARE, *Hamlet*

Who is this that looks forth like the dawn,
fair as the moon,
bright as the sun,
terrible as an army with banners?
— SONG OF SOLOMON, 6:10

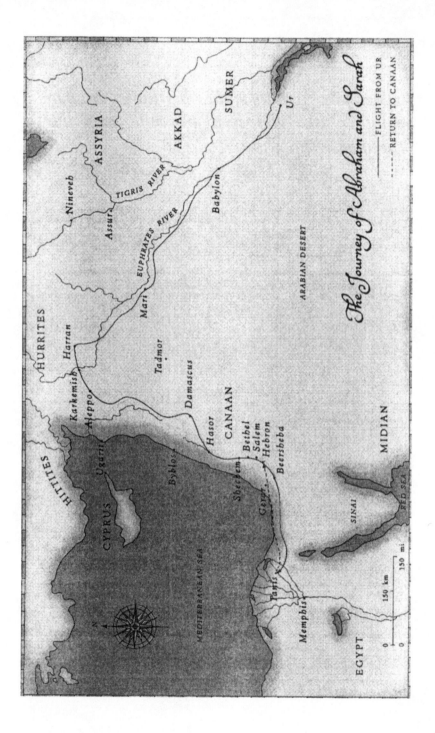

The Journey of Abraham and Sarah

——— FLIGHT FROM UR
- - - - RETURN TO CANAAN

Prologue

Twice during the night, my chest stopped filling with air. Twice, it was empty, and as dry as a leather goatskin. Although my mouth was wide open to the dawn wind, I could not drink it in. I lifted my shaking hands in the darkness. Pain ran through my bones, greedy as vermin.

And then it stopped. Twice, the air returned to my lips, flowing over my tongue as cool and sweet as milk.

It's a sign. I know how to recognize the signs. After so many years, so many trials and tribulations, Yhwh, the invisible god, is going to separate Sarah from Abraham. Tonight, tomorrow night, very soon. He will take my life.

That's the way things are. That's the way they must come to pass. There's no point protesting, no point being afraid. Yhwh will mark out my route away from this land that still bears my steps. An old woman's steps, so light the grass hardly bends beneath my weight.

That's the way things are, the way they're meant to be. The next time the air refuses to come into my mouth, I won't be so scared.

This morning, as dawn was spreading over the meadows and dusty cliffs around Hebron, I left the mothers' tent, but instead of going to wait outside Abraham's tent with bread and fruit, as I've done thousands of times since he became my husband, I came here, to the hill of Qiryat-Arba, and sat down on a stone at the mouth of the cave of Makhpela. It took me a while to climb the hill. But I don't care how hard it is. If Yhwh decides to take my breath from me in broad daylight, this is where I want my body to collapse, here, in this garden, in front of this cave.

This place fills me with peace and joy. A white cliff surrounds the mouth of the cave like a well-constructed wall. From beneath the shade of a huge poplar, a spring runs down into a vast semicircular garden. Its slope, like a palm open in greeting, descends toward the plain, marked with long low walls built by the shepherds, planted with thick trees, and fragrant with sage and rosemary.

From here, I can see our tents drawn close around Abraham's black-and-white tent. There are too many to count. Hundreds, I suppose. The sheep stretch as far as the eye can see, their wool brilliant white against the grass, which is greener than the water of a pool. It's the end of spring. The rains were mild and came at the right time. I can also see the smoke rising vertically from the fires, which is a sign that the east wind, heavy with sand and dryness, will spare us again today. Even from up here, I can hear horns, dogs barking as they gather the sheep, occasionally the cries of children. My hearing is no weaker than my sight. Sarah's body still holds out!

Youth knows nothing of time, old age knows nothing but time. When you're young, you play hide-and-seek with the shade. When you're old, you seek out the warmth of the sun. But the shade is always there, while the sun is fleeting. It rises, crosses the sky, and disappears, and we wait impatiently for its return. These days, I love time as much as I love Isaac, the son I waited so long to see.

For a long time, the cycle of seasons left no trace on me. One day followed another, and my body showed no sign of them. That lasted many years. My name wasn't yet Sarah, but Sarai. They said I was the most beautiful of women. My beauty was a beauty that inspired as much fear as desire. A beauty that seduced Abram as soon as he set eyes on me. A beauty that never faded, troubling and doomed, like a flower that would never bear fruit. Not a day went by that I didn't curse this beauty that wouldn't leave me.

Until Yhwh at last wiped out the terrible act that was the cause of everything. A sin I committed as an innocent child, for love for the man who was then called Abram. A sin, or a word I wasn't able to hear, for we knew so little then.

The sun is high now. Through the fine needles of the cedars and the dancing leaves of the great poplar, it warms my old body. I'm so thin now, I could wrap myself in my long hair, which has never turned white. Such a little body, but one that harbors so many memories! So many images, scents, caresses, faces, emotions, and words that I could populate the whole land of Canaan with them.

I love this place. Here, the memories gush from me like a waterfall cascading into a river. The cool air from inside the cave brushes my neck and my cheek with the tenderness of a familiar whisper. At moments it seems to me it's my own breath, the breath that Yhwh withheld from me last night.

In truth, this place is a nail in the pillar of time, like the pottery nails used to mark the presence of the souls in the splendid walls of my city, Ur.

Two nights ago I received another sign from Yhwh. I had a dream with my eyes wide open. I was still breathing peacefully, but my body was stiff and cold. In the darkness of the tent, without even the moonlight filtering through the canvas, I suddenly heard the banging of metal tools on stone and the voices of men at work. I wondered what kind of work they could be doing in the middle of the night, so close to the mothers' tent. I wanted to get up and look. But before I could lift myself up on my elbow, I saw. I saw with my eyes what only the spirit of dreams can make us see.

It was no longer night but day. The sun shone down on the white cliff and the mouth of the cave of Makhpela. That was where men had been working since the first light of dawn, building walls, thick, solid walls. A beautiful facade, complete with door and windows. A house of stone as splendid as any palace in Ur, Eridu, or Nippur. A dwelling I recognized immediately.

They were building our tomb.

The tomb of Abraham and his wife, Sarah.

I shall be the first to take my place in it. My beloved Abraham will lay my body there so that at last I can attain the peace of the other world.

My dream faded. The blows of hammer on stone ceased. I opened my eyes. The tent was dark, and Rachel and Lesha were sleeping beside me, breathing peacefully.

But the meaning of the dream remained with me. All of us to whom Abraham's invisible god revealed Himself, this now numerous people to whom He offered His covenant for all eternity, we know only cities of tents, cities of desert and wind and wandering. Yet I, Sarah, was born in a house with thirty rooms, in a city that contained a hundred similar houses, its most beautiful temple as high as the hill of Qiryat-Arba, its outer walls thicker than an ox.

In my whole life, following Abraham into the mountains where the Euphrates rises, walking beside him in search of the land of Canaan, or even as far as Egypt, I have never seen a city as splendid as the Ur I knew as a child. And I have never forgotten it.

Nor have I forgotten what I was taught there: that the strength of the people of Sumer and Akkad lies in the beauty of their cities, the solidity of their walls, the perfection of their irrigation systems, the magnificence of their gardens.

So, when day had broken, I went to see Abraham. While he ate, I told him what I had seen in my dream.

"It's time for our people to build walls, houses, and cities," I said. "Time for us to take root in this land. Remember how we loved the walls of Salem. How dazzled we were by Pharaoh's palaces. But in this camp, the camp of the great king Abraham, the man who hears the word of Yhwh and is heard by Him, the women still weave canvas for tents as they did when your father Terah's clan camped beneath the walls of Ur, in the space reserved for the *mar.Tu*, the men with no city."

Abraham listened, never taking his eyes off me. "I know you've always missed the walls of your city," he said, smiling, and his beard quivered.

He took my fingers in his, and for a long moment we remained still. Two old bodies linked by our hands and by the thousands of tender words we no longer need to speak.

At last, I said what I had been wanting to say since my dream had faded. "When I've stopped breathing, I want you to bury me in the cave of Makhpela, on the hill of Qiryat-Arba. The gardens around it are the most beautiful I've seen since the gardens of my father's palace. They belong to a Hittite named Ephron. Buy them from him; I know he won't refuse. Once you've buried me, bring masons from Salem or Beersheba. If they're as skillful as Pharaoh's masons, so much the better. Ask them to build walls at the mouth of the cave, the most beautiful, most solid walls they can build, for the tomb of Abraham and Sarah. It will be our people's first house, a place for them to gather, in all their great number, happy and confident. Isaac and Ishmael will be with them. The two of them together. Isn't it up to us, with the help of Yhwh, to ensure the future?"

Abraham had no need to promise me he would carry out my wishes. I know he will, for he always has.

Now, I can wait in peace for my breath to leave me. Wait and remember. There is no wind and yet, above me, the leaves of the poplar tremble, filling the air with a noise like rain. Under the cedars and acacias, the light dances in patches of molten gold. A fragrance of lily and mint comes to rest on my lips. Swallows play and sing above the cliff. Just like that day. The day the blood flowed for the first time between my thighs. The day the long life of Sarai, daughter of Ichbi Sum-Usur, daughter of Taram, began.

16

Part One

UR

The Bridal Blood

Sarai clumsily pushed aside the curtain that hung in the doorway and ran to the middle of the brick terrace that overlooked the women's courtyard. Dawn was breaking, and there was just enough light for her to see the blood on her hands. She closed her eyes to hold back the tears.

She did not need to look down to know that her tunic was stained. She could feel the fine woolen cloth sticking wetly to her thighs and knees.

Here it was again! A sharp pain, like a demon's claw moving between her hips! She stood frozen, her eyes half closed. The pain faded as suddenly as it had come.

Sarai held out her soiled hands in front of her. She should have implored Inanna, the almighty Lady of Heaven, but no word passed her lips. She was petrified. Fear, disgust, and denial mingled in her mind.

19

Only a moment ago, she had woken suddenly, her belly ringed with pain, and put her hands between her thighs. Into this blood that was flowing out of her for the first time. The bridal blood. The blood that creates life.

It had not come as she had been promised it would. It was not like dew or honey. It flowed as if from an invisible wound. In a moment of panic, she had seen herself being emptied of blood like an ewe under the sacrificial knife.

She had reacted like a silly child, and now she felt ashamed. But her terror had been so great that she had sat up moaning on her bed and rushed outside.

Now, in the growing light of day, she looked at her bloodstained hands as if they did not belong to her. Something strange was happening in her body, something that had obliterated her happy childhood at a stroke.

Tomorrow, and the day after tomorrow, and all the days and years to come, would be different. She knew what awaited her. What awaited every girl in whom the bridal blood flowed. Her handmaid Sililli and all the other women in the household would laugh. They would dance and sing and give thanks to Nintu, the Midwife of the World.

But Sarai felt no joy. At that moment, she

wished her body was someone else's.

She took a deep breath. The smell of the night fires floating in the cool air of early morning calmed her a little. The coolness of the bricks beneath her bare feet did her good. There was no noise in the house or the gardens. Not even the flight of a bird. The whole city seemed to be holding its breath, waiting for the sun to burst forth. For the moment it was still hidden on the other side of the world, but the ocher light that preceded it was spreading over the horizon like oil.

Abruptly Sarai turned and went back through the curtain into her bedchamber. In the dim light, it was just possible to make out the big bedstead where Nisaba and Lillu lay sleeping. Without moving, Sarai listened to her sisters' regular breathing. At least she had not woken them.

She advanced cautiously to her own bed. She wanted to sit down, but hesitated.

She thought of the advice Sililli had given her. Change your tunic, take off the sheet, roll the soiled straw in it, go to the door and take some balls of wool dipped in sweet oil, wash your thighs and genitals with them, then take some other balls, scented with essence of terebinth, and use them to absorb the blood. All she had to do was perform a few simple actions. But she couldn't. She didn't know why, but she couldn't bear even the thought of touching herself.

Anger was beginning to replace fear. What if Nisaba and Lillu discovered her and roused the whole household, crying out across the men's courtyard, "Sarai is bleeding, Sarai has the bridal blood!"

That would be the most disgusting thing of all.

Why did the blood running between her thighs make her more adult? Why, at the same time as she gained the freedom to speak, was she going to lose the freedom to act? For that was what was going to happen. Now, in exchange for a few silver shekels or a few measures of barley, her father could give her to a man. A stranger she might have to hate for the rest of her days. Why did things have to happen that way? Why not another way?

Sarai tried hard to dismiss this chaos of thoughts, this mixture of sadness and anger, but she couldn't. She couldn't even remember a single word of the prayers Sililli had taught her. It was as if a demon had banished them from her heart and mind. Lady Moon would be furious. She would send down a curse on her.

Anger and denial swept through her

again. She couldn't stay here in the dark. But she didn't want to wake Sililli. Once Sililli took charge, things would really start.

She had to flee. To flee beyond the wall that enclosed the city, perhaps as far as the bend in the Euphrates, where the labyrinth of the lower city and the reedy lagoons stretched over dozens of *ùs*. That was another world, a fascinating but hostile world, and Sarai wasn't brave enough to go there. Instead, she took refuge in the huge garden, which was full of a hundred kinds of trees and flowers and vegetables and surrounded by a wall that in places was higher than the highest rooms. She hid in a tamarisk grove clinging to the oldest part of the wall, where sun, wind, and rain had, in places, dissolved the stack of bricks and reduced it to a hard ocher dust. When the tamarisks were in bloom, their huge pink flowers spread like luxuriant hair over the wall and could be seen clear across the city. They had become the distinguishing feature of the house of Ichbi Sum-Usur, son of Ella Dum-tu, Lord of Ur, merchant and high-ranking official in the service of King Amar-Sin, who ruled the empire of Ur by the will of almighty Ea.

"Sarai! Sarai!!"
She recognized the voices: Lillu's piercing

shriek and Sililli's more muted and anxious tones. Some of the handmaids had already searched the garden, but finding nothing, had gone away again.

Silence returned, except for the murmur of the water flowing in the irrigation channels and the chirping of the birds.

From where she was, Sarai could see everything but could not be seen. Her father's house was one of the most beautiful in the royal city. It was shaped like a hand enclosing a huge rectangular central courtyard, which was reached through the main entrance. At either end, the courtyard was separated by two green-and-yellow brick buildings, open only for receptions and celebrations, and by two smaller courtyards, the women's and the men's. The men's quarters, with their white staircases, overhung the temple of the family's ancestors, the storehouses, and the room where her father's scribes worked, while the women's chambers were built above the kitchens, the handmaids' dormitories, and the chamber of blood. Both opened onto a broad terrace, shaded by bowers of vines and wisteria, with a view of the gardens. The terrace allowed the men to join the women at night without having to cross the courtyards.

From her grove, Sarai could also see a

large part of the city, and, towering over it like a mountain, the ziggurat, the Sublime Platform. Not a day went by that she did not come here to admire the gardens of the ziggurat. They were a lake of foliage between earth and sky, full of every flower and every tree the gods had sown on the earth. From this riot of greenery emerged the steps, covered in black-and-white ceramics, that led up to the Sublime Bedchamber, with its lapis lazuli columns and walls. There, once a year, the king of Ur was united with the Lady of Heaven.

Today, though, she had eyes only for what was happening in the house. Everything seemed to have calmed down. Sarai had the impression they had stopped searching for her. When the handmaids had appeared earlier in the garden, she had been tempted to join them. But now it was too late for her to leave her hiding place. With every hour that passed, she was more at fault. If anyone saw her in this state, they would scream with fright and turn away, shielding their eyes as if they had seen a woman possessed by demons. It was unthinkable that she could show herself like this to the women. It would be a blemish on her father's house. She had to stay here and wait until nightfall. Only then could she perform her ablutions in the garden's irrigation basin. After that, she would go and ask Sililli for forgiveness. With enough tears, and enough terror in her voice, to mollify her.

Until then she had to forget her thirst and the heat that was gradually transforming the still air into a strange miasma of dry dust.

She stiffened when she heard the shouts.

"Sarai! Answer me, Sarai! I know you're there! Do you want to die today, with the shame of the gods on you?"

She recognized the thick calves, the yellow-and-white tunic with its black border instantly.

"Sililli?"

"Who else were you expecting?" the handmaid retorted, in an angry whisper.

"How did you manage to find me?"

Sililli took a few steps back. "Stop your chattering," she said, lowering her voice even more, "and come out of there right now before anyone sees you."

"You mustn't look at me," Sarai warned.

She emerged from the copse, straightening up with difficulty, her muscles aching from her long immobility.

Sililli stifled a cry. "Forgive her, almighty Ea! Forgive her!"

Sarai did not dare look Sililli in the face. She stared down at her short, round shadow on the ground, and saw her raise her arms to heaven then hug them to her bosom.

"Almighty Lady of Heaven," Sililli muttered, in a choked voice, "forgive me for having seen her soiled face and hands! She is only a child, holy Inanna. Nintu will soon purify her."

Sarai restrained herself from rushing into the handmaid's arms. "I'm so sorry," she said, in a barely audible whisper. "I didn't do as you told me to. I couldn't."

She did not have time to say more. A linen sheet was flung over her, covering her from head to foot, and Sililli's hands clasped her waist. Now Sarai no longer needed to hold back, and she leaned against the firm, fleshy body of the woman who had not only been her nurse, but had also been like a mother to her.

"Yes, you silly little thing," Sililli whispered in her ear through the linen, the anger gone from her voice, the tremor of fear still there, "I've known about this hiding place for a long time. Since the first time you came here! Did you think you could escape your old Sililli? In the name of almighty Ea, what possessed you? Did you think you could hide from the sacred laws of Ur? To go where? To remain at fault your whole life? Oh, my little girl! Why didn't you come to see me? Do you think you're the first to be afraid of the bridal blood?"

Sarai wanted to say something to justify herself, but Sililli placed a hand on her mouth.

"No! You can tell me everything later. Nobody must see us here. Great Ea! Who knows what would happen if you were seen like this? Your aunts already know you've become a woman. They're waiting for you in the chamber of blood. Don't be afraid, they won't scold if you arrive before the sun goes down. I've brought you a pitcher of lemon water and terebinth bark so you can wash your hands and face. Now throw your soiled tunic under the tamarisk. I'll come back later to burn it. Wrap yourself in this linen veil. Make sure you avoid your sisters, or nobody will be able to stop those pests from going and telling your father everything."

Sarai felt Sililli's hand stroking her cheek through the cloth.

"Do what I ask of you. And hurry up about it. Your father must know nothing of your escapade."

"Sililli."

"What now?" Sililli said.

"Will you be there, too? In the chamber of blood, I mean."

"Of course. Where else should I be?"

Washed and scented, her linen veil knotted over her left shoulder, Sarai reached the women's courtyard without meeting a soul. She had gathered all her courage to approach the mysterious door she had never gone anywhere near.

From the outside, the chamber of blood was nothing but a long white wall with no windows that took up almost the entire space below the quarters reserved for the women: Ichbi's wife, sisters, daughters, female relatives, and handmaids. The door was cleverly concealed by a cane portico covered with a luxuriant ocher-flowered bignonia, so that it was possible to cross the women's courtyard in all directions without ever seeing it.

Sarai went through the portico. Before her was a small double door of thick cedarwood, the bottom half painted blue and the top half red: the door of the chamber of blood.

Sarai had only a few steps to take to open this door. But she did not move. Invisible threads were holding her back. Was it fear?

Like all girls her age, she had heard many stories about the chamber of blood. Like all girls her age, she knew that once a month women went and shut themselves in there for seven days. During full moons, they would gather there to make vows and petitions that could be said nowhere else. It was a place where women laughed, wept, ate honey and cakes and fruit, shared their dreams and secrets — and sometimes died in agony. Occasionally, through the thick walls, Sarai had heard the screams of a woman in labor. She had seen women go in there, happy with their big bellies, and not come out again. No men ever entered, or even tried to peer inside. Anyone curious or foolhardy enough to do so would carry the stain of their offense down with them to the hell of Ereshkigal.

But in truth, she knew very little of what went on there. She had heard the most absurd rumors, whispered by her sisters and cousins. *Unopened girls* did not know what happened to those who entered the chamber of blood for the first time, and none of the *munus,* the *opened women,* ever divulged the secret.

Her day had come. Who could go against the will of the gods? Sililli was right. It was time. She could not remain at fault any longer. She must have the courage to open that door.

★ ★ ★

Her eyes, dazzled by the bright daylight outside, took some time to accustom themselves to the darkness. A mixture of strong odors floated in the enclosed air. Some she recognized: the scent of almond and orange peel oils, the smell of sesame oil, which was used in lamps. After a moment, she noticed another smell — thicker, slightly nauseating — that she had never smelled before.

Shadows took shape within the shadows, figures moved. The chamber of blood was not completely dark. A dozen candles in brass disks diffused a yellow, flickering brightness. The chamber was both larger and higher than Sarai had imagined, with other, smaller rooms off to the sides. The brick floor was cooled by a narrow channel of clear water. At the far end, the gentle murmur of a fountain could be heard.

A handclap made Sarai jump. There before her were three of her aunts, and behind them, standing slightly to one side, Sililli and two young handmaids. They all wore white togas with broad black stripes, and their hair was held in place by dark-colored headscarfs. They were smiling affectionately.

Her aunt Egime, the eldest of her father's sisters, took a step forward. She clapped again, then folded her arms over her chest, keeping her palms open. Sililli handed her a pottery pitcher filled with scented water, and with a graceful gesture Egime plunged her hand in it and sprinkled Sarai.

Nintu, mistress of the menstrual blood,
Nintu, you who decide on life in the wombs of women,
Nintu, beloved patroness of childbearing, welcome Sarai, daughter of Taram and Ichbi, Lord of Ur, into this chamber. She is here to purify herself, and to entrust her first blood to you. She is here to become pure and clean again for the bed of childbirth!

After this prayer of welcome, the other women clapped three times, then took turns throwing the scented water over Sarai, until her face and shoulders were streaming. The scent was strong, so strong that it penetrated her nostrils and her throat, making her feel slightly intoxicated.

When the pitcher was empty, the women surrounded Sarai, took her hands, and pulled her into one of the alcoves, where a high, round, narrow basin stood. Sililli untied her linen veil, and she was pushed naked into the basin. It was deeper than she had supposed: The freezing water reached to just below her barely formed breasts. Sarai shivered, and hugged herself in a childish gesture. The women laughed. They emptied phials into the water, then rubbed her vigorously with little linen bags filled with herbs. The air was filled with new scents. This time, Sarai recognized mint and terebinth, as well as the curious smell of weasel bile, sometimes used for smearing the feet as a protection against demons.

The oil softened the water. Sarai became accustomed to its coolness. She closed her eyes and relaxed, and soon, the tension and the fear faded under all the rubbing and stroking.

No sooner was she used to it than Egime was already ordering her out of the bath. Without wiping her, or covering her with even a small cloth, Egime led Sarai to another part of the room, where a brightly colored carpet had been rolled out. She made her stand with her legs apart and placed a wide-necked bronze vase between her thighs. Sililli took Sarai's hand. Egime, her eyes fixed on the vase, started speaking in a loud voice.

Nintu, patroness of childbirth, you who received the sacred brick of childbearing from the hands of almighty Enki, you who hold the scissors to cut the birth cord,

Nintu, you who received the green lazulite vase, the silagarra, *from almighty Enki, gather the blood of Sarai.*

Make sure that it is fertile.

Nintu, gather the blood of Sarai like dew in a furrow. Make sure that it is making its honey. O, Nintu, sister of Enlil the First, make sure that Sarai's vulva is fertile and as soft as a Dilum date and that her future husband never tires of it!

A strange silence followed.

Sarai could feel her heart beating against her temples and in her throat. The skin on her legs, buttocks, shoulders, belly, and forehead was beginning to prickle with heat, as though it had been stung with nettles.

Then, in the same sharp, commanding voice, her old aunt repeated the prayer. This time, the other aunts recited it in unison with her.

Once finished, they started all over again.

Sarai realized that this would continue until her blood ran into the bronze vase.

The ceremony seemed to go on for ever. With each word that Egime uttered, Sililli's hand squeezed Sarai's fingers. All at once, a cold pain froze her back and thighs. She was ashamed of her own nakedness and the position she was in. Why was it taking so long? Why was the blood taking so much time to flow now, when only this morning it had been flowing so abundantly?

The prayer was repeated twenty times. Finally, the water was tinged with red. The women applauded. Egime seized Sarai's face between her rough fingers and planted her lips on her brow.

"Well done, child! Twenty prayers, that's a good number. Nintu likes you. You should be pleased and thank her." She took the bronze vase and placed it in Sarai's hands. "Follow me," she ordered.

At the far end of the chamber of blood, against a red-and-blue mud wall, stood a terra-cotta statue, taller than Sarai. It was a statue of a woman with a round face and thick lips, her curly hair held in place by a metal ring. In one of her hands she held a tiny vase, identical to the one that Sarai was carrying. With the other hand, she held high the scissors of birth. The altar below the statue was covered with food, as if laid for a feast.

"Nintu, Midwife of the World," Egime whispered, her head bowed, "Sarai, daughter of Taram and Ichbi, salutes you and thanks you."

Sarai looked at her, uncomprehending. With an irritated pout, Egime seized her right hand, dipped her fingers in the blood, and rubbed them over the belly of the statue.

"Now you do it," she ordered.

Pursing her lips in disgust, Sarai obeyed. Egime then took the bronze vase and poured a few drops of menstrual blood into the small dish held by the statue of Nintu. When she stood up again, her face was wreathed with a big smile, quite a change from her usual expression.

"Welcome to the chamber of blood, daughter of my brother. Welcome among us, future *munus!* If I've understood Sililli's muddled explanations correctly, it seems you haven't eaten since this morning. You must be hungry."

There was a great burst of laughter behind Sarai. It was Sililli. Sarai let herself be drawn into her arms, finding it surprisingly comforting to lay her head on her handmaid's ample bosom.

"You see," Sililli whispered, with a touch of reproach in her voice, "it wasn't so terrible. It wasn't worth making so much fuss over."

That evening, before her meal — cakes

36

and fruit and barley and honey biscuits and fresh ewes' cheese — she was given a new tunic, a fine linen tunic with black stripes, like the one worn by her aunts and the handmaids, and a shawl for her hair. Then the women taught her what to do when her periods came: how to make little wool tampons dipped in a special oil, the one whose strong, slightly disagreeable odor had greeted her when she first opened the door.

"It's olive oil," Egime explained. "A rare and precious oil produced by the *mar.Tu,* the men with no city. You can thank your father for that: He has it brought for the king's wives and sets a few amphoras aside for us. When there's none left, we use flatfish oil. Believe me, that's much less sweet and really stinks. After we've used that, we have to soak our buttocks in cypress oil for a whole day. Otherwise, when our men come to our beds, they might think our vulvae have turned into fishing baskets!"

The joke was greeted with gales of laughter. Finally, Sililli explained to her how to fold the linen that she had to wrap around the area between her thighs.

"You must change it every night before going to bed and wash it the next day. I'll show you the sink, at the other end of the chamber."

In fact, the chamber of blood contained everything women might need during their seven days of confinement: comfortable beds, plenty of food — fruit, meat, cheese, cakes — supplied by women from outside, and lots to do. There were baskets overflowing with spun wool, and weaving frames full of work in progress.

As Sililli was only there because of Sarai's initiation, she could not spend the night. Before she returned to the women's courtyard, she prepared an herb tea, which she gave to Sarai in a steaming goblet.

"That way you won't have a stomachache tonight," she said, kissing Sarai gently on the head. "Now, I'm not allowed back in here until twilight tomorrow. If anything's the matter, just ask Aunt Egime. I know she's a bit abrupt, but you can see how much she loves you."

She must have put something else in the drink besides herbs for the stomach, for not long after she had left, Sarai fell into a deep sleep untroubled by dreams.

When she woke, her aunts and the handmaids were already busy, weaving with just as much dexterity in the semidarkness as they would in broad daylight, chattering all the while like birds, and only breaking off to laugh or to swap good-natured jibes.

Egime ordered Sarai to thank Nintu and offer some food on her altar. Then Sarai washed herself in the basin, while a hand-maid poured oils into the water and smeared her belly and thighs with a scented pomade.

When she was clean, Egime asked if she was still bleeding regularly. After that, Sarai had a breakfast of ewes' milk, slightly cur-dled cow's cheese mixed with honey, and barley bread soaked in meat juice and spread with crushed dates, apricots, and peaches.

But just as she was about to help with the weaving, and to learn how to pass the spin-dles between the thinnest threads, her young aunts approached, bearing a tall sheet of bronze.

Sarai, surprised, looked at them uncomprehendingly.

"Take off your tunic, we're going to tell you what you look like."

"What I look like?"

"Exactly. You're going to look at yourself naked in the mirror and we'll tell you what your future husband will see when he puts the marriage ointment on you."

These words sent a chill through Sarai far greater than the morning's bath. She glanced at Egime. Without interrupting her work, her old aunt nodded and smiled, with a smile as imposing as a command.

Sarai gave a disdainful shrug, though she was far from feeling as calm as she pretended. She regretted the fact that Sililli wasn't here. If she had been, her young aunts would never have dared to mock her.

With an abrupt movement, she took off her tunic. While the women sat down around her, chuckling, she tried to appear as indifferent as she could.

"Turn around slowly," one of the aunts ordered, "so that we can see you properly."

Her moving figure was reflected in the bronze mirror, though she could hardly see herself in the dim light.

Egime was the first to comment on the spectacle. "The bridal blood may be flowing from her womb, but the fact is, she's still only a child. If her bridegroom wants to taste her honey cake as soon as he puts the ointment on her, he's going to be disappointed."

"I'm only twelve years and two seasons old," Sarai protested, feeling hot with anger. "Of course I'm a child."

"But her thighs are slim and well shaped," one of the handmaids said. "She's going to have beautiful legs, I'm sure of it."

"She'll always have small feet," another

said, "and small hands, too. That should be quite graceful."

"Is a husband interested in his wife's feet and hands the day he puts the ointment on her?" Egime muttered.

"But look at her buttocks, sister. He'll have his money's worth there. See how high and hard they are. Like golden little gourds. What husband could resist taking a bite of those? And the dimple at the top. I tell you, sisters, in a year or two, her husband will get plenty of milk to drink there."

"Her belly's quite nice, too," the youngest of the aunts said, "and her skin as delicate as you could wish. A real pleasure to pass your palm over it."

"Lift your arms, Sarai!" another ordered. "What a pity, sisters! Our niece's arms are less graceful than her legs."

"She has elbows like a goose, but they'll do. The shoulders are pretty. I'd say they're going to be broad. What do you think, Egime?"

"Big shoulders, big breasts, that's what they say. I've seen that dozens of times."

They all burst out laughing.

"For now, though, the bridegroom won't have anything to get his teeth into!"

"But they're coming out, they're taking shape."

"Hardly! You can see her bones more clearly than her breasts."

"Yours weren't much bigger at her age," Egime said to her younger sister, "and look at them now: We have to weave you double-length tunics to cover them!"

They laughed again, not even noticing that tears were running down Sarai's cheeks into her mouth, she wiped them away with her wrist.

"What the groom definitely won't see, the day of the ointment, is the sweet forest. Not even a shadow! He'll have to be content with the furrow and, in my opinion, wait for the field to grow before he can plow it!"

"Enough!" cried Sarai, kicking over the bronze mirror and covering herself with her tunic.

"Sarai!" Egime roared.

"I won't listen to any more of your wicked comments! I don't need anyone to tell me I'm beautiful, and I'll be even more beautiful when I've grown up. I'll be more beautiful than all of you. You're all jealous, that's what you are!"

"Proud and snake-tongued, that's what *you* are!" Egime replied. "If your bridegroom doesn't pull a long face when he sees you, he will when he hears you. I hope my brother Ichbi has made careful plans. I wouldn't like him to get a rejection."

"My father hasn't decided to get me married. Why do you keep saying that? I have no bridegroom. You're all old and you're saying stupid things!"

She had almost screamed the last words. They echoed off the damp walls of the chamber of blood and subsided to the brick floor. The laughter ceased, and there was an embarrassed silence.

"How do you know you have no bridegroom?" Egime asked, with an even deeper frown.

A shiver ran through Sarai. The fear that had knotted her stomach the day before had returned.

"My father has told me nothing," she breathed. "He always tells me what he wants me to do."

Her aunts and the handmaids averted their eyes.

"Your father has no need to tell you about things that happen as they should," Egime retorted.

"Yes, my father tells me everything. I'm his favorite daughter —"

Sarai broke off. She had only to speak the words to realize what a lie they were.

Egime let out a brief sigh. "Childish nonsense! Don't invent something that isn't real! The laws of the city and the will of almighty Ea must be respected. You'll stay with us for four days, and on the seventh you'll leave the chamber of blood and be prepared for your wedding. The month of plowing is a good month for it. There will be meals and chanting. The man who is to be your husband must already be on his way to Ur. I'm sure your father has chosen someone rich and powerful. You'll have no cause for complaint. By the next moon, he will have put the ointment of cypress on you. That is what will happen. That is how it must be."

Abram

After seven long days and seven nights full of dreams she did not dare tell anyone about, Sarai left the chamber of blood. It was a moment she dreaded as much as she had wished for it.

The daylight was so bright that she could hardly open her eyes. She heard, more than she saw, Sililli greet her with chuckles of contentment and kiss her, while Egime gave her a few last pieces of advice.

Before Sarai could even say a word, Sililli pulled her over to the staircase leading to the women's quarters, whose white walls were even more dazzling than the walls of the courtyard. Sarai let herself be led like a blind girl. There seemed to be more steps going up than she remembered. She did not open her eyes until they reached the upper terrace, where Sililli opened a cedarwood door, its wood so new it still smelled of resin.

"Go in!"

Shielding her eyes, Sarai hesitated. There seemed to be nothing beyond the door but a gaping shadow.

"Come on now, go in!" Sililli repeated.

The room was spacious, its length greater than its breadth. There was a square window, through which the morning sun entered, and a window seat covered with a mat. The floor was of oiled red bricks and the high ceiling was made of thin reeds carefully attached to squared-off beams. Everything was new. There were two beds, one large and one small, as well as a huge painted chest reinforced with silver studs. Against one wall was a weaving frame, also new. The vases, bowls, and goblets on a rack in a corner of the room had never been used, nor had any flame ever licked the terra-cotta fireplace.

"Isn't it magnificent? It was your father who wanted things to be like this."

Sililli was flushed with excitement. In a flood of words, she told Sarai how Ichbi Sum-Usur had urged on the carpenters and masons so that all these wonders should be ready for the day when his daughter left the chamber of blood.

"He took care of everything! He even decided how high the walls should be. He said: 'She's the first of my daughters to be married, and nothing can be too beautiful for her. I want her bridal chamber to be the highest and most beautiful in the women's courtyard!' "

Sarai felt a strange tightening in her chest. She wanted to share Sililli's joy, but she was finding it hard to breathe. She could not take her eyes off the big bed. Sililli was right; it was the most beautiful she had ever seen. The plane-wood bedstead stood on broad feet that bore delicately carved figures of the zodiac. On the wide dark board, its end covered with immaculately white sheepskins, a red silhouette of Nintu had been painted.

"All the months of the four seasons are here," Sililli said, running her index finger over the drawing of the Goat-Fish, the constellation of *Mul.suhur*. "So that all of them can bring you luck." She pointed to the small bed in another corner of the room. "And that's for me. It's new, too. Of course, I'll only sleep here on the nights when you're alone."

Sarai avoided her gaze. But Sililli hadn't finished yet. She went to the big chest and lifted the thick wooden lid with its silver hinges, revealing a heap of fabrics and shawls.

"A full chest, that was another thing your father wanted! Look how beautifully these are woven! Linen *rakutus* as smooth as a baby's skin. And this . . ."

She opened a leather bag and emptied its contents on the sheepskins: a collection of wooden and silver clasps, bracelets, and brooches. Then she took one of the lengths of material from the chest and in a few deft movements draped Sarai in a perfectly folded toga, leaving her left shoulder bare, as was the custom.

Sililli took a step backward to admire her work, but Sarai did not give her time. She removed the toga and dropped it on the bed.

"Do you know who he is?" she asked, in a voice that shook more than she would have liked.

"Sarai . . . What are you talking about?"

"Him. The man my father has chosen to be my husband. The man who'll sleep with me in this big bed."

Sililli frowned and gave a deep sigh that shook her bosom. Mechanically, she picked up the fabric Sarai had dropped and carefully folded it.

"How should I know? Your father doesn't confide things like that to a handmaid."

"But is he already here?" Sarai asked, annoyed. "You must at least know that."

"It isn't customary for the bridegroom and his father to come to the bride's house before she has taken part in the first meal for the guests. Didn't Egime teach you anything in those seven days?"

"Oh, yes! She taught me how to sing, how to wash my linen, how to weave fine but solid-colored threads. She taught me what a wife must do to make sure her husband is never hungry. How he must be fed morning and night. What to say to him and what not to say to him. She taught me how to add color to my feet, how to wear a shawl, how to put pomade between my buttocks! My head is still spinning with all the things she taught me!" As Sarai's voice rose, tears sprung into her eyes, tears she could not hide. "But she didn't tell me who my husband would be."

"Because she doesn't know."

Sarai looked into Sililli's eyes, hoping to catch her out in a lie, but all she saw in those eyes was a sad, slightly weary tenderness.

"She doesn't know, Sarai," repeated Sililli. "This is how it is, my child. A daughter belongs to her father, her father gives her to her husband. This is how things are!"

"That's what you all say. But I'm going to ask my father."

"Sarai! Sarai! Open your eyes! To-morrow, the whole house will be cele-brating. Your father will give the first banquet and show off your beauty to his guests. Your bridegroom will come to offer his nuptial platter and his silver ingots, and then you'll know who he is. The day after tomorrow, he'll put the bridal scent on you and you'll be his. There! That's what's going to happen. Nothing can change that, for that is how the daughters of the lords of Ur are married. And you are Sarai, the daughter of Ichbi Sum-Usur. In two nights, your husband will come to sleep in this beautiful chamber, in this beautiful bed. For your greater happiness. I'm sure your father hasn't made a bad choice . . ."

Her hands over her ears so she couldn't hear any more, Sarai rushed to the door, only to be brought up short by Kiddin, her elder brother, standing on the threshold.

He was fifteen, but seemed two years older. Although his beard was still only a light down, he was as handsome as a young lord of Ur, eldest son of a great house, ought to be, with regular features and strong mus-cles, like a warrior's. Kiddin loved fighting, and practiced every day. He was always well groomed, always very aware of the way he looked, the way his voice sounded. Sarai

50

had long since noticed how careful he was to ensure that the cloth of his toga, against his bare right shoulder, emphasized the smoothness of his skin and made women want to stroke it. In the household, his chief concern was to make sure that everyone respected his rank as the firstborn. Even Sililli, although she seemed to fear nobody but Ichbi Sum-Usur, took care never to offend him.

"Good morning, sister," Kiddin said, in a cold voice. "Our father wants you to join him. He is about to sacrifice some sheep to learn your future as a wife. The *barù* is already in the temple, drinking and scenting himself."

Sarai opened her mouth to ask the question that was nagging at her, but nothing came out except "Good day, brother."

"Get ready," Kiddin said, with a gleam in his eyes, and a mocking smile that gave a glimpse of the young boy that he really was. "I'll be back for you in a little while."

He turned his back and left the room, like a great lord who liked to let his words hang in the air.

The little room where Sarai's father was working was quite cluttered. Two of the walls were completely covered with shelves piled high with clay tablets. Letters, contracts, and accounts by the hundreds. All the important things that made Ichbi Sum-Usur a feared and respected man.

On a long ebony table, a servant was pressing a ball of clay into a wooden mold with the help of a pestle. Beside him were small boxes of fresh clay covered with damp linen, bronze knives, pots filled with large and small styli: everything required for writing. Sitting at the other end, a scribe was meticulously sculpting words in the paste.

Sarai heard her father dictating: ". . . the bridegroom will be able to come into my house and stay there like a welcome son . . ."

She let the curtain over the door fall behind her.

"My daughter!" her father cried, and beneath his long, black, perfectly waved beard, his double chin swelled with pleasure. With a gesture, he dismissed his servants. The scribe and his assistant quickly covered their unfinished work with a cloth and withdrew, bowing several times to Sarai.

Ichbi Sum-Usur opened his arms wide. "My daughter," he repeated, as if the words were like honey in his mouth. "The first to marry!"

"I'm so happy to see you, Father."

And it was true. She was always happy to see him. He was not much taller than she was, and his corpulence bore witness to his lack of exercise as well as the extravagant meals he was constantly organizing. But she loved his imposing bearing, the distinction only power could bestow and only the noblest citizens of Ur possessed. His eyes, underlined thickly with kohl, had the self-confidence of those who knew themselves to be above the common herd. And today he was draped in a magnificent tunic, with colorful embroidered hems and little silver tassels, the finery of a high-ranking official. Sarai's dress, although of very fine material, seemed quite plain in comparison.

She was proud of her father, proud to be his daughter, and although Kiddin, her elder brother, was of course Ichbi Sum-Usur's firstborn, she had no doubt she was the first in his heart. And she loved nothing better than to make sure of it.

She bowed respectfully, perhaps a little excessively, but it brought a satisfied grunt from her father. He approached, put a finger under her chin, and lifted her head.

"You're looking beautiful, my child. Egime tells me you were a good girl in the chamber of blood. I'm pleased with you. I

53

hope you're pleased with me."

Inhaling the scent of myrrh, with which he had liberally sprinkled himself, Sarai merely batted her eyelids in reply.

"Is that all? I build you the most beautiful bedchamber in the house and that's all the thanks I get?"

"I'm very pleased with the bedchamber, Father. The bed in particular is very beautiful. Everything is very beautiful. The chest and the dresses. Everything. And you are still my beloved father."

"But?" Ichbi Sum-Usur sighed: He could read her as well as if she were a tablet from the royal scribes.

"But, my beloved father, I know nothing of the husband who will join me there. Depending on who he is, I may find my bed less beautiful and my bedchamber worse than a hovel in the lower city."

Ichbi Sum-Usur raised an eyebrow in surprise. "Sarai!" he said, with a sigh that was half a laugh. "Sarai, my daughter! Will you never change?"

"My father, all I want to know is who you've chosen as my husband and why. Don't I have the right to know that?"

Sarai's voice was neither tearful nor submissive. On the contrary, Ichbi Sum-Usur could sense a familiar resonance in it: the resonance his own voice had when he expected his orders to be obeyed without question.

He looked at her through narrowed eyes, letting the silence hover in the air, as he did when he wished to impress his subordinates. Outside, in the courtyard, there were voices, shouts of greeting. The guests were starting to arrive. Sarai put her small hand on her father's broad wrist. He rose to his full height, with all the solemnity he could muster.

"A father chooses the man who will take his daughter for a wife for reasons that suit him. The man I have chosen for you suits me. If he suits me, he will suit you."

"I only want to see his face."

"You'll have all your married life to see it."

"What if I don't like it?"

"A marriage is not a whim. A husband isn't chosen because he has a nice nose."

"I'm not talking about his nose. Wasn't it you who taught me to recognize a man's destiny by observing his face and his walk?"

"In that case, trust me. I've made the right choice."

"Father, please!"

"That's enough!" Ichbi Sum-Usur said,

finally losing patience. "What do you think? That I'll go with you to his house so that you can size him up? Almighty Ea, protect me! Perhaps I should also send messengers all over the city to announce that Ichbi Sum-Usur has changed his mind about the marriage of his daughter the goddess because the husband he chose isn't to her taste! Sarai, Sarai! Please don't offend the gods with any more of this nonsense."

He turned, angrily seized the tablet of fresh clay on which the scribe had been writing earlier, and brandished it in front of Sarai's face.

"This tablet is your contract as a wife. There are still seven days, seven days before another one exactly the same comes back to me, carrying the imprint of your bridegroom and his father. Seven days of banquets, chanting, and prayers that are going to cost me two thousand minas of barley! Seven days during which my favorite daughter has but one right and one duty: to be beautiful and to smile."

His voice had risen, the last words spoken with such anger that they must have been heard from the courtyard. He threw the tablet on the table and carefully readjusted his tunic, which had slipped from his shoulder.

"The soothsayer is waiting for us. Let's hope he doesn't discover some disaster in the entrails."

The soothsayer was an old man, so thin that there seemed to be almost nothing of his body beneath his toga. His hair and beard, perfectly combed and oiled, covered his shoulders and chest. All that could be seen of his face was his black pupils, as luminous as polished stones.

Sarai was standing between her father and Kiddin. She could feel their warmth against her shoulders and hear their breathing. From time to time, Kiddin glanced at her, but she averted her eyes. He made no secret of the fact that he had heard their father's outburst. When he had joined them on their way to the temple, his smile had spoken volumes. In any case, there was no need for him to speak his thoughts out loud. Sarai could guess them as well as if he had whispered them in her ear: "This time, sister, our father has held out. He isn't giving in to your whims! It was about time! Do you still think you're his favorite?"

All that remained was to hope that the gods would be good to her, and that her father hadn't chosen for her a husband as arrogant and boastful as Kiddin! She wouldn't be able to stand someone like that for a single day!

Sarai banished these thoughts. She mustn't think bad things while the *barù* was beginning the ceremony. On the contrary, she must open her heart to the soothsayer and the Lords of Heaven. Let them see how much good she had inside her. Let them make sure that her husband was a man capable of cultivating all that was best in her.

She straightened her back, relaxed her fingers, and slowly lifted her face, as if to be seen better. She fought against the acrid smell coming from the cedarwood shavings that the soothsayer was throwing on the embers of a little hearth. It was hard to see anything because all the openings in the temple had been sealed. Only two torches of beeswax illuminated the bench seat that supported the statues and the altars of the family's ancestors. The soothsayer had placed three sheep livers at the feet of Ichbi Sum-Usur's ancestors. Turning his back, he mumbled words that nobody understood. But the congregation was doing its best not to disturb his concentration.

A few paces behind the front row occupied by Sarai, her father, and her brother were half a dozen close relatives and two or three guests. When Sarai had entered the temple, she had avoided their smiles and encouragements, still furious at failing to make her father yield. Now, like her, they were trying hard to breathe and not to cough, despite the smoke that stung their eyes and irritated their throats.

Suddenly, the *barù* put the three livers together on a thick wicker tray. He turned and walked straight toward Sarai and her father. Sarai could not help but stare at the entrails, still dripping with hot blood.

"Ichbi Sum-Usur, faithful servant," the soothsayer said, his voice echoing loud and clear through the temple, "you whose name means 'Son who saves his honor,' Ichbi Sum-Usur, I have placed a liver before your father, I have placed a liver before your father's father. I have placed a liver before your great-grandfather. I have asked all three to be present for the oracle. What they know, you will know, Ichbi Sum-Usur."

The soothsayer's emaciated face was so close to Sarai that she could smell his milky, slightly sour breath, which made her recoil. Kiddin's pitiless hand forced her to resume her place. In deep silence, the *barù* examined every part of her face, his lips curling with concentration, like a wild beast's. Sarai stared in fascination at his gums, which were too white, his teeth, which were too yellow, and the many gaps between them. She did her best not to show her disgust and apprehension. Around her, was dead silence. No shuffling of feet, no clicking of tongues. Only the crackling of the shavings on the embers.

Without warning, the *barù* pushed the tray containing the entrails against Sarai's chest. She seized the edges. It was much heavier than she had imagined. She avoided looking down at the dark flesh.

The *barù* moved away from her, and took several steps back. Without taking his eyes off her, he stopped next to the brick hearth. Beside it, he had placed the statuette of his own god on a stone table. His beard began to shake, although his mouth was not moving. Slowly, slowly, he lifted his eyes to the dark ceiling. Then he turned toward his god. He opened his arms, and leaned forward.

"O Asalluli, son of Ea, almighty Lord of Divination," he thundered, making them all shudder, "I have purified myself in the odor of the cypress. O Asalluli, for Ichbi Sum-Usur your servant, for Sarai your handmaid, accept this *ikribu*. Reveal your presence, O Asalluli, listen to Ichbi Sum-Usur's anxiety as he gives his daughter as a wife. Listen to his question and deliver a favorable oracle. From this month *kislimù*, in the third year of the reign of Amar-Sin, until the hour of her death, will Sarai be a good, fertile, and faithful wife?"

Silence again fell over the temple like thick smoke.

Nothing happened. Nobody moved. Sarai felt the muscles of her shoulders grow hard, then fill with tiny needles. The back of her neck was becoming as painful as if the point of an arrow had been planted there. The discomfort spread to the small of her back, her thighs, her arms! Her whole body was stiff from the weight of the tray with the livers, and so inflamed that she thought she would cry out in pain.

The soothsayer again approached her and placed his hands on hers. Icy hands, the flesh barely covering the bones. Abruptly, he took the tray from her. She took a deep breath, and the pain flowed out of her limbs like receding water. Behind her, there were sighs of relief. But neither her father nor Kiddin batted an eyelid.

The *barù* placed the livers on three terracotta cylinders surrounding the statuette of his god. From a large leather bag he took a number of written tablets and a sheep liver made out of glazed pottery. He went quickly and removed the curtain that obscured the opening nearest the table. The curling blue smoke, as thick as seaweed, danced in the daylight that flooded the room.

The soothsayer was on his way back to the table when a strange noise made him stop in his tracks. A kind of hissing sound, almost like a whistle. Everyone stiffened, eyes wide with anxiety. The soothsayer looked intently at the livers. A bubble was forming on the left-hand one. Slowly, blood flowed over the lobe. Again the hissing sound was heard. A murmur of fear ran through the assembly. Sarai felt her father trembling against her arm.

The soothsayer took a cautious step forward. The liver slid off the cylinder that was supporting it. Folding like a wet rag, it fell to the floor. A cry of terror filled the temple, followed by a frozen silence.

Sarai did not dare look at her father. Her throat and the small of her back were tight with fear. Without saying a word or looking at the assembly, the soothsayer went to the table, bent his aged body, seized the liver that had fallen to the floor, and placed it in an empty basket next to the cedarwood shavings. Then, without any explanation, he bent over the remaining entrails and listened.

A sigh of relief went through the audience

and everyone prepared for a long wait.

Sarai knew she would need both courage and patience. The process could take a long time: several hours by the water clock. A soothsayer might begin his analysis of the oracle at noon and not finish until twilight. Each part of the liver had to be examined carefully. The *barù* would touch them, rub them, slice them. He would count the cysts, the fissures, the pustules, then check their location and significance against the terracotta liver and what was written on his tablets. He might also write down his observations on fresh tablets.

This time, however, it did not take long. An hour at the most. The soothsayer lifted his frail body, washed his bloody hands, and carefully wiped them. Ichbi Sum-Usur stiffened. Sarai heard him breathing more heavily. Her own heart was beating faster. Anxiety once again gripped the small of her back.

Without so much as a glance at her, the *barù* came back and planted himself before her father.

"The examination is over, Ichbi Sum-Usur. As you've seen, your great-grandfather refuses his oracle. This is what I found in the others. Two livers: an elevation on the left of the spleen. One liver: a perforation.

63

One liver: a cross on the finger. One liver: two fissures at the base of the throne. One liver without any fissure. Tomorrow I will let you have the tablets confirming all this. The oracle is favorable to your daughter. A good and even willing wife. A faithful wife, even though it is not in her character. As for her fertility: two children. Possibly boys."

Sarai's father laughed, and at the same time she heard her relatives' exclamations behind her. But before she could be sure whether the oracle was good or bad for her, her father raised his hand.

"*Barù*, why does my father's grandfather refuse his oracle?"

"Your great-grandfather refuses to answer your question, Ichbi Sum-Usur," the *barù* said, with a glance at Sarai.

"Why?" Ichbi Sum-Usur asked again, raising his voice. "Have I made the wrong choice?"

The soothsayer shook his head. "The question was: Will Sarai be a good, fertile, and faithful wife? This is not about your choice, but about your daughter, Ichbi Sum-Usur. Your ancestor says: I want nothing to do with this wedding."

A heavy silence ensued. Sarai's heart was pounding. Beside her, Kiddin was clenching his fists nervously.

"Must I refuse my daughter to the man who wants her for his wife?" her father asked. "I don't understand."

"No. Two livers and two ancestors are sufficient. The oracle is still valid. However, as you are a good client, I shall tell you this for free, and I shan't write it down on the tablet. Your great-grandfather says this. Your daughter pleases Ishtar. She can be a wife without a husband. She is the kind of woman who provokes violent acts. That can be disastrous as well as glorious. The gods will decide her fate: queen or slave. However, for the sake of your family as well as that of the man who is taking her as a wife: Let her get children without delay."

"Queen or slave!" Sarai said.

"But also fertile and faithful, that's the most important thing," Sililli said approvingly, seemingly unconcerned by what she had heard. "Your father must be relieved! I'm certainly relieved. And you see, I told you the truth. He couldn't possibly change his mind."

Sarai refrained from answering. They were in her new bedchamber, and Sililli was carefully washing her hair, anointing it with an oily scent, and gathering it into dozens of braids.

"Tomorrow," Sililli went on, "you will be a queen. That, too, I know. As well as any *barù*."

Her long ram's horn comb in her hand, she bent down to judge the straightness of the part she had just traced in Sarai's hair.

"Do you think the *barùs* always tell the truth?" Sarai asked, after a moment's silence.

Sililli took her time before replying. "They sometimes make mistakes. Sometimes, too, the gods change their minds. But when a soothsayer is sure he's right, he writes it down on a tablet. What he doesn't write down should only be listened to with one ear. I, too, can tell your future by looking right in your eyes. Especially as I know them by heart. Queen of a good husband, with beautiful children. I see nothing but good."

She laughed without waiting for Sarai to laugh. Her fingers worked with astonishing agility, forming one braid after another, while Sarai looked through the little window, watching night fall and thinking: I shall be here every evening, preparing food for my husband. Sleeping in the bed so that he can become a father. In just a few days. For years and years. Until I'm older than Sililli.

How was it possible?

66

However hard she tried, she could not form any image of these moments in her mind. It wasn't only that she had no idea what her bridegroom looked like. She couldn't see herself — skinny and flat-chested, as her aunts had commented — lying in this bed beside a man's big body. And not only beside him.

"Sililli, do you think he'll do that?" she asked. "Try straightaway to make me have children?"

Sililli grunted and stroked her cheek.

Sarai pushed her hand away. "It isn't possible, is it? Look at me: I'm only a child! How could I have children?"

Sililli broke off from her work, her cheeks as red as if she were standing in front of a fire. "Don't worry so much. He won't do it straightaway. He's probably only a big awkward lump. You'll have plenty of time."

Sarai knew the intonations of Sililli's voice well enough to know that her words lacked conviction. "You're lying," she said, though without spite.

"I'm not lying!" Sililli protested. "It's just that you never know exactly how things are going to turn out. But a man would be mad to sow his seed in a girl as young as you."

"Unless a soothsayer advises him to hurry up and make children."

To that, there could be no reply. They said nothing more while Sililli finished with her hair.

The next day, as soon as there was sufficient light, the house filled with noise as the servants completed the preparations for the first of the seven banquets A bamboo dais had been erected in the big central courtyard, where the bride and bridegroom and their closest relatives would sit, looking down on the rest of the guests spread around the courtyard: women to the left, men to the right. Mats, carpets, cushions, and little wicker seats were put out for them, and low tables were set up, bearing arrangements of flower petals and branches of myrtle and bay, as well as goblets of water scented with orange and lemon. Cane canopies were stretched between the terraces so that the area where the banquet was to take place would remain cool even during the hottest part of the day.

The statues of the ancestors were carried from the temple and placed in an arcade leading to the men's courtyard. There the altars were carefully reconstructed, and made fragrant with food and scents. Ichbi Sum-Usur himself supervised the arrangement of the rare potted plants from Magan and Meluhha, and the placing, here and there in the courtyard, of kittens on leashes, doves in cages, and snakes in baskets to entertain and impress the guests.

Finally, dishes by the dozen were brought out, plates of cakes, baskets full of loaves of barley or wheat bread. Jars of wine and beer were opened.

When the sun was at its highest, Kiddin came to fetch Sarai. Sililli cried out when she saw him. His oiled and curled hair was held in place by a finely woven ribbon. A line of kohl emphasized the whiteness of his eyes. The ceremonial toga he wore, although it lacked the silver tassels, was at least as magnificent as his father's. He was as resplendent as a god, so much so that he could have been taken for the bridegroom.

He seized Sarai's hand and they crossed the women's courtyard. She heard the excited chuckles of the handmaids, who had stopped their work to wonder at the beauty of their young master.

Kiddin did not let go of his sister's hand until they reached the dais. She climbed it and sat down on a little sculpted seat, surrounded by her aunts.

Old Egime gave her a thorough inspection. But Sililli had done her work to perfection, and Egime could find no fault with it.

Sarai's hair was so perfect, it could pass for a diadem held in place by silver clasps. Every fold of her tunic was as it should be. The woolen belt woven for the occasion emphasized the tininess of her waist. For this first banquet, the Presentation, she wore no makeup except for a fine layer of kaolin, which gave her face the pallor of a full moon. The lack of adornment, the delicacy of her features, and the slightness of her figure all made her look more strange than beautiful.

Sarai sat stiffly on her little seat, looking straight ahead of her, waiting for the sun to reach its zenith and the first guests to come through the double door of the palace.

There were more than a hundred of them. The whole of Ichbi Sum-Usur's large family had been invited. Some came from Eridu, from Larsa, and even Uruk. Ichbi Sum-Usur had obtained safe-conducts from King Shu-Sin so that they could travel to Ur. This favor was the finest gift the sovereign could give his faithful servant. Sarai's father was blushing with pride.

The guests advanced along the aisle between the tables, the seats, and the cushions, and crossed the courtyard to the dais. There, they each greeted Ichbi Sum-Usur and his eldest with many fine words and

70

much laughter before plunging their hands into a bronze basin. The water in it was scented with a mixture of benzoin, amber, and myrtle. The guests sprinkled their faces and their bare shoulders and armpits, left or right depending on whether they were men or women. Next, a slave handed each of them a white cloth with yellow stripes with which they wiped themselves before draping it over their tunic.

Finally, the men separated from the women and took their places at table, their distance from the dais depending on their rank. None looked at Sarai, or paid her the least attention. The women, though, all passed before her. They did not so much salute her as look her up and down, reserving their lengthy comments on her appearance for later. The ceremony lasted two long hours. When they were all seated, Ichbi Sum-Usur and Kiddin went to the altar of the ancestors to make libations and prayers. Then Sarai's father returned to his guests and, opening his arms, welcomed everyone in a loud voice and declared that the gods in the heaven of Ur wanted them to quench their thirst and take their pleasure in honor of the thirst and the pleasure that his daughter Sarai would soon know, as a true *munus*.

★ ★ ★

A chorus of a dozen young women sang tirelessly at the foot of the dais, dancers twirled between the guests and the tables, musicians beat drums and blew into flutes. All of them seemed impervious to the heat, although the canopies that protected the guests from the burning sun also trapped the air inside the courtyard. There was not a breath of wind to displace the powerful odors of scents and food. Sarai found it impossible to eat, and she had already drunk as much as she could. The kaolin on her cheeks and forehead grew heavier as it absorbed her sweat. She felt suffocated.

Next to her, her aunts, like the rest of the guests, were consuming large amounts of beer, honeyed wine, and food. Fanning themselves with wicker fans, they chattered and guffawed at the tops of their voices. On the men's side, it was the same. In fact, nobody was paying the slightest attention to the endless chants, whose words seemed all too obviously intended for Sarai alone.

Abruptly, the chants stopped. The dancers froze, and the slaves put down the jars. Ichbi Sum-Usur dismissed his court with an abrupt gesture. Only the music of the drums and flutes continued to ring out as all eyes turned to the entrance.

72

Sarai saw him as soon as he entered the courtyard.

Him, the man who wanted her as his wife.

Without realizing it, she had sat up to get a better look at him. It was hard to see him clearly in the shade of the canopies. He was advancing slowly behind an older man, presumably his father. At first sight, he looked quite tall and moved with a self-confident gait.

She opened her mouth, but felt suddenly as though her body had forgotten to breathe. Her heart was hammering against her ribs, and her hands were shaking. She hid them in the folds of her toga.

The bridegroom's father seemed to be taking pleasure in advancing with exasperating slowness. All the guests, both men and women, were saluting them respectfully as they passed. Sarai thought she heard a murmur of approval, but perhaps it was only the blood humming in her ears.

And yet, as the two men approached, a joyful smile spread over her face. She could see him better now. He had a strong neck and broad shoulders on a slender body. His hair was thick and curly and gathered in a bun held in place by a silver clasp. He already had a beard; quite a bushy one, too. He was a man. The way he swung his arms, the confident way he moved: yes, a man. Not a child, not even a boy like Kiddin.

Sarai heard the barely contained praises of her aunts as father and son presented themselves before the basin of scent. With measured gestures, the two men sprinkled their faces.

She could see him quite clearly now. Straight eyebrows, a thin, hooked nose, mouth as distinct as a line between the curls of his beard, long lashes that almost veiled his eyes, calves and feet clearly visible below his linen toga with its threads of red and blue, solid ankles elegantly gripped by the leather straps of his sandals: Everything about him was noble. He was everything a man was supposed to be in the land of Sumer and Akkad.

A hand gripped Sarai's elbow, gripped it like a claw. She jumped, half turned, and received Egime's drunken breath in her face.

"There he is, your husband!" Egime whispered passionately. "Take a good look at him, child. And salute him as he deserves. He's a king. I tell you that. All of us would beg him to lie with us!"

Sarai really wanted to smile. She wanted her heart to beat with impatience, joy, and pleasure, not with fear. It did indeed seem that her father had found the noblest, strongest, handsomest of men for his beloved daughter!

Ichbi Sum-Usur was now greeting the two men, and Kiddin was already making a fuss of his future brother. It was clear from the way he was smiling, laughing, bending his head, and exchanging his shawl with him how much he admired the newcomer, how much he wanted to please him.

Yes, Kiddin wouldn't have hesitated to marry the man!

As Sarai watched him, doubt twisted in her stomach like a snake.

She had been so busy staring at the man who was to be the master of her days and nights that she had not thought about the ritual platter that the bridegroom was supposed to offer the bride's family. But now, four slaves were carrying it up onto the dais. There were shouts and applause. The guests were no longer holding back their admiration.

The platter was the size of a man's torso. It was made of precious wood from Zagros and covered in leather, bronze, and silver. In the middle, carved from the same piece of wood, stood a bull with golden horns, a silver muffle, and lapis lazuli eyes, a chest inlaid with ivory and ebony, and a huge, erect bronze penis.

The cries of acclaim continued. Kiddin's eyes gleamed with excitement.

Sarai shuddered.

Ichbi Sum-Usur stepped forward, said something out loud that Sarai did not understand, put his hand on the bull, and stroked its horns.

Laughter swept through the courtyard. Sarai realized that her bridegroom was laughing, too. His mouth was open, revealing his white teeth. In a flash, she saw his face in her chamber, in her bed. Laughing like that, his mouth wide open above her. As if about to bite or tear.

At that moment, the groom grasped the bull's bronze penis with one hand. With the other, he dismissed his slaves with a peremptory gesture. As one of them appeared not to understand, he kicked him in the thigh and sent him tumbling head over heels off the dais, to further gales of laughter. With one arm, barely swaying under the weight of the platter, he brandished his offering above his head. The women let out shrill cries, and the men rose from their seats to cheer him.

Egime, who had not let go of Sarai's arm, yelped and squeezed it so tightly that Sarai in her turn cried out. From the chorus of singers a new chant arose.

Then, in the midst of the din, he turned toward her and for the first time looked at her.

She saw his eyes move all over her, then return to her face.

She saw his expression.

She saw what he discovered and what he thought.

A thin, graceless child. A girl without breasts or hips, with shaking hands, the bones of her wrists protruding. A little child with a ridiculous face under a layer of kaolin cracked like the soil at the end of summer. Not a woman with high cheekbones, full lips, and gentle eyes.

She saw it in his eyes and the tension of his mouth as he relaxed his exertions and let the nuptial platter fall back into the hands of the slaves. And what she saw was not even disappointment. It was contempt. It was the expression of a man disgusted at the thought of the effort he would have to make even to look again at the woman who was going to be his wife.

The following day, two hours after daybreak, even more guests streamed into the courtyard. Even though the servants had removed the seats, there was still not enough room for everybody, and some were waiting patiently in the lane in front of the house. The chants, the flutes, and the drums were almost smothered by the din of voices.

At noon, the statues of Ichbi Sum-Usur's ancestors were carried onto the dais and placed beside those of the bridegroom's family. The nuptial platter was placed before them, and the bull disappeared under a mountain of flower petals and jewels and offerings of finely woven cloth. Silence fell when the two fathers, after throwing cedarwood shavings into the terracotta hearths, addressed their gods and their beloved ancestors in singsong voices.

Some twenty slaves lifted a large bronze basin onto the dais, and young girls in white togas emptied into it jars of cedar and amber ointment diluted with the water of the Euphrates.

Then the slaves unfolded a cane-and-wicker screen from one wall to the other, hiding the basin and the ancestors from the guests in the courtyard. Sarai was led by Egime to the end of the dais reserved for the women.

She was wearing her nuptial toga, fringed with silver tassels and held in at the waist by a woven scarlet belt. Both her shoulders were bare. The area around her eyes was covered, from the brows to the cheekbones, with a thick layer of kohl, out of which her eyes shone like those of an animal surprised in the dark. Her lips had been smeared with a paste that made them seem fuller. Despite this, her aunts noticed how pale her cheeks were, as pale as if Sililli had not removed all the kaolin from the day before.

Opposite her, on the other side of the dais, stood the groom and his father, surrounded by her father, Kiddin, and her uncles. They were all staring at her, but not only did the smoke from the herbs and the cedarwood blur their faces, Sarai was also doing her best not to look at the man who would soon share her bed.

From the crowd of unseen guests on the other side of the screen came the sound of flutes. Sweet, tremulous music that wrapped itself tenderly around Sarai's heart, rose through her chest, and calmed her like a caress. All the thoughts that had made her body feel so tight since morning vanished. The muscles of her shoulders and her stomach relaxed. She felt calm, sure of herself. Ready to do what had to be done.

And now, it all began. And to her, it all seemed to happen at the same time.

Behind the screen, the singers joined in with the flutes.

When for the wild bull I have bathed,
When with amber I have anointed my
mouth . . .

Ichbi Sum-Usur crossed the dais, the smoke from the cedarwood shavings swirling around him.

When I have painted my eyes with kohl . . .

With a jolt, Egime pushed Sarai toward her father, who led her into the heart of the smoke, facing the ancestors, and thanked them, congratulated them, while the singers, now accompanied by the voices of all the guests, took up the nuptial chant:

When I have adorned myself for him,
When my loins have been molded by his
hands . . .

Ichbi Sum-Usur seized the cords of her bridal belt and untied them. Then he pulled on the toga and slid it off her body until she was naked.

When with milk and cream he has
smoothed my thighs . . .

His hand on the small of her back, he

pushed her into the basin where the oint-
ments had been poured. A slave girl handed
him a wooden bowl, which he filled with
scented water from the basin. He raised his
hand high above Sarai, then poured the
water over her chest. She bent her knees a
little as the cold water ran over her belly and
down as far as her thighs.

The chant was becoming more and more
fervent. She knew without seeing him that
he was there, behind her. Him, the bridegroom. She saw her father pass the wooden
bowl to him, and she thought her heart
would burst.

In his turn, the groom bent to fill the
bowl, and his naked shoulder brushed
against Sarai's hip. She could smell the
strong odor of the myrtle oil on his hair. The
fingers that were going to touch her were reflected in the scented water.

She leaped out of the basin. Dripping
with water, she picked up her tunic from the
ground and ran to the end of the dais where
the women were. Egime was the only one to
stand in her way. Sarai pushed her aside
roughly. She heard cries, the noise of something falling. She ran through one room,
then another. The chanting had stopped.
She saw the astonished face of a handmaid.
She kept running until she reached the

garden. She knew which way to go: across the canals and basins. She could jump from one to the other, until she got to the streets of the city outside the walls of the palace.

She went straight on, without any other aim than to get as far away as she could. The streets between the high brick walls were narrow and dark, sometimes just wide enough to let two or three people pass side by side, or an ass carrying a saddlepack. Under the astounded eyes of the passersby, she weaved quickly between the sacks and baskets of the street vendors.

She was out of breath by the time she at last reached the great canal that ran alongside the outer wall of the royal city of Ur. Through a thousand branches, it distributed the water of the Euphrates to the temples, the royal palaces, and the dwellings of the lords. Flowing eventually into the river at the western and southern harbors, it encircled the noble city, making it an island, separating it and purifying it of the stains of the lower city, where the common people lived.

Standing in the shade of a wall, Sarai looked at the crowd to see if among them were any servants or slaves her father might have sent out to find her. But there were none. They must have been taken so much by surprise that she was already a long way away before they set off in pursuit of her.

Now she must get to one of the gates as quickly as possible. But she hesitated. Would the gods allow her to get through the outer wall?

What a sight she must be! Her tasseled toga, thrown on in haste, was now in complete disarray; her eyes were still black with kohl, and the diadem of her hair had collapsed as she ran. She was sure the guards, who kept a close watch on everyone entering and leaving the noble city, would be just as surprised as the people she had passed so far.

For a moment, she thought: What if I returned home? Sililli could help me slip into my chamber. She must be worried sick and crying her eyes out. She'll be only too pleased to see me. Obviously there couldn't be a wedding now. She was sure the noble bridegroom her father had chosen for her, humiliated and insulted by her escape, had already left. The house must be echoing to Ichbi Sum-Usur's rage.

No, she couldn't go back. It was over. Ever since she had seen that man, her bridegroom, on the dais, her mind had been made up. Never again would she see Sililli, her sisters, her father, or even Kiddin, whom she would hardly miss. She had made her gesture in front of everyone, and now she was a girl without a family. All that mattered now was to get away from the soldiers, whose task, as evening fell, was to clear the streets of the noble city and make sure that everyone went home. She would find shelter for the night outside the walls. This wasn't the moment to feel sorry for herself. On the contrary, she had to harden her heart and show how brave she was. Tomorrow she would have plenty of time to think, to think long and hard.

Walking as naturally as she could, she retraced her steps and plunged into the red shade of an almost deserted alley. While she was running, she had noticed a dead-end street, almost blocked by a half-crumbled wall. Sarai found it now and edged her way in.

Hidden from prying eyes, she undid her hair, then took out the horn needles around which Sililli had rolled her locks. It would have been preferable to untie the braids, but there was no time for that now, so she simply pushed them onto the back of her neck. With the bottom of her toga, she wiped the makeup off her lips and eyes. Then she undressed, tearing the hems of her tunic to take off the bridal tassels that still hung from it. Aware that she was doing something she could not reverse, she threw them away among the bricks.

Sarai quickly turned the tunic inside out so that the coarser part of the material was on the outside, then wrapped herself in it and covered her head. She hoped the guards would think she was just a handmaid, noble, but not noble enough to attract their attention. With a newfound confidence, and even a touch of excitement, she climbed back out through the wall, walked back to the canal, and reached the north gate.

But a moment later, that newfound confidence wavered.

The outer wall of Ur, more than a thousand years old, was as thick as fifty men and as high as a hundred. In all the kingdom of Shu-Sin, son of Shlugi, only Nippur had such formidable ramparts. There were gates at the four cardinal points, gates reinforced with bronze, so heavy they needed fifty men with oxen to move them. Now that Sarai was quite near, she could see the guards walking up and down, keeping a watchful eye on everyone entering or leaving. They wore helmets and leather-lined capes and carried lances.

But the gods decided to make things

easier for her. A noisy procession approached, on its way back to the lower city from one of the great temples, the temple of Sin or of Ea. There were musicians at the head of the procession, followed by men bearing flower-bedecked litters on which statuettes of their ancestors sat enthroned, and young priestesses, dressed in the simple toga of the lesser temples, without belts and without jewelry in their hair, carrying perfume burners from which arose the acid smoke of reeds and *bidurhu* gum. Bringing up the rear, a crowd of people pushed and shoved. Sarai slipped easily into the crowd, unobserved except by a young girl her own age, who looked somewhat surprised to see Sarai fall into step beside her.

The procession crossed the wooden bridge over the canal. The guards were at their places on either side of the gate. Sarai held her breath as she plunged into the cool darkness. It was so thick, they seemed to be walking through a tunnel. Nobody shouted, nobody called out after her.

There were gardens on the other side, and an old wall with zigzagging steps cut into it. Suddenly, the vast lower city came into view. Hundreds of tangled streets stretched for dozens of *ùs* into the distance. The whole bend in the river was covered with roofs.

Once outside the walls of the royal city, the procession was less orderly. Young boys left the line, squabbling among themselves. On either side, bystanders sang, danced, and clapped their hands in time to the music. Some gathered around the litters and flung petals and bowls of perfume or beer at the statuettes. Shouts and laughter drowned the chanting. Sarai took advantage of the confusion to turn into the first street she came to.

She kept on walking, recognizing nothing around her. The houses here were nothing but overlapping cubes, with single-leaf wooden doors or sometimes just curtains over the entrance, and walls covered with white cob.

There were many people on the streets, common people wearing tunics or loincloths, with wicker sandals on their feet, their calves gray with dust. They chatted, laughed, called to one another. Some carried baskets or sacks, goaded asses, pushed carts loaded with rushes or watermelons. A few people, both women and men, looked at Sarai in surprise, but with no real curiosity. For her, everything was strange and astonishing.

In the whole of her young life, she had left

the royal city a mere half dozen times, crossing the river in a boat with her father, heading west to the great temples of Eridu. But the lower city, the northern city, was somewhere the lords never went. They felt nothing but contempt and distrust toward it. The handmaids told stories about how at night the streets swarmed with black-skinned demons, animals with more than one body, fierce jaws, and claws, and other horrors straight out of the caves of the underworld.

The men and women of the lower city were the subjects of the Lords of Ur, but never saw their faces. Whenever Ichbi Sum-Usur needed craftsmen or merchants from among them, he would ask his scribes, his foremen or his regents to find them.

Sarai just had to look around her to realize that she would find neither help nor shelter. Who would welcome a girl from the royal city, a runaway, moreover, without fearing the wrath of the lords? It wouldn't stay secret for long, because there were no secrets in the lower city. People spent as much time on the streets as they did inside their own homes. The doors of the houses were usually left open, and the inner courtyards could be seen by anyone passing by. The streets and alleys were cluttered with children, geese, dogs, and even pigs, and strewn with refuse. But nobody seemed to mind. They all went about their business, their mouths wide open, bustling unconcerned about the stalls where everything was bought and sold: food, rope, fabrics, sacks of grain, even asses. All around was the smell of rotting vegetables, of meat and fish exposed to the heat, mingled with the stench of excrement — the excrement of asses and children — not yet absorbed by the dusty ground. A stench so suffocating that Sarai had to hold her veil over her mouth to breathe. She was the only one doing so, but everyone was too busy to pay her any attention.

She was suddenly startled by a cry: "Child, child!" An old woman sat in a doorway, smiling — or grinning — at her, her face nothing but wrinkles, her eyes almost invisible, her lack of teeth revealing a disgustingly pink tongue. She wagged a crooked finger at Sarai, beckoning her to come closer.

"Herbs, my child, herbs! Do you want any of my herbs?"

A dozen small baskets were lined up along the wall beside her, crammed with leaves, seeds of all colors, stones, crystals of gum. Sarai wanted to run away, but the old woman's eyes held her back.

"Herbs or something else? Come here, child, don't be afraid!"

Her voice became softer. There was even a touch of kindness in it. Were luck and the gods smiling on her? Sarai wondered. Perhaps the old woman could find her shelter for the night? What could a woman like her fear? But her next question froze Sarai's blood.

"Do you need something, goddess? Anything you want, Kani Alk-Nàa can sell it to you . . ."

Why did the woman call her "goddess"? Had she guessed she was from the royal city? Or was she simply mocking her? Feigning indifference, Sarai bent over the baskets. They not only contained herbs and seeds, but animal skeletons, fetuses, skulls, dried entrails, and the gods knew what else! She was outside the lair of a witch, a *kassaptu!*

The old woman noticed her expression of disgust and let out a piercing laugh. "You're a long way from home, goddess! Make sure the demons of the night don't eat you!"

Sarai straightened up, fear in her belly, and ran away.

Behind her, the high walls of Ur towered like mountains, their tops bathed in the ocher light of dusk: impossible to get back inside now until dawn. Above the walls, only the upper terraces of the ziggurat were visible, the dark crown of the gardens, the Sublime Bedchamber with its lapis lazuli reflecting the sun like a daytime star. There was no more beautiful sight in all the world.

Sarai ran without looking back, thinking of her garden, her new bedchamber, the softness of her bed. She slowed down. Night was coming on fast, like the sea coming to drown the shore.

She knew that if she had stayed in her father's palace, she would by now be with a husband who didn't care about her and would be in a hurry to get it over with, and there would be nothing beautiful about her chamber or her bed. Yet tears welled up in her eyes. She felt a good deal less brave now.

"Make sure the demons of the night don't eat you!" the old woman had cried. The warning still echoed in Sarai's ears. The sun was disappearing beneath the rim of the world. She was finding it increasingly difficult to keep going. Her legs felt heavy. She had lost her beautiful kid sandals in the mud. Water slapped beneath her bare feet. The bottom of her tunic was soaked. Bulrushes struck her arms and shoulders.

She was wading along the riverbank without knowing how she had got there. She had followed an alley; the houses had become less frequent. She had hurried straight on, exhausted, too terrified to stop, still hoping to find something — a hut made out of bulrushes, a boat, a tree trunk, a hole in the ground — anything that could protect her. The cold and the night were pressing against the back of her neck.

Suddenly, her foot hit something hard. She felt a blow against her thigh, thought of the demons, and screamed in terror. Headfirst, she tipped over in the water. Her fingers sank into the mud. The torn fabric of her toga almost strangled her. Sarai pushed herself up until she was sitting, ready to face the most horrible of deaths.

But what she saw, standing outlined in the dim light, was not a monster but a man.

Perhaps not even a man: a boy. A head crowned by a halo of curly hair, a long, thin, but muscular body, naked but for a raw linen loincloth, legs black with mud up to the knees. In his left hand he carried a kind of cylindrical wicker basket, with animals moving about inside it. Sarai could barely make out his features. Only the gleam in his eyes as he stared at her.

He made a furious gesture with his arm,

pointed at the river, and said something in a language she did not understand. Then he stopped speaking and took another, closer look at her.

She wiped the mud from her cheeks with her hand. Her tunic was torn, so she knelt in the water, covered herself as best she could with the soaked cloth, then finally stood up.

The boy was a head taller than her. He was watching her calmly, staring at her braids without a smile although she must have been a horrible sight.

"What are you doing here?" he asked, in her language this time. There was no harshness in his voice, only surprise and curiosity.

With the back of her wrist, Sarai again wiped her cheeks and eyelids. "What about you?" she asked in return.

He raised his basket and shook it. Inside it, two frogs with swollen necks blinked. Now she could see his face clearly, a narrow face with a high forehead and very arched eyebrows that almost met above a big curved nose. The slightly greenish brown of his eyes was translucent in the last light of day. His checks were covered with a sparse down. He had beautiful lips — big, full, shaped like wings — a prominent chin, and a thin neck. The skin between his shoulder blades was damp.

"I was fishing," he said with a smile, and glanced at the river, which seemed to grow bigger as the night deepened. "It's the best time for frogs and crayfish. If nobody steps on you and screams."

Sarai was sure of it now: He was a *mar.Tu*. One of those Amorites from the borders of the world, where the sun disappeared. A man who worshiped lesser gods and was never allowed to set foot in the royal city.

She shivered, the skin on her arms bristling in the cold. The wind rose, making the wet cloth cling to her body. Without knowing why, she felt a desire to tell the truth, to let this boy know who she was.

"My name is Sarai," she said, in a low, frail voice, hardly pausing to take a breath. "My father, Ichbi Sum-Usur, is a lord of Ur. Today was the day a man was supposed to take me as his wife. He, too, is a lord of Ur. But when he looked at me, I knew I would never be able to live with him, in the same bed and the same chamber. I knew I would rather die than feel his hands on me. I thought I could hide in my house. But it wasn't possible. The handmaid who takes care of me knows all my hiding places. I wanted to throw myself from a wall and break my legs. I wasn't brave enough. I ran away. Now my father probably thinks his daughter is dead . . ."

The boy listened, looking now at her mouth, now at her braids. When she had stopped speaking, he said nothing at first. The darkness of the night seemed to rush toward them, transforming them into mere silhouettes under the countless stars.

"My name is Abram, son of Terah," he said at last. "I am a *mar.Tu*. Our tents are five or six *ùs* farther north. You mustn't stay here, you'll catch cold."

As he took a step toward her, she heard the noise of the water and jumped. He held out his hand. Palm to palm, he squeezed her hand with his own warm, slightly rough hand.

Firmly, but with a strange gentleness, he drew her after him. His gentleness made Sarai's whole body feel iridescent, from her thighs to deep in her chest.

"We have to find you a dry place, and make a fire," he said, and his words brought tears of gratitude to her eyes. "The nights are cold at this time of the year. I don't suppose you know where to go. It isn't every day that the daughters of the lords of Ur get lost in the bulrushes by the river. I could take you to my father's tent. But he'd think I was bringing him a bride, and my brothers would be jealous. I'm not the eldest. Never

95

mind, we'll find somewhere else."

The "somewhere" was just a sandy hillock. But the sand was warm and the hillock offered protection from the wind.

Abram seemed to be able to see in the dark. It did not take him long to collect some dry reeds and dead junipers, and he lit a fire by rubbing lichens and juniper twigs skillfully between his palms. The sight of the flames warmed Sarai just as much as their heat.

Abram continued to bustle about, constantly disappearing and coming back with more armfuls of reeds and dry shrubs. When there were enough of them, he crouched down without a word.

Now they could see each other much better. But as soon as their eyes met, they looked away again, embarrassed. For a long time they said nothing, warming themselves at the flames and watching the swirling sparks fly upward.

Sarai estimated that the young *mar.Tu* was about the same age as Kiddin. Probably not so strong, she thought, used more to running than fighting, her brother's favorite exercise. His hair made him look quite different, less noble, less proud, but she liked that.

Suddenly, Abram stood up, jolting the exhausted Sarai out of her torpor. "I'm going to the tents," he said.

Sarai leaped to her feet. Abram laughed at the sight of her terrified face. He picked up his wicker basket and shook the frogs.

"Don't worry. I'm just going to find something to eat. I'm hungry, and you must be, too. What I've caught here isn't enough to feed us."

As Sarai was sitting down again, annoyed at having shown fear, he smiled, mockingly. "Are you able to put wood on the fire?"

She merely shrugged.

"Perfect," he said.

He examined the sky for a moment. The moon was already up. Sarai noted that he often looked up at the sky, as if he were looking for traces of the sun in the stars. Then he took a few steps, and vanished into the night. All Sarai could hear now was the wind in the bulrushes, the lapping of the river, and, far in the distance, from the lower city, the barking of dogs.

She was once more stricken with fear. The boy could easily leave her here. The fire would attract the demons. She peered into the darkness, thinking she might see a sniggering crowd. But then her pride regained the upper hand. She was ashamed of herself. She must stop being afraid. She only feared what she did not know. Tonight, everything was completely unknown. The night, the fire, the river, the sky above her in its infinity. Even the name of this *mar.Tu* boy, Abram.

What a strange name! Abram. She liked the way the syllables coiled in her mouth.

Abram certainly wasn't afraid of the night. He moved about in it as if it were broad daylight. He didn't even seem to dread the demons.

Perhaps that was what being a *mar.Tu* meant?

In truth, she liked everything about this boy. It may simply have been because she had been scared of being lost and alone in the night. Or it may have been because he wasn't anything like Kiddin. Or the bridegroom her father had chosen for her.

It amused her to think how horrified they would all have been if they had seen Abram take her hand so unceremoniously! A *mar.Tu* daring to touch the daughter of a lord of Ur! What a sacrilege!

But she had not even thought of withdrawing her hand. She had felt no shame, no repulsion. Even his smell, so different from the scents with which the lords of Ur anointed themselves, did not disgust her.

Even the fact that he was a barbarian, a *mar.Tu,* pleased her!

Sarai wondered what he thought of her. She must be a dreadful sight, she knew, yet Abram had shown no reaction. Perhaps that was the way these *men without a city* behaved. Both her father and Sililli claimed that they were crude, cunning, inscrutable people. It didn't matter: This one hadn't hesitated to come to her aid.

Unless Sililli and her father were right and she never saw him again.

She hated herself for thinking such a thing. She put more wood on the fire and forced herself not to let her mind wander again.

He woke her by dropping two thick white sheepskins and a big leather bag by her side.

"It took me a while because I didn't want my brothers to see me," he explained. "They might have thought I wanted to sleep under the stars in order to get an early start hunting, and they would have followed me. They always follow me when I go hunting. I've already killed ten lynx and three stags. One day I'll face a lion."

Sarai wondered if he was boasting or trying to impress her. But he wasn't. Abram unrolled the sheepskins, took a coarse dress from his sack, and handed it to her.

"To replace your toga."

He himself had swapped his loincloth for a tunic held in at the waist by a belt. The handle of dagger protruded from a leather sheath hanging from the belt.

While Sarai withdrew into the shadows to change, he ostentatiously turned his back on her, stoked the fire, and took food from the bag.

When she came back and squatted again by the fire, he looked at her with a slightly ironic smile, which made his cheeks seem rounder. In the shifting light of the flames, the brown of his eyes was even more transparent.

"This is the first time you've worn a dress like that, isn't it?" he asked, amused. "It suits you."

Sarai also smiled. "Are my eyes still black?" she asked.

Abram hesitated, then burst out laughing: a laugh he had been holding back for a long time, which made his whole body shake. "Your eyes, yes!" he said, catching his breath. "Your cheeks and temples, too. In fact, when I first saw you, if I hadn't seen your stomach, I'd have thought you were black all over. They do exist, you know — women who are black all over — far away to the south, by the sea."

Sarai felt her cheeks burning with rage and shame. "It's the kohl they put on brides."

She seized her toga furiously and tried to tear the bottom of it, but the cloth resisted.

"Wait," said Abram.

He took out his dagger. It had a curved blade of very hard wood. Sarai had never seen one like it before. It sliced easily through the damp cloth. When he held it out to her, she seized his hand.

"Will you do it?" she asked, her voice shaking more than she would have liked. "You can see in the dark," she added, trying to sound more confident.

He shook his head, embarrassed. So that they should both feel less awkward, she closed her eyes. Kneeling before her in the luminous warmth of the fire, he cleaned her eyelids, her cheeks, her forehead. Gently. As if it was something he had always known how to do.

When he had finished, Sarai opened her eyes again. He smiled, and the wings of his beautiful lips seemed to fly away.

"Do you think I'm pretty now?" she dared to ask.

"Our girls don't have such beautiful hair," he said simply. "Or such straight noses."

Sarai did not know if that was a compliment.

Then, to dispel their embarrassment and assuage their hunger, they threw themselves on the food Abram had brought: still-warm kid, whitefish, cheese, fruit, fermented milk in a skin gourd. Strong-tasting dishes, without the sweet flavors preferred by the lords of Ur. Sarai ate as heartily as Abram, showing nothing of her surprise.

At first they ate in silence. Then Abram asked what Sarai planned to do when morning came. She said she didn't know, but perhaps she could find refuge in the great temples of Eridu, where girls without families were allowed to become priestesses. But her voice lacked conviction. The fact was, she had no idea. Tomorrow seemed so far away.

Abram then asked if she wasn't afraid her gods would punish her for refusing the husband her father had chosen for her and running away from home. She said no, this time with such confidence that he stopped eating and looked at her in surprise.

"No, because if they'd wanted to punish me, they'd have sent demons instead of making me fall over you."

The idea greatly amused Abram. "The

lords of Ur are the only people who believe the night is populated with demons. All I've ever seen at night were bulls, elephants, lions, or tigers. They're fierce, but a man can kill them. Or run after the gazelles!"

Sarai did not take offense. The fire crackled, the embers were getting hotter and hotter, the sheepskins were soft to the touch. Abram was right. The night no longer frightened her.

All at once, she was aware of happiness suffusing her body, from the ends of her hair to the tips of her toes, and calming her mind. She felt warm, and there was laughter in her chest that did not need to cross her lips. The flames danced for her, time stood still, and this boy she had not even known when the sun was up, Abram, who was so close to her she could have brushed his shoulder, was going to protect her from everything. She knew it.

So they kept talking, kept asking each other questions. Abram told her about his two brothers, Haran, the eldest, and Nahor, and about his father who made clay statues of ancestors for people like Ichbi Sum-Usur, statues with heads so lifelike you'd think they could speak.

Sarai wanted to know if he liked living in a tent. He explained that the clan of which his

103

father, Terah, was the head, reared great flocks for one of the lords of Ur. Every two years, when it was time for the royal taxes, they took their animals to Larsa to be counted by Shu-Sin's officials.

"Then we either come back here with just a few animals or start a completely new flock. One day, my father will earn enough from his statues, and we won't need to bother with rearing sheep anymore."

He questioned her, too. Sarai told him about her life in the palace. She spoke about Sililli, Kiddin, her sisters, and, for the first time in a long while, the vague but painful memories she had of her mother, who had died giving birth to Lillu. So carried away was she by the excitement of confiding all this, she even mentioned the chamber of blood and the *barù*'s strange prophecy: Queen or slave . . .

Abram was a good listener, patient and attentive.

They talked for so long that the wood on the fire burned down completely and the moon crossed more than half the night sky. Sarai said her people feared that one night the Lady Moon would vanish forever and that the gods, in their anger, would take the sun away. It would then be horribly cold.

"In a tent," she said, "it would be even

more terrible than in a house."

Abram shook his head, poked the embers, and replied that he didn't believe in any of that. There was no reason for the moon and the sun to disappear.

"Why are you so sure?" Sarai asked, surprised.

"Nobody can remember it ever happening. Why should something that's never happened since the beginning of the world suddenly happen one day?" He paused. "Just because you sleep in a tent doesn't mean you can't think. It doesn't mean you can't learn by observing the things around you."

For the first time, Sarai heard a proud, combative tone in his voice, which he immediately tempered by admitting that he could not read or write words in clay like the lords of Ur, who knew many things he didn't.

Suddenly he held out his hand to Sarai. "Come and see."

He walked away from the fire. Stiff all over, Sarai hurried after him, vaguely worried she would lose him in the darkness, even though the moon was quite bright.

He came to a halt on the crest of the dune. Before them, as if suspended between the darkness of the earth and the sky swarming with stars, hundreds of torches glowed in the night, forming the outline of a tiara. It was the ziggurat, whose immense staircase and platforms were lit up every night. But she had only ever seen it like that from the roof of her house, and never from such a distance. Only here was it possible to understand how perfectly it was designed, and how its scale was not human but divine.

"You can cross the river," Abram said, "you can walk far out into the plains, two, three days of walking, and you can still see it."

He turned to her and seized her face in his hands, which were soft and burning hot. Sarai shuddered, thinking he was going to kiss her, wondering if she was going to surrender or resist the *mar.Tu*'s impertinence. But all he did was slowly tip her face up toward the stars.

"Look at the fires of heaven. They're more amazing than the ziggurat. See how many there are, how far away! Do you believe a god lives in each one of them?"

How could she answer that? She said nothing, and placed her lips on Abram's wrist.

He gave a mocking laugh. "Do you really think the daughter of a lord of Ur can leave the city and her father's house without being found and punished?"

It was as if he had poured cold water over her body. Her happiness vanished at a stroke, to be replaced by tears and anger. She ran down the side of the dune and went and huddled on the sheepskin, making an effort to swallow her sobs. When he knelt behind her and placed his hands on her shoulders, she wanted to get up and slap him. But instead, she leaned against him, gripping his arms and hugging them with all her might against her chest. So it was that they collapsed side by side, her face buried in the sheepskin, and lay motionless.

"Forgive me," Abram whispered in her ear. "I didn't mean any harm by what I said. I wouldn't want anyone to hurt you. If tomorrow you still want to run away, I'll help you."

She wanted to ask why he would do that, but not a word passed her lips. It was enough that he was close to her, that she could inhale his strange smell, feel the heat of his body and his breath on the back of her neck. That was all that mattered.

They lay there, not moving. Her tears ceased, but something else, something disturbing, took their place. Abram's palms were pressed against her breasts. They suddenly seemed very hot to her, and so did the tips of her breasts. Against her buttocks, she could feel Abram's penis swelling. There was a quivering in her belly that had nothing to do with fear or anger. She remembered the man who had almost become her husband grasping the penis of the sculpted bull on the nuptial platter. This was still her wedding day. Her wedding night. She wanted to reach out her hand and touch Abram's penis. To turn to him and place her lips on his beautiful mouth.

At that moment, Abram loosened his embrace and moved away from her, saying that they had to sleep. That she was going to need all her energy for tomorrow.

He picked up the second skin to cover them, lay down flat on his back, and offered his outstretched arm as a pillow. She laid her head on it.

"You smell good," he whispered. "I've never smelled such a good scent on a girl before. I know I'll always remember your smell. Your face, too — I'll always remember your face."

It was as if these words took away the heat of her desire. A moment later, exhaustion overcame Sarai, and she fell asleep without knowing if she had really kissed Abram or if she had dreamed it.

When she awoke, she was alone among

the sheepskins, surrounded by soldiers with javelins and shields in their hands. Their leader kneeled before her and asked her if she was the daughter of Ichbi Sum-Usur, Lord of Ur.

The Herb of Infertility

Ichbi Sum-Usur's anger lasted four moons. During all that time, nobody was allowed to speak Sarai's name, to meet her gaze, to eat, laugh, or scent themselves in her company. She herself was not allowed to braid her hair, walk about without a veil over her head, paint her face with kohl and amber, or wear jewelry.

Sililli, who was still her handmaid, had to observe all these prohibitions to the letter, and was also given orders to watch Sarai night and day.

"If that girl leaves this house again without my permission," Ichbi Sum-Usur told her, "you will die. I'll hang you by the feet, open your belly, and put scorpions inside."

Sarai found there was a good side to these punishments. They meant she did not have to bear her aunts' pitying or furious looks, or the innuendo-laden chatter of her sisters or the handmaids.

What she did have to bear for a whole week was Sililli's constant whining and sniffling, morning, noon, and night, her tearful prayers to almighty Inanna for forgiveness.

Sarai also had to attend a sacrifice of seven ewes, watched by her ancestors and all the members of the family. She had to perform a thousand ablutions in the temple, washing and purifying herself over and over again.

Sililli and Egime plied her endlessly with questions. They wanted to know what she had done during her flight, what demons had assailed her during her solitary night on the riverbank. After all, it must have been demons who had urged her to leave the nuptial bath as her bridegroom was about to anoint her with scents.

Sarai replied calmly, as many times as they wanted to hear it, that no demon had ever approached her, either here in the house, or there by the river.

"I was lost and alone."

She said nothing about Abram.

Neither Sililli nor Egime believed a word of what she said. Sarai did not have to meet their gaze to realize that. Their sighs and grimaces were eloquent enough. Egime next decided to check her niece's virginity. Cold with anger, Sarai lay down on her bed and parted her legs.

While her aunt screwed up her furrowed face to examine the evidence, Sarai thought about the desire she had felt for Abram during their night on the riverbank. She thought about his palms cupping her breasts and his penis growing hard against the small of her back. At such a humiliating moment, the thought was like a soothing caress. In the most secret parts of her heart and mind, she thanked Abram for having been wise enough to resist her innocence.

When they were done, she faced the two women, forcing them to lower their eyes. "From now on," she said, in an icy tone fully the equal of her father's, "I shan't answer any more of your questions. Nobody's allowed to speak Sarai's name in this house. Well, Sarai won't open her mouth either to gratify your stupidity."

But the two women's suspicions were not allayed. To safeguard what could still be safeguarded, they hung a large number of amulets on the door of Sarai's bedchamber, on the wooden parts of her bed, and even around her neck.

And the days passed.

Sililli's tears ceased. Everyone learned to

live with Sarai as if she were only half there. They sometimes even told jokes in her presence, and pretended not to see her smile.

Sarai herself grew quite used to this life, because it allowed her to be alone with her thoughts. In her mind, she summoned Abram to her side. As in a waking dream, she could hear his voice and smell his *mar.Tu* smell. Often at night, before she drifted into sleep, she would sing silently to him, to Abram, the words she would never have agreed to sing to the man who had wanted to become her husband.

She had matured enough in the past few weeks, though, not to have any illusions about these imagined joys. With every day that passed, she became more aware of how quite extraordinary and ephemeral her encounter with the young *mar.Tu* had been. A few questions still remained: Why wasn't Abram beside her when the soldiers had woken her? Had he been bidding her farewell without her realizing it when he told her he would always remember her face? Was he still thinking about her, or did he think it was better to forget this girl from the royal city, a girl he should never have met? A girl from whom he could expect nothing, for never, as far back as any inhabitant of Ur could remember, had an Amorite barbarian dared to lay his hand on the daughter of a lord of Ur, unless it was to rape her?

Sometimes, after night fell, she would escape Sililli's vigilance, walk to the upper part of the garden, and stand for a long time looking at the torches illuminating the ziggurat. Perhaps, she thought, at that very moment Abram was on the riverbank, lying among the reeds, a basket full of frogs and crayfish beside him, also looking at the fiery diadem of the staircase of heaven. Perhaps at that very moment he was thinking about her.

One night, when a melancholy mist hung over Ur, heralding the rainy season, and Sarai had just returned from one of these walks, Sililli finally revealed to Sarai what was really troubling her.

"You've told us there was no demon with you the night you spent alone by the river. But the guards who found you said you were sleeping on new sheepskins next to a big fire that had burned out. There were also traces of food. Not to mention something we ourselves noticed: When you ran away you were wearing a fine tunic, and when you came back you had a dress on, such a coarse dress I'm sure it was never woven in Ur. Even a slave girl in this house would have refused it!"

114

It was not exactly an interrogation, but it was clear that it grieved Sililli not to know the truth. Listening to her, Sarai realized that keeping her secret to herself grieved her, too. So, in a voice so low that Sililli had to take her in her arms and put her ear up against her mouth to hear, she told Sililli everything. She told her about Abram: his beauty, his kindness, his smooth brown skin, his smell. And his promise not to forget her face.

By the time she had finished, Sililli's cheeks were bathed in tears. The handmaid finally drew apart from her and shook her head. "A *mar.Tu!*" she whispered. "A *mar.Tu!* A *mar.Tu!* . . ."

They said nothing more until Sililli clasped Sarai to her ample chest, clasped her so hard, it was as if she wanted her to disappear into it.

"Forget him, forget him or he'll bring you more misfortune than you can imagine! Forget him as if he were a demon, my Sarai!"

They both realized immediately that Sililli had done something wrong: She had spoken Sarai's name. They laughed through their tears.

"My Sarai!" Sililli repeated, carried away with emotion. "Your father vowed to have me eaten by scorpions if I disobeyed him. But I love you, and I know you need me to help you forget this *mar.Tu*. Promise me we'll never talk about him again."

One morning, when Lady Moon was still visible, full and round, in the dawn sky, the blood once again flowed between Sarai's thighs. For the second time, she entered the chamber of blood. Egime was there, making sure that the aunts and the handmaids observed Ichbi Sum-Usur's wishes to the letter. For seven days, they took care not to share a bath with her, to keep their distance when she helped with the weaving, and only to address her indirectly.

In addition, to impress on her the kind of punishments that awaited rebellious women, they told stories about the sad fates of those who had flouted the laws of the gods, as well as their fathers, and their husbands, of women who had profaned their duties as wives, either swallowing herbs of infertility in order not to bear children, or bearing children after giving a welcome between their thighs to men who should never have laid a hand on them, sometimes foreigners, or even demons. In truth, the madness of lustful women knew no bounds; it was like an icy, burning wind blowing straight from hell.

"Yes," Egime said, "we women can be our own worst enemies, if we're not careful. The worst time of all is when we're young and we can't tell the difference between good dreams and bad dreams, the ones that make our hearts beat and our private parts go all wet and carry us off to Ereshkigal's lair as surely as an Elamite soldier rapes and kills. Ea is great, for he has given us fathers and husbands to protect us from ourselves."

Sarai would listen in silence, giving nothing away.

What Egime and the others did not know was that at night, when everyone was asleep in the thick darkness of the chamber of blood, Sarai did not dream. No, the thoughts that came to her, the images that floated in the darkness, were not cunning illusions but very real memories: She thought about Abram's lips, the lips she had not had the courage to kiss.

She thought about the kiss she had neither given nor received. Both of them had remained pure. Her father may have had good reason to be furious, but Sarai had in no way offended the gods, and they had no reason to be angry. She felt it.

She felt it deep in her stomach as she

made offerings to Nintu, Midwife of the World.

She felt it deep in her chest as she prayed to almighty Inanna.

Sometimes she thought there could well exist other punishments from the gods quite different than those imagined by the women of the house. This pain, for example, which tormented her more and more every day, this awareness that she had not felt the soft lips of the *mar.Tu* Abram on her own lips. A gentle, almost soothing pain, which had to be kept secret. Wasn't that a punishment, too?

When she emerged from the chamber of blood and they saw her wandering sadly and submissively through the house and the garden, everyone thought that the daughter of Ichbi Sum-Usur was on the road to repentance.

The weeks passed. Twice more, Sarai went into the chamber of blood. Egime was less distant this time, and even though her young aunts still refused to meet her gaze, they had no hesitation in chatting with her as they used to, and even complimented her on how well she carded and spun wool.

Having been patient for all these moons, Sililli could no longer conceal her joy. Sarai had not only changed, she had also obeyed her to the letter: Since that night she had confessed, she had never again spoken about the *mar.Tu.*

"Your father is pleased with you," Sililli said suddenly one day, when the rain was falling like a flood and everyone was indoors. "He's been observing you for days. I can see from his face that he's no longer angry. I'm sure he'll soon forgive you."

Sarai nodded her head slightly to acknowledge that she had heard. But it was some time before she spoke.

"Do you think my father is planning to find me another husband?" she asked, in a level voice.

In the dim light of the rain-darkened day, Sililli's smile was more luminous than a rainbow. "We all want what's best for you!"

This time, Sarai was much better prepared. She wore the kind of toga that was worn to visit the great temples, had an offering basket full of flowers, and wore her hair arranged in the style of a handmaid. She had left nothing to chance. Around her neck hung a little woven bag containing three shekels' worth of brass and silver rings, in case she had to bribe the guards. She would do it if she had to. She felt as strong and determined as a soldier facing

119

the raised lances of the enemy lines.

She had left her bedchamber before dawn, while Sililli was still asleep, and waited in the garden until the light of day allowed her to cross the irrigation basins. Sure of the way, she headed for the outer wall. The streets were almost empty. It was no longer raining, but the city still smelled of damp dust and the brick walls were darker than usual. The guards had just opened the gates of the royal city, and the first carts laden with food were coming through the entrance.

The soldiers watched her as she approached. She saw at once that they took her for what she had hoped they would: a handmaid from a good house in the lower city, returning from the temples after spending the night there and carrying a basket of sacred flowers. Their eyes still swollen from their long watch, they seemed quite happy to see a pretty girl so early in the morning and answered her smile with a friendly salute.

Once in the lower city, Sarai walked quickly. She lost her way once or twice, but it did not matter. All she had to do was walk to the river.

When she arrived at the reedy lagoon, she had the impression it was at the same place where she had met Abram. It had the same wretched, half-ruined houses, the same patches of sandy ground, some fallow, some planted with melons and fragrant herbs. Nevertheless, she had to go upstream for *ùs* before she came in sight of the tents of the *mar. Tu.* The tents were low and round, barely higher than the reeds, which meant that the wind slid over their curved roofs. There were hundreds of them, made of thick brown or beige canvas, some as vast as real houses, others arranged lengthwise around enclosures of bulrushes containing the small livestock.

At the sight of this huge encampment, already alive with half-naked children and women in long robes, Sarai halted, her heart pounding. If the gods disapproved of what she was doing, now was the time for their anger to strike her.

She walking along the sandy path that led into the encampment. She had hardly reached the first tents when the women broke off from their work and the children from their games. Blushing with embarrassment, Sarai hoped to be greeted by smiles, but none came. The women gathered in silence in the middle of the path. The children approached her. Eyes bright with curiosity, they pressed around her, examining her hair, her belt, her basket — which she had quite forgotten to empty of its flowers. Was this the first time they had seen an inhabitant of the royal city?

Mustering her courage, Sarai greeted them respectfully, in her most neutral tone, invoked the protection of almighty Ea on all of them, and asked the way to the tents of the clan of Terah, the idol maker who produced statues of ancestors.

The women appeared not to understand. Sarai was afraid she had not pronounced the name of Abram's father correctly. "Terah, Terah . . ." she repeated, trying to find the right intonations. The oldest of the women said a few words in the *mar.Tu* language. Two other women answered her, shaking their heads. The old woman looked at Sarai again, her pale gray eyes surprised but benevolent.

"Terah isn't here anymore," she said. "He and all his people have gone."

"Gone?" Sarai's surprise was so great, she nearly cried out.

"They've been gone two moons already," the old *mar.Tu* went on. "It's winter. They've taken the flocks of the lords of Ur to be counted for the tax."

She had been prepared for anything, but

never for a moment had she imagined that Abram and his family would not be there.

She had thought of how angry Abram might be when he saw her. Or how happy she would be to see him smile at the sight of her.

She had thought of the words she would say to him: "I've come to you so that you can place your mouth on mine. My father is going to find me a new husband. This time, I shan't be able to refuse. If he asked me what I wanted, I'd choose you, though I know that no lord of the royal city has ever given his daughter to a *mar.Tu*. But for the past three moons, not a day has passed that I haven't thought about you. I've thought about your lips and the kiss I wanted from them the night you protected me. I've thought long and hard. I've prayed to holy Inanna, made offerings to Nintu and the statues of our ancestors in my father's temple. I waited for them to speak to me, to tell me if these thoughts of mine were bad. They said nothing. They let me leave the city without showing their anger. Now I'm here before you, for I know that your kiss will purify me, just as well as the icy water in the chamber of blood, and better than a basin full of scent or a sacrifice of ewes. Give me that kiss, Abram, and I'll return to my father's house and become the wife of the man he's chosen for me. I'll accept him. When he comes to my bed, the breath of your kiss will be on my lips to protect me."

She had thought he would laugh. Or get angry. She had thought that perhaps he would not be satisfied with just a kiss. She was ready for that. Nothing that came from him could soil her. Nothing that he took from her — denying it to her future husband — could diminish her.

But perhaps he would say, "No! I don't want you to leave. I don't want a stranger to come to your bed. Come, let me introduce you to my brothers and my father. You will be my chosen wife. We'll go far away from Ur."

For that, too, she was ready.

She had imagined so many things!

But never had she thought that he might have left the riverbank and be far away, unattainable.

Now she was running, far from the tents of the *mar.Tu*, running until she was out of breath in order not to cry, and wondering what to do next.

Sililli must be looking for her in every corner of the house, heart pounding with terror. Hiding from everyone the fact that Sarai was gone, for fear of Ichbi Sum-Usur's rage. Begging the gods for Sarai's return.

Sarai could do what Sililli and her father wanted. She could return and say, "I went to pray in the great temple to purify myself." Sililli, in her relief, would believe her. Everyone would be delighted with how sensible she was being.

The next time she emerged from the chamber of blood, her father would announce that he had finally convinced a man from the royal city to take her as his wife. A lord of Ur, not as rich or as handsome as the man she had humiliated, but whose fault was that?

Sarai would bow her head, go to the temple, listen to the soothsayer. There would be no guests this time, no chanting, no dancing, no banquets. But the groom would still come impatiently to her chamber and her bed.

He would touch her, and Abram's kiss would not protect her. Abram's lips, words, and caresses would not be with her through her married life.

It was then that she heard the words. Words that no lips uttered, as if a god or a demon had breathed them.

"Do you need something, goddess? Kani Alk-Nàa will sell it to you!"

Sarai stopped running, her chest on fire,

tears stinging her eyes.

"Do you need something, goddess?" she heard again.

The old witch! The *kassaptu* who had shouted at her the day she met Abram! It was her voice Sarai was hearing in her head. And, as if in echo, she remembered the stories her aunts had told in the chamber of blood: "There's one woman who drank the herb of infertility. She didn't bleed for three whole moons. Her husband didn't want to touch her anymore, or even hear anyone speak her name. Her husband or any other man. Who'd want a woman capable of stopping her own blood?"

Sarai caught her breath. A smile as gray as the sky clouded her features. The gods were not abandoning her. They wouldn't let her spoil like dead meat in the arms of a husband.

"The herb of infertility?" the *kassaptu* muttered. "Are you sure that's what you want?"

Sarai merely nodded. Her heart was pounding. It had been less difficult to find the witch's lair again than to go inside. Everyone in the lower city seemed to know Kani Alk-Nàa. But before she could find the courage to cross the threshold of the one room that served as her lair, Sarai had walked up and down the street a dozen times.

"You're quite young to want the herb of infertility," Kani Alk-Nàa went on. "It can be dangerous at your age."

Sarai resisted the desire to reply. She clasped her hands together; she didn't want the witch to see them shaking.

"Are you at least a wife?"

Once again Sarai did not reply. She stared at the dozens of baskets piled up in every corner of the room, giving off a smell of dust and rotting fruit. A thin chuckle made her turn her head. The old woman was laughing, her little pink tongue wriggling between her bare gums like a snake's tail.

"Afraid, are you? Afraid that Kani Alk-Nàa will cast a spell on you, lord's daughter?"

Without a word, Sarai took off the purse that hung around her neck and emptied the contents in front of the witch.

"Three shekels," the old woman calculated, gathering the copper and silver rings avidly; she was not laughing now. "I don't care if you're a wife or not. But I need to know if it's already happened."

Sarai hesitated, uncertain if she had understood correctly.

The old woman sighed. "Has the bull been between your thighs?" she asked, with irritation. "Are you an opened woman? If not, come back and see me after the man has parted your thighs."

"I am an opened woman," Sarai lied, in a hoarse voice.

The *kassaptu*'s eyes, barely visible between the folds of her eyelids, remained fixed for a moment. Sarai was afraid she would guess the truth.

"Good. And how long has the man's milk been inside you?"

"Almost . . . almost one moon."

"Hmmm. You should have come earlier." The old woman stretched her puny hand toward the baskets. She took out five little packets of herbs wrapped in dried reeds and handed them to Sarai. "Here's your herb of infertility."

"How many times is it for?" asked Sarai, without daring to look up.

"How many times will your bleeding stop? That depends on the woman. Two moons, maybe three, as you're young. You'll see. Put each of these packets in a *silà* of boiling water, without opening them, and leave them to soak for half a day. Then take the packets out and drink the infusion three times between the zenith and twilight. Do as

I tell you, lord's daughter, and everything will be fine."

Sarai had guessed right. She found Sililli hiding in her bedchamber, her face bathed in tears, her voice shrill with reproach, relief, anger, and tenderness. She had been so afraid that she had said nothing. Nobody in the house knew that Sarai had been gone since morning.

"I said you were sick, you had a bad stomach, and I'd given you herbs to help you sleep. You weren't to be disturbed, in order to let the herbs do their work. May all the Lords of Heaven forgive me, I've been telling lies all day!"

"No, no. Your herbs always do me good! I'll be up tomorrow, and they'll see me and say that Sililli knows more about herbs than any other handmaid in the city!"

The compliment, and Sarai's promise to show herself to the whole household the next day, made Sililli smile through her tears. But her moaning soon resumed.

"You'll be the death of me, my girl, the death of me! Either your father will kill me with his scorpions, or the gods will tear my heart out for my lies!"

"It's only a little lie," Sarai jested bitterly. "Almost the truth."

"Don't blaspheme, I beg you! Not on a day like today." She lowered her voice to an almost inaudible whisper to ask the question that was tormenting her. "Were you with him? With the *mar.Tu?*"

Sarai thought of telling the truth. But then she thought of the *kassaptu*'s little packets rubbing against her skin under the belt of her tunic, and she lied again. After all, what was one lie more or less?

"No, I went to the great temple of Inanna. I wanted to make offerings and ask the protection of the Almighty One so that my father should make a good choice for the man I am to marry."

"The great temple? Is that where you were?"

"I need to be prepared. I don't want to be afraid again."

"Without telling me — even though you know your father has forbidden you to leave the house?"

"The idea came to me while you were still asleep. Everyone was asleep, even my father. And I wanted to be alone before holy Inanna."

Sililli shook her head. "You'll be the death of me, my girl," she said again, "the death of me!"

Sarai summoned the strength to smile

and to hug her, pressing her cheek against hers, until Sililli abandoned her questions with a sigh of resignation.

"Anyway, you're here. And we all have to die one day."

But she never again let Sarai out of her sight. She would wake her in the night to make sure she had not run away. Because of this, Sarai was unable to prepare the herb of infertility until just before it was time for her to go back to the chamber of blood. Nor was she able to follow Kani Alk-Nàa's instructions to the letter.

She stole a pitcher of boiling water from the kitchen, put the five packets of herbs in it to soak, and hid it in the garden. But thanks to Sililli's vigilance, she could not drink the infusion as quickly as she wanted. It was not until the next day that she managed to escape her handmaid's eyes, slip out into the garden, and take the infused packets of herbs from the pitcher. They had become white and shriveled. Did it really matter that they had soaked for so long? Sarai doubted it. The important thing was to hide them until she had an opportunity to destroy them!

Recalling the disgusting stench of the witch's lair, she dreaded the taste of the potion, but she was pleasantly surprised:

The infusion was sweet, almost as sweet as honey, with a slightly acid but refreshing aftertaste. It was far from unpleasant, and she would even have drunk it for pleasure. Fearing that she would have little free time in the hours to come, Sarai decided unhesitatingly to swallow the entire pitcher.

When she returned to the women's quarters, she felt calm for the first time in days. At last, it was done. At last, the herb of infertility was inside her. The blood wasn't coming to flow between her thighs.

She knew what would happen. After two, or three, or five days with no blood on her linen, Sililli, her aunts, and her father would think she was ill; it would not occur to any of them that she had been brave enough to enter the lair of a *kassaptu*. They would make a large number of offerings to Nintu, but the blood still would not flow. Two moons would pass, perhaps three.

Long enough for her father to postpone the bridegroom's arrival, perhaps even to renounce the idea of offering his daughter to anyone at all.

Long enough for the *mar.Tu* Abram to return.

That night, taking advantage of Sililli's brief absence, Sarai quickly hid the five packets of the herb of infertility under her bed. Then she stood before the red silhouette of the goddess Nintu at the foot of her bed, opened her arms and the palms of her hands, and turned her face up to heaven. Without her lips moving, without anyone hearing her, she implored Nintu's mercy.

> *O Nintu, patroness of childbirth, you who received the brick of childbearing from the hands of almighty Enki, you who hold the scissors of the birth cord,*
> *Consider your daughter Sarai, be patient with her,*
> *Look down on my weakness,*
> *Look at the blood that is in my heart:*
> *It is cold for the husband I have not chosen.*
> *The herb of infertility is like a cloud in the sky,*
> *It does not long stop the sun from shining.*
> *O Nintu, forgive Sarai, daughter of Ichbi Sum-Usur.*

It was toward morning, while she was fast asleep, that hell entered Sarai's belly.

She saw it first in her dream. Dancing flames penetrated her body like a man. She tried to ward them off, but her hands went right through the fire without lessening it.

She saw her own body become red and swollen, while the *kassaptu*'s face creased with pleasure and she shouted in a loud voice: "You see, now it's true: You are an opened woman." Sarai's body cracked open, her entrails split and burned. She saw them fall to the ground, black and shriveled. She twisted in pain. Her belly, like an emptied gourd, made her weep and cry out. The cries became her name and woke her.

"Sarai! Sarai! Why are you shouting like that?"

Sililli was leaning over her, holding her hands, her face distorted with fear in the dim light of the oil lamp.

"Are you sick?" Sililli was asking. "Where does it hurt?"

Sarai could not answer. The fire in her belly was sucking the air from her lungs. She could hardly breathe.

"It's only a nightmare," Sililli said, imploringly. "You must wake up."

The fire made her limbs ice cold. She could feel them becoming hard and brittle. She opened her mouth wide, trying desperately to breathe. Sililli seized Sarai around the waist and supported her back, which was arching as if it would break. Suddenly, everything inside her became soft, dusty, like something rotten reduced to ashes. The air finally entered her lungs, sweeping away the ash and what remained of the fire. She saw blackness coming. An immense, welcoming darkness. She was happy to vanish into it.

She did not hear Sililli's screams, which woke the whole of Ichbi Sum-Usur's household.

Until daybreak, they thought she was dead.

Sililli filled the women's courtyard with weeping. Ichbi Sum-Usur ordered all the fires to be extinguished. Shutting himself away in the temple of the house, he prostrated himself before the statues of his ancestors with a fervor that astonished his eldest son. Kiddin watched the tears streaming down his father's cheeks with a mixture of disappointment and disgust. When he saw him lie down on the floor and empty a goblet of cold ashes over his noble head, the thought occurred to him that the gods were infinitely wise: They had taken his sister from the world. A sister incapable of abiding by the laws and duties of women. An ill-fated sister who attracted demons but could still melt the heart of an overfond father. Had she lived a few more years, he and his father would both have become the laughingstocks of Ur.

Just before dawn, Egime let out a cry.

"Sarai's alive! She's alive, she's breathing!"

She repeated it until Ichbi Sum-Usur rushed to the women's quarters and a stunned silence ensued.

Replacing Sililli, who could not bear to approach the corpse of the girl she considered her own child, Egime had been about to wash, purify, and dress Sarai for her journey to the underworld. But doubt had stayed her hand.

"She isn't cold and she isn't stiff," she explained. "And parts of her stomach are burning hot. I put my hand on her chest and listened to her mouth: She's breathing."

As they stood there before Sarai's inert body on her beautiful bridal bed, Egime called them to witness. She held a dove's feather close to her niece's cracked lips. The feather shook, and slowly bent, first in one direction then the other. There was no doubt about it: Air was entering and leaving Sarai's body.

"She's alive," Egime said. "She's just sleeping."

Sililli yelped like a ewe being slaughtered, and collapsed on the floor. Ichbi Sum-Usur was shaken by a long, nervous laugh.

Kiddin shot him a fierce look, and he managed to stifle it. He ordered all the fires to be relit, one hundred *silà* of cedarwood shavings to be burned, and Sarai's young aunts to purify themselves and go to the great temple of Inanna to offer half a flock of small livestock in his name.

When the sun had reached its zenith, Sarai was still asleep. She was still asleep at twilight. Sililli, who had been watching over this stubborn sleep as if she were watching a pot of milk on a fire, turned to Egime.

"It isn't possible. She can't be asleep."

"She is. I know what happened. The punishment finally came. Her intended husband's gods asked Ereshkigal for justice, and Ereshkigal sent his great demon Pazzuzzu to take her last night and drag her down to hell. But Sarai must have found a way to move him. You know how she is. The demon finally let her go. She was so exhausted when she came back, she needs many hours' sleep."

Sililli thought for a while, then shook her head. "Things may have happened that way. . . . But did Pazzuzzu let her go just so she could sleep?"

"That's what she's doing."

"No. I know what sleep is. You move, your limbs twitch. She hasn't moved a muscle since this morning."

"It'll come," Egime replied, with a touch of irritation. "The way you sleep when you come back from the underworld is no ordinary sleep."

"It isn't sleep at all!" Sililli went on, stubbornly. "She's still sick. That's what I think."

"She's asleep. It doesn't really matter what you think."

"What do you mean? I'm almost like her mother. Her life is my life! She's as much part of me as if she had come out of me."

"Some use that's been! We've all appreciated the kind of behavior you taught her!"

Soon, the two women were arguing so violently that they had to be separated. Egime left Sarai's bedchamber in a furious temper, which she took out on anyone who approached her.

Alone with Sarai's thin, motionless body, Sililli was more than ever confirmed in her opinion. How was it possible to sleep with two women screaming by your side? No sleep could be as deep as that.

With a terrible sense of foreboding, she decided to give Sarai another wash. In the middle of changing the bed, she came across the five little packets of dried leaves.

Evil herbs, the kind the *kassaptus* made!

White and cracked from being left for a long time in boiled water!

"Great Ea! O Great Ea, protect us!"

Now she knew why Sarai had been gone from the house a whole day. Egime could shut her eyes to the truth as much as she liked. Sarai was definitely not asleep.

But she might as well be dead.

By the next day, Sarai had still not opened her eyes and everyone was of Sililli's opinion: She was not asleep.

But Sililli, her skin gray and her eyes red from lack of sleep, kept her secret deep inside her. With her own hands, she had burned the packets, destroying the last traces of the sacrilege. She was sure Ichbi Sum-Usur would prefer to go to his tomb unaware that his daughter had obtained herbs from a witch. She was strong enough to bury Sarai's secret so deep in her heart that she managed to perform her daily purifications and her interminable petitions to Inanna with almost as much faith and purity as before.

Not that she had any better idea than anyone else how to bring Sarai back to the land of the living. While Ichbi Sum-Usur was spending a fortune on offerings to all the gods and goddesses who could care for the welfare of the family, Sililli did her best to keep Sarai from dying of hunger and thirst before the work of the underworld could be undone.

She made a gruel of barley and peach water and, with infinite patience, spooned it into Sarai's mouth. Sometimes, with a jolt that was like a hiccup, her throat would take it in. More often than not, though, it would stay there until Sililli pulled it out with her fingers.

Egime, watching from the threshold of the bedchamber, could not help admonishing her to use just the peach water. "You're going to end up choking her with that gruel of yours! What's the point in feeding someone who's asleep?"

"To let them dream," Sililli replied, unswayed.

When evening fell, Ichbi Sum-Usur entered Sarai's bedchamber with the soothsayer who had performed the oracle before she was due to get married.

The *barù* was told in detail how Sarai had fallen unconscious. As best she could, Sililli described her cries and her sufferings. The *barù* questioned her about the days and hours that had preceded that terrible moment. Sililli did not tell the truth, but she was not too afraid about misleading the *barù*. After all, the soothsayer had his own ways to distinguish true from false; that was his task, that was what he was paid for.

The soothsayer had his instruments — the hearths, the cedarwood shavings, the oils, the lamps, the finely written clay tablets, the sheep's livers, hearts, and lungs — brought into Sarai's bedchamber and arranged on wicker tables at the foot of her bed. Then he asked to be left alone and for the door to be closed.

Late that night, he appeared suddenly on the threshold of the brightly lit chamber, waking those who were waiting on the terrace. Sarai's father let out a cry that terrified the women. The *barù* raised his hands to calm them.

"Ichbi Sum-Usur's daughter has her eyes open," he declared, and there was a touch of surprise in his voice. "She's no longer asleep."

Sililli was the first to rush to her. The soothsayer was right. Sarai had even sat up in bed, trembling like a leaf. She recognized Sililli, smiled vaguely, and fell back again.

Sililli caught her hands, begging almighty Ea not to let her say anything in her confused state that might compromise her.

"What happened to me?" was all Sarai asked.

Sililli hugged her and whispered in her ear that she knew everything, that the most important thing was to keep silent.

"I've said it before and the examination confirms it," the *barù* said. "The daughter of Ichbi Sum-Usur pleases Ishtar. The Lady of War is asking for her. The daughter of Ichbi Sum-Usur is made for the temple. She will have to renounce the bridal blood, or she will die."

Part Two

THE TEMPLE OF ISHTAR

The Sacred Handmaid

There were about a hundred of them, standing in four rows in the great courtyard of the temple. A hundred young men in leather capes and leather helmets, with spears and shields in their hands. In the darkness before the dawn, the gold borders on their helmets, the insignia of the officers, were invisible, as were their faces. Around them huge statues stood guard, statues of Enki and Ea, of Dumuzi, the god who died and rose again, ancestor of all the Almighty Ancestors of Ur, and, glowing in the dark, the gold statue of Ishtar, the Lady of War.

There they stood, motionless. They had been waiting for this moment since twilight.

One by one, the naphtha fires that illuminated the walls and staircases of the ziggurat were extinguished. For a brief instant, the night returned, made up of stars and the milk of the gods. Then the sky gradually grew brighter, and the light of day obliterated the stars. The gold borders on the young officers' helmets began to shine. Their eyes shone, too, with a pained stillness.

Up above them, the sacred columns, lapis lazuli slabs, bronze corbels, and silver reliefs of the Sublime Bedchamber captured the first rays of the sun.

A sigh quivered in the air. The noise of horns and drums rang out. On the platform of the temple, the singers of Ishtar, dressed in purple togas, launched into their prayer:

> *O illustrious lady,*
> *Star of the warlike clamor,*
> *Queen of all inhabited places, you who*
> *   open your immense arms of light . . .*

With deep-throated fervor, the young officers joined in the chant:

> *You who set brother against brother,*
> *You who make the gods waver, who*
> *   terrify the living by your mere ap-*
> *   pearance,*
> *Grant us your grace,*
> *O shepherdess of the multitudes . . .*

The great doors of the temple opened, and two wagons entered the courtyard, each pulled by a team of four horses. Between the wagons, a dozen soldiers held a bull at bay with their lowered spears. An agate-and-crystal wig rested between the bull's horns, and its flanks were covered with a rug embellished with brass rings and bronze and ivory beads.

Slowly, as the sun descended the Staircase of Heaven, the wagons and the bull took up position before the warriors.

It was then that she appeared, up on the sacred platform.

She was unrecognizable in a diadem surmounted by three golden flowers with carnelian hearts, a white toga gathered at the waist by a gold belt in the shape of intertwined ears of barley, which underlined the beauty of her figure, and an impressive necklace of turquoise pearls and gold and bronze balls. Kiddin recognized her from the way she walked.

He was there, in the very front row of the young officers. And it was definitely her, as astonishingly beautiful as he had heard she was: Sarai, the Sacred Handmaid of the Blood!

Without realizing it, he beat his spear against his shield, and a hundred hands imitated him. Startled by the noise, the bull bellowed.

Sarai advanced between the singers and the priests. Her steps seemed to be supported less by the platform than by the muffled beating of the spears. Her hands held in front of her, palms out, she took up the chant that poured from their ardent throats:

> *O Star of the warlike clamor,*
> *Celestial light that blazes against our*
>   *enemies,*
>   *O quick-tempered Ishtar, ruin of*
>   *the arrogant!*

A prayer of flesh and blood attempting to shake the heavens. The sun, in its eternal motion, reached the dense foliage that encircled the middle of the ziggurat.

Kiddin tried to catch his sister's eye. But between the thick lines of kohl, Sarai's gaze remained fixed, her pupils dark and distant. As he looked at this woman who was almost a stranger, Kiddin could not help briefly recalling the image of the rebellious, destructive girl who had brought their house close to disaster.

Seven or eight years had passed since the time his sister had nearly died, years that had sculpted her figure and her face until they were perfect. With her finely drawn lips, reddened now with amber, her high cheekbones, her strong shoulders, she had the authority, the passion, the heavenly remoteness of Ishtar herself.

At last the sun reached the lower steps of the Staircase of Heaven, and Sarai raised her arms.

Instantly, there was silence. The priests stopped their drumming and the handmaids their chanting. The warriors no longer smote their shields, and their throats were stilled. They watched, agog, as Sarai's toga slipped from her right shoulder, baring a breast as luminous as the orb of the moon.

The bull lifted its head in surprise, making its finery rattle, and rolled its bulging eyes, as if the better to see the priestess in her white toga as she glided to the edge of the platform. Like the warriors, he shuddered when the Sacred Handmaid of Blood launched into her petition:

I invoke you, O almighty princess Ishtar,
*   You whom I serve night and day,*
Listen to the request of your chosen
*   daughter,*
Listen to the petition of one whose blood
*   you held back,*
Show mercy to the warriors of your son
*   Shu-Sin . . .*

Sarai turned her back on the bull and the warriors, and faced the golden gaze of the statue of Ishtar. Like mirrors, the golden flowers of her diadem blazed in the sun.

You who straddle the great Powers,
You who reduce shields to dust,
Show grace to these warriors who have
waited for you to wake,
Keep their bodies free from wounds,
The tears of death and the shame of defeat.

Her prayer came to an abrupt halt. Time stood still. The silence weighed on the warriors, as heavily as the shadow of the ziggurat had weighed on them during the night.

Slowly, Sarai's body began to sway.

The drums began to beat.

A muffled drumbeat accompanied each step the priestess took, giving rhythm to her dance and accentuating the undulation of her hips.

The warriors beat their spears against the shields, and cried, "Ilulama! Ilulama!"

Step by step, still dancing, the Sacred Handmaid descended toward the beast. The bull lowered its muzzle and pointed its horns at her. Sarai continued to advance, hips swaying to the swell of the drums and the cries of the warriors.

The bull clawed the ground, bellowed, and retreated, panting. Kiddin's voice shook. Sarai writhed in front of the bull, her gold belt glittering in its pupils. Kiddin's fist teased on his spear. Sarai clapped her hands. Simultaneously, ten spears sank into the bull's neck. The blood spurted, spattering the young officers. Sarai spoke the final words:

> *O my sovereign,*
> *You who hold the sacred sleeve,*
> *With your foaming mouth*
> *Drink the blood of the angry bull, eat his*
> *   raging heart*
> *And support their fight . . .*

"I don't like you going so close to the horns," Sililli muttered; it was clear from her voice that this was one of her bad days. "It isn't necessary. I know: I asked the priests. They all said the same thing: 'The Sacred Handmaid of the Blood can stay on the platform while the bull is being killed.' "

Sililli had followed the ceremony in silence, but now, as she unfastened the clasps of Sarai's toga, she gave vent to her anxiety.

"There's no risk," Sarai replied. "My Sovereign protects me."

Sililli pulled a face. "One of these days you may have to deal with a bull who's fiercer than the others. One thrust, and it'll cut you in two."

"Why would Ishtar allow that to happen? No priestess in this temple is more devoted to her than I am. I've counted: Since the war with the *Gutis* resumed, I've offered blood eighty-seven times for the officers."

"Oh, I know! I know you're good at arithmetic, as you are at so many other things! It makes no difference. You're going closer and closer to the bulls. They don't like it, and neither do I."

"Well, I like it!" Sarai laughed, taking off the last of her clothes. Her pale skin was glistening with sweat; with her fingertips, she wiped a few drops from between her breasts. "If I didn't, it'd be boring. And all these handsome warriors wouldn't be so eager."

With a mockingly lascivious swivel of her hips, she stepped into the scented bath. Predicting more disasters, Sililli went over to the statue of Inanna that sat enthroned in the center of the vast room and put the golden diadem, the necklace, the belt, and the toga on it.

They were in one of the countless chambers of the *giparù*, the huge residence of the priestesses of Inanna, which stood within the sacred walls of the temple, next to the ziggurat. The walls of the chamber were hung with rugs; daylight entered through great arched windows, and aromatic incense was burning. Pure water gurgled through a succession of basins covered with glazed bricks. It was a place where the Sacred Handmaids would sometimes gather to purify themselves, or where King Shu-Sin's sister, the High Priestess of Inanna, would invite one or other of them to join her for a peaceful chat and a rest from the long prayers. But whenever Sarai faced the bull and offered its blood to the warriors, she had the privilege of purifying herself alone.

She closed her eyes and abandoned herself voluptuously to the water, which was only slightly warmer than body heat. The argument with Sililli was not a new one. With the years, Sililli had not only grown fatter and slower. Her temperament had changed, too, and she was constantly worrying about the very things that made Sarai feel strong and powerful. After all, what did the most respected Sacred Handmaid of the Blood in the whole temple have to fear?

"There's no reason for you to worry about me, Sililli," Sarai said, in a calm voice.

She heard sandaled feet shuffling across the brick floor, and Sililli's fingers, softened by the scented ointment, closed on her shoulders and began their delectable massage.

"You know perfectly well there are always reasons to worry," Sililli grumbled. "And besides, there are other things I don't like about the way you dance."

"Please don't spoil the best moment of the day."

"Is it really necessary for you to show your breasts to these hotheaded young men? Do you think they're indifferent to the sight? You're beautiful enough to inflame them fully clothed! There's no need to arouse them before they've even left for the war."

Sarai had no time to reply. The bronze bell at the entrance of the room chimed, and two young handmaids appeared and bowed.

"Sacred Handmaid," they said, in perfect unison, "an officer who is also a lord wishes to speak with you. He received your blessing this morning and wants to thank you."

"You see," Sililli muttered, sourly.

"Who is he?"

"The eldest son of Lord Ichbi Sum-Usur."

Sililli's fingers tightened on Sarai's shoulders.

"Kiddin?" Sarai said, her eyes wide with surprise. "Was he there this morning? Well, let him wait in the little courtyard, if he has the patience. I'll join him when I'm ready."

He was standing in the middle of the courtyard, without his spear or his shield, but still wearing his cape and his gold-festooned helmet. He had his back to her, watching the handmaids arranging the innumerable dishes for the meal of the idols on palanquins of bulrushes in front of the kitchens. It had been a very long time since brother and sister had been face-to-face. His shoulders were broader. Sarai was sure he had become a formidable and promising warrior. He turned to greet her, and beneath the abundant hair and beard, his face and smile were as she had always known them. Kiddin bowed, with all the respect of which he was capable.

"May Ea be gracious to you, Sacred Handmaid."

Without awaiting her greeting in return, he launched immediately into a flowery speech, telling her how strongly he had felt the presence of Ishtar, thanks to the invocation of the Sacred Handmaid of the Blood, and how protected and encouraged he had felt, who would soon be leading the soldiers of Ur against the invaders from the mountains.

"And all of us who were present this morning will carry in our memories your courage before the bull. If we were to weaken in battle, we have only to remember you. Just as you defied the bull's horns, so we shall defy the swords of our enemies."

Sarai smiled. Kiddin — proud, haughty, handsome Kiddin, who cared as much for his body as his rank — was making a huge effort to please her and even, in his way, to appear humble.

"Good day, brother," she replied, her tone distant rather than affectionate. "I'm pleased that the invocation was of benefit to you."

"It was, Sacred Handmaid, be sure of that."

Kiddin rose to his full height and looked Sarai up and down. There was nothing humble in his gaze. Nothing brotherly, either. It was the kind of look that made Sililli's hackles rise. The look of a young animal, inflamed by Sarai's beauty and heavy with desire.

Kiddin put his hand inside his leather cape and took out a necklace of gold beads, carnelians, and silver rings.

"Accept this gift. May it enhance your

beauty, the greatest my eyes have ever contemplated."

Sarai laughed, so loudly that the handmaids turned their heads. "Gratitude, soft words, a necklace . . . I can't believe my eyes or my ears! What's happening to you, Kiddin? Has the prospect of battle sweetened your character, dear brother?"

"We aren't children anymore!" Kiddin retorted, curling his lips. "The time for squabbling is over. You have been enhancing our father's name in this temple for many moons now, and I am grateful to you. I may have been unfair toward you in the past. Who could ever have guessed that your whims were ruled by the hand of Inanna? You're right, though: I have a duty to be humble before you. My words and my gift are sincere. And my pride is great: Like everyone in our house, I've heard the news, Sacred Handmaid of the Blood."

Once again, he bowed respectfully, holding his hand out for Sarai to take the necklace, which she had still not touched.

"The news?" she asked, frowning.

"Oh . . . Didn't you know? True, our father only found out about it yesterday. Our almighty sovereign has named you to be his sacred spouse in the Sublime Bedchamber when seedtime next comes around."

The shock of it took Sarai's breath away. Emboldened, Kiddin stepped forward and placed the necklace in his sister's hands.

"Don't be surprised," he said, in a low but excited voice. "We'd been expecting this choice for a long time. Who could lay greater claim to such an honor? There is no priestess in all the temples of Ur, Eridu, or even Larsa who has been free of the bridal blood for as long as you. Seven years! Not to mention your beauty . . . Never before has Inanna been so present in a priestess, or so powerful. Now that war is looming, who better than you to replace the Lady of War in the king's sacred bed?"

Sarai wanted to free her hands, but Kiddin would not let go of them.

"You are doing our house an enormous honor. My one wish is to become your equal. Once you have been united with him, the mighty Shu-Sin will entrust me with one of his four armies. Rightly so. Thanks to your blessing this morning, I shall fight like a lion as soon as battle begins. Think, sister, how important our family will soon be in Ur! You, the Priestess of the Sublime Bed-chamber, and I the Bull of War."

"We haven't reached that point yet," Sarai replied, coldly. "There's nothing certain about the king's choice. Don't trust rumors. In the temple, words spread like flies!"

"Oh, no! You can be quite certain of what I'm telling you. But that isn't the reason I'm here. I've come to inform you that my father desires your presence in our house. He has refurbished our temple to make it worthy of the Sacred Handmaid of the Blood, and he wishes you to make the first offerings to the new statues of our ancestors."

Sarai hesitated. Kiddin was aware of it.

"If you refused," he went on, effortlessly resuming his old tone, which had lost all trace of tenderness or humility, "nobody would understand. Since you started living in the temple, I can't recall you setting foot in our house more than three times. If you didn't come to salute our ancestors, it would be an insult to the living and the dead."

A few days later, Sarai entered Ichbi Sum-Usur's house with an escort of handmaids, including Sililli. The whole household had gathered in the courtyard. Behind her father and brother stood her aunts, uncles, and cousins, as well as the handmaids, gardeners, and slaves. The family wore ceremonial togas with tasseled and embroidered hems, and had put on their wigs and jewelry.

Kiddin was right, Sarai thought, as she advanced across the petal-strewn mats and rugs. It was so long since she had last been here that she barely recognized the place. Ichbi Sum-Usur had had the communal rooms surrounding the courtyard decorated with massive columns, on which the sunlight formed geometric shadows. On all of them, there were splendid bas-reliefs of glazed brick, carved with scenes from the lives of the gods. The colors, the forms, the subtlety of the contours were remarkable: It was as though the Lords of Heaven were about to leap into the courtyard, as alive as humans.

Ichbi Sum-Usur, too, had a new solidity about him. At the waist, his toga bulged with rolls of flesh, and the jowls of his face ended in a self-satisfied double chin. His natural hair was covered with a heavy, oiled wig. His joy at seeing his beloved daughter again was sincere. Gently, with a new deference, he bowed to her, offering his palms to heaven, in a mark of respect she had only ever seen him grant the most powerful. His eyes dimmed with emotion.

"Sacred Handmaid of the Blood, welcome to my house. May Enlil, Ea, and the Lady of the Moon be thanked."

While their father was speaking, Kiddin

bowed deeply, as did the rest of the household. As a sign of his new rank, he wore the symbolic ax of the king's officers in his belt. When he straightened up again, a smile as white as salt in the sun shone through his dark beard.

Sarai approached her father. She took his hands in hers, brought them to her forehead, and bowed in her turn.

"My father! Here I am only Sarai, your daughter. You used to call me 'my beloved daughter.' "

She was unable to continue. Abruptly tearing his hands from hers, Ichbi Sum-Usur stepped back. "No, no, Sacred Handmaid! That cannot be! Now Ea is your only father and Inanna your sweet mother. I, Ichbi Sum-Usur, am merely the humble mortal who led you into this life so that they could choose you."

Sarai opened her mouth to protest.

"My father is right!" Kiddin said, forestalling her, in a voice loud enough to be heard by everybody. "The daughter and sister we knew died six years ago, during those days when she slept with a sleep that was not human and Ishtar revealed to her the Heaven of the Lords. The woman who opened her eyes again is forever our beloved Sacred Handmaid of the Blood. To call her otherwise would be to offend the Lords of Heaven."

Sarai felt a coldness in her chest, a coldness as icy as a winter wind. She was on the point of reminding Kiddin of the words he himself had used when he had come to ask an audience of her in the *giparù,* words he was now forbidding everyone to use: "Sarai," "my sister," "my very dear sister."

But she remained silent. Kiddin may not have been sincere, but the same could not be said of her father or the others, who were looking at her with intense respect — respect and fear.

Yes, for them she was the Goddess of War made flesh! The capricious girl, the rebel who needed constant supervision, had disappeared. The gods had chosen her. The sadness of it seized her by the throat. She had never felt so alone in her life.

With resignation, she did what was expected of her until the sun reached the zenith. The temple was newly decorated; altars of precious wood had been set up and strewn with petals, ready to welcome new statues of the ancestors. She uttered prayers, sang the praises of the dead, burned perfumes, gave and received offerings. She did all with a mechanical indifference that passed for the usual detachment of a priestess accustomed to such ceremonies. From time to time, she sensed how pleased her father and the household were, and she forced herself to find a kind of satisfaction in that.

When at last the sun was at its zenith, they returned to the great courtyard, where tables and cushions had been arranged for a banquet. Tradition demanded that all the members of the family had to sit down to a meal to which the statues of the ancestors would be invited, like relatives returning from a long journey. Until they had taken their places among the living and been served large portions of the richest dishes, nobody would be allowed to drink or touch any of the food.

Everyone sat down according to their rank. Handmaids placed a seat for Sarai in the center of a small dais, between Ichbi Sum-Usur and the aunts. As soon as she was seated, a strange stillness seized everyone. Nobody said a word. The house froze, as if it was populated by statues. The only sign of life came from the birds flying overhead and casting strong shadows.

A shiver ran down Sarai's neck and her shoulders. Discreetly, she clenched her fists to stop her fingers from trembling. She felt

163

fear in the small of her back, like a wave of pain.

Suddenly, she no longer saw the tense faces of her relatives sitting at the banquet tables, but instead another dais that had been set up on this very spot, one day long ago. She no longer heard the heavy silence as they waited for the ancestors, but rather, the din of wedding chants. At her feet, she saw a basin of scented water. She saw herself standing naked before her father and the man who wanted her as his wife, and felt once again the contact of the oily water on her skin as she slipped into it with despair in her heart.

It was so long ago! So long since she had last thought of all that! So long since she had dreamed of a *mar.Tu* who would come and take her far away from Ur through the power of a single kiss!

A long creaking, like a moan, made her jump. The great door of the house was finally opening. Freshly painted and resplendent, Ichbi Sum-Usur's five ancestors appeared, carried on cane palanquins.

They crouched life-size on purple, black, and white cushions. Their curly wigs swayed on their shoulders, and their togas were perfectly pleated. Their severe faces were wrinkled with age and their ivory and lapis lazuli eyes seemed to pierce the souls of the living as surely as arrows. Each of them held in one hand a golden sheaf of barley or corn; in the other, a sickle or some writing tablets.

These were statues of rare perfection. Murmurs of approval were heard in the courtyard. The stillness suddenly broke, and the assembly raised their arms and broke into a fervent chant.

> *O Fathers of our fathers,*
> *Seed of the damp earth,*
> *Sperm of our destinies,*
> *O beloved fathers . . .*

Ichbi Sum-Usur and Kiddin stood up and held out their hands. Their faces were red, and their eyes shone. The slaves moved the palanquins close to the dais and carefully placed the statues between the perfume burners. Standing behind them, Sarai recognized his face.

It all happened so slowly, it was as if the laws of nature had been suspended. In reality, it took but a fleeting moment.

Two men entered the courtyard, a few steps behind the ancestors. When the statues were put down, they both came to a

165

halt. One of them was old, the other in the full flower of his youth. They were wearing the thick gray linen robes of the *mar.Tu,* which was what had attracted Sarai's attention. The older one had a wrinkled face and hands made white by kneading clay. Their postures were reverential, even slightly anxious. The younger one stood stiffly and frowned as he peered about him more in surprise than in admiration. His eyes took in the sun-drenched bas-reliefs, then turned to the dais. Luminous brown eyes, that came to rest on Kiddin and on Ichbi Sum-Usur. It was him.

It seemed as though he did not dare to meet her gaze; admiring only her toga, her figure. She did not realize that she was slowly moving forward on the dais. A voice inside her repeated: "It's him, I know it's him."

He had grown taller, his shoulders broader, his neck thicker. His mouth was framed by a finely curled beard, slightly glossy in the sun. The voice inside her said, "I recognize his lips, it really is him."

He raised his eyes to hers, intrigued, not recognizing her, yet unable to turn his gaze from her.

The voice inside her repeated: "These are his lips. They haven't changed, and I'll never forget them. But how will he possibly be able to recognize me?"

The chants and the music became a painful din. She felt as if she were calling out above the noise: "Abram! Abram! Abram, I'm Sarai . . ."

He gave a start. The old man looked at him anxiously.

A hand closed over Sarai's arm.

"What are you doing?"

Kiddin pulled her back roughly. She realized that she had been standing right at the edge of the dais. Her feet were almost touching one of the statues. From the courtyard, faces turned toward her in alarm.

She continued to stare at Abram. She detected a smile on his lips. He had recognized her. She was sure of it.

"What's gotten into you?" Kiddin said, angrily.

Ichbi Sum-Usur intervened. "How dare you lay a hand on the Sacred Handmaid, my son?"

"Who are those two *mar.Tu* in the courtyard?" Kiddin asked, ignoring his father's question. "What are they doing here?"

"It's the potter and his son, who made the statues. They did such a good job that I gave them permission to accompany our ancestors to the temple."

Sarai was barely listening. Perhaps she hadn't even spoken Abram's name out loud. And yet, she was sure that he had heard it.

"I want them out of the courtyard!" Kiddin ordered, pointing to the strangers.

"Son!"

"Do what I ask of you, Father. I want these *mar.Tu* out of our house at once!"

Abram understood Kiddin's gesture. He seized his father's arm and pulled him toward the door. As they were about to disappear, Sarai spoke his name in a loud, clear voice: "Abram."

This time, Kiddin and Ichbi Sum-Usur heard her. But her father, carried away by the power of the ceremony, the chanting, and the music, was already holding out to his daughter the first platters of offerings.

Before she took them, Sarai looked at Kiddin, who was still shaking with rage.

"Don't you ever dare raise your hand to me again, son of Ichbi Sum-Usur," she said, in a calm voice, "or the bull's blood could well become your own."

Sililli, as plaintive as if the roof of the temple had fallen on her shoulders, was spouting her usual nonsense: "You're mad, Kiddin will never forgive you for this insult . . . The *mar. Tu* is back and already the trouble is starting . . . I thought you had changed, I thought you had forgotten! Why haven't the gods taken these memories from you?"

None of what had happened in the courtyard of Ichbi Sum-Usur's house had escaped her. But she had managed to keep silent until they had returned to the temple. It was only when Sarai had asked for her help that the torrent of complaints and terrors had poured out.

Patiently, Sarai took her hands, and, without raising her voice, repeated her request: that Sililli go to the tents of the *mar. Tu* and thank Terah the potter for the beauty of the statues. "Tell him I apologize for Kiddin's roughness and the way he insulted them. Tell him that to make amends, I, the Sacred Handmaid of the Blood, invite his son Abram to share my dawn meal, the day after tomorrow."

Sililli rolled her eyes. "You can't ask him to come here! It's blasphemy to bring a *mar. Tu* here! It will be a blemish on the temple! What will happen if the others find out? I know: The high priestess will tell the king. And that will be the end of it; he won't want you in the Sublime Bedchamber anymore."

"Stop this nonsense and use your brain!" Sarai said, exasperated. "It's quite normal for a potter to come to the temple. They're always coming here to bring their work."

"But not here, in the *giparù*. Not to share a meal with a priestess. Kiddin's right, you're leading us straight to disaster." Sarai moved away, her face as hard and arrogant as if she were facing the bull. "All right. I'll manage without you."

With a gesture, she ordered Sililli to leave her. But Sililli did not move. With her plump fingers, she wiped the tears that were forming on her eyelids.

"What are you going to say to your *mar.Tu?*" she asked, in a weary, tremulous, and barely audible voice. "That no blood has flowed between your thighs for six years? Even the *mar.Tu* want women with fertile wombs."

Sarai went red, as if Sililli had slapped her. But the handmaid had no intention of keeping silent.

"Haven't you understood yet? You are the Sacred Handmaid of the Blood. And that is what you will remain. Here, you're respected and envied. The warriors love you because they hope that, thanks to you, they won't be wounded in battle. But outside this temple, Sarai, you're nothing but a woman with a barren womb."

"You have no right to talk to me like that."

"I have every right," Sililli said, her face distorted with sorrow. "It was I who kept silent for you all these years. It was I who burned the witch's herbs. The gods have already forgiven you once. Don't demand too much of them."

Sarai's anger faded as abruptly as it had come. In a long-forgotten impulse, she crouched by Sililli, embraced her, and rested her head on her shoulder.

"All I ask is to see and hear him once," she whispered. "Just once. To know if he, too, has thought about me all these years."

"And then?" Sililli asked.

"Then everything will be as it was before."

Sarai did not think he would come. Sililli had not brought back any reply to her message.

"He looked at me as if I was a crazy old woman. Which means that he at least is sensible. He simply waited for me to leave. His father thanked me, and that was it."

It was agreed that Sililli would wait for him at dusk by the door in the outer wall, behind the *giparù,* a narrow door normally used by those bringing in animals, carts laden with grain, and all the supplies needed for the offerings. In the early hours of the morning, nobody would notice a *mar.Tu* among the busy crowd of servants and slaves.

During the night, with Sililli's reluctant help, Sarai had discreetly arranged lamps, cushions, and trays of food in one of the small rooms where spare togas and finery were stored in preparation for the great seedtime ceremony. It was reached through a narrow corridor within the huge wall surrounding the *giparù*, which only the handmaids used. Once Abram had arrived, Sililli would have to stand in the corridor, keeping guard.

But now, as she waited in silence between these narrow walls, Sarai began to have her doubts. She had to admit that Sililli was right about many things. Cruel truths that she tried to ignore, as you try to ignore an intense but incurable pain.

But just as she had been convinced as a young girl that a kiss from Abram would purify her for the rest of her married life, so now, too, she hoped for a kind of miracle from their meeting.

Not that she had lied to Sililli. It might be true that all she wanted was to know that during all these years, he, too, had not forgotten her.

But what if he didn't come?

She dismissed the question. She had to be patient. Time was passing very slowly, and outside the sun had barely risen.

The shuffling of sandals made her jump. There he was, standing in the flickering light of the oil lamps.

There was a brief moment of embarrassment. Then he bowed ceremoniously. His first words were to apologize for not knowing how a Sacred Handmaid of the Blood in the temple of Ishtar ought to be addressed. His voice had not changed. He still had his *mar.Tu* accent.

"With a lot of respect and even more fear," she replied.

They both laughed. A laugh such as Sarai had not had for a long time, a laugh like cool water, which dispelled some of their awkwardness.

They sat down on the cushions, with a low table between them. Apart from his bushy hair and beard, he had hardly changed. His mouth was still just as beautiful, just as perfect. His cheekbones were perhaps more prominent. It was the face of a determined man who had already confronted trials in his life.

Sarai poured an infusion of thyme and rosemary into brass goblets. "I was afraid you wouldn't come," she said.

"My father and brothers didn't want me to. They're terrified at the thought that my presence here is a blasphemy. They're afraid of your father and your brother. We *mar. Tu* are like that. We fear many things."

His self-assured tone was as she remembered it. There was a new element to it now: a calm amusement, the detachment of a man who liked to reflect about ideas before he made them his. He drank some of the infusion.

"I left our tents in the middle of the night, without them seeing me. I took some pottery from my father's kiln so they would think that I was bringing it to the temple. I gave it to your handmaid. My offering to your goddess!"

Sarai could feel her heart beating faster. These words were like the first glimpse of what was to come: He, too, was cheating and lying for her.

"That last time, when we met on the riverbank, you also had to sneak out to bring food and skins."

Abram nodded and smiled. "Yes . . . It was so long ago . . ."

"But you haven't forgotten."

"No."

The embarrassment returned all at once. They ate dates and honey cakes. Abram clearly had a healthy appetite. As she watched him making these simple gestures, Sarai felt a strange new pleasure — new and also disturbing. Above the collar of Abram's tunic, the skin at the base of his neck seemed to her extremely smooth. She wanted to touch it.

"That morning," she said, "the soldiers found me and took me back to my father's house." She gave a little laugh. "He was very angry. But a few moons later, I managed to escape again. I went to your camp. I wanted to . . . to thank you for your help. But they told me your family had gone."

"We'd left for the North, and we stayed there."

Abram told her how, after leading the flocks to the huge royal tax center at Puzri-Dagan, Terah had decided to settle in Nippur to sell his pottery.

"There are temples everywhere there. The lords want new statues of their ancestors every year," Abram said, amused.

While his father's workshop prospered, he and his brothers, Haran and Nahor, had raised herds of small livestock for the great families of Nippur. In three or four years, thanks as much to the livestock as to his father's pottery, they had grown sufficiently prosperous to have their own herds. Soon they had so many animals that each time they left the tax center at Puzri-Dagan, they would move the herds from one city to another, from Urum to Adab, hugging the mountain slopes where the grass grew in abundance.

"My father, Terah, has become the chief of our tribe. A large tribe, numbering more than five hundred tents . . . But last winter, war broke out again with the people of the mountain. On the way to Adab, the *Gutis* pillaged our homes and storehouses and stole our herds. That's what always happens: Whenever a war breaks out between cities, they start by stealing our animals and raping our women, and nobody comes to our aid. We aren't made for war, so my father decided to return to Ur." Once again, his eyes creased in an amused smile. "The lords of Ur are very happy we're back. They all like the *mar.Tu* Terah's pottery. Your father, for one."

"I like it, too. It's beautiful."

Abram laughed, ate a date, and waved his hand as if her words were smoke. "And you," he said, his eyes still smiling, "how is it that you've become the most beautiful of women, and yet in all this time no lord of Ur has taken you as his wife?"

Sarai felt her throat go dry and the blood burn her cheeks. Abram was like that. He did not beat about the bush, and knew how to catch her off guard, answering questions he had not yet been asked. She had thought about the words she would say to him. Now they all seemed to sound contrived.

Sililli's words echoed in her head: "Even the *mar.Tu* want women with fertile wombs!" Hers was barren, and had been barren for so long that she doubted she would ever again see the blood flow between her legs. But could she explain to Abram that she had taken a *kassaptu*'s drug in her despair at not having received a kiss from him? That she had been an irresponsible child, incapable of grasping the consequences of her acts?

"No, no man can marry a handmaid of Ishtar," she finally stammered.

Abram's face froze. Avoiding his gaze, Sarai told him briefly how she had become "sick" soon after their encounter, and how the soothsayer had understood the significance of her sojourn in the underworld and had encouraged her to become a daughter of the temple.

He listened without batting an eyelid while she explained, with a certain pride, how for five long years she had learned all the skills of the priestesses: writing on tablets, poetry, chanting, dancing, preparing offerings, and, finally, dominating the bull.

"The bull?" he said in surprise.

That was his only interruption.

"Yes, that's what it means to be the Sacred Handmaid of the Blood: to salute the bull and then offer his blood to the goddess of war."

She explained how the bull's blood that flowed before the warriors leaving for battle protected them from injury and death. The gods, once their thirst was quenched, would breathe a little of their omnipotence into the arms of the human beings who had made the offering. She omitted that the priestess did not menstruate, and was as dry as dust under the feet of a conqueror.

When she stopped, Abram thought for a moment, and shook his head. "You spill a bull's blood to please your gods so that they should support you? But what if the warriors on the other side do the same? How can the gods choose which side to support? Perhaps they support both sides, and there's no winner and no loser. Perhaps they support neither side, and the winner is simply the stronger or more cunning of the two? While the gods eat your offerings —"

Once again, his voice was full of irony, but colder and harder this time.

"No, you don't understand!" Sarai interrupted him, tenderly. "The gods of the lords of Ur aren't anyone else's gods! We are the only ones who can invoke them!"

"And you think, do you, that your gods took you off to the underworld? That they chose you to dance before the warriors until a bull dies, a bull my brothers and I have patiently reared?"

Sarai hesitated. Abram's cleverness impressed her. Indeed, how could she herself believe what the soothsayer and the priests said when she knew the true cause of her sickness? Even Sililli, who was always ready to see the presence of the gods in all things, trod very carefully whenever she touched on the subject.

"I don't know," she replied. "Sometimes, I think I was only sick. But the priests say it's the gods who decide our sickness and health. And besides . . . it wasn't the usual kind of sickness. Who can know the will of the gods?"

"Yes. Who can know?"

Abram looked skeptical. He became pensive, and ate and drank in silence. Sarai watched him, loving his every gesture: the grip of his fingers on the brass goblet, the movement of his chest as he breathed, the flexing of his shoulder muscles beneath the tunic. Her desire for him to touch her as he touched the objects and the food, the desire for his kiss — buried for so many years — came flooding back to her.

"Who can know if these gods exist?" Abram said suddenly. "The gods of the lords of Ur, the gods of all the cities I've visited. That's an awful lot of gods! Almost as many as there are men on earth. Where are they? What proof do we have of their presence? How are we to know if they help humans or threaten them? People say the gods are in everything. Whatever they do, even if they keep silent, there's supposed to be a reason for it. A stone falls on a donkey and kills it: It's the will of the gods. Why? Nobody knows, but they know, or their priests do. A woman dies giving birth, and her child dies at the same time: the will of the gods. But the woman is as pure as spring water, and her child has barely been born. Where's the justice in that? Where's the goodness of the gods? Why should these people suffer? The priests will say the woman's husband or father-in-law or uncle or someone else forgot one day to salute a lord. Or had a bad thought. Or ate mutton when there was no moon . . . And there you have it, that's the reason for the gods' anger!"

He had raised his voice, which echoed in the small room. Suddenly aware of how outspoken he was being, he let out a great laugh.

"Forgive these words in this place, Sacred Handmaid! Perhaps Ishtar will strike me dead when I leave here . . ."

He fell silent, as if waiting for Ishtar herself to hear his laughter and respond. Perhaps it was also to give Sarai time to take offense, to protest, even to drive him away. But she remained impassive.

Abram leaned forward, serious again. "The city of Urum is built on the banks of a river as wide as the Euphrates, called the Tigris because it can be as fierce as a tiger. I met an old man there who'd followed the river to its source, far away in the mountains of the north. He was looking for precious stones, but all he brought back was brass and diorites. But on the other side of the mountains, he met peoples who weren't barbarians and who believed in just one god. A god whose one task and one wish was to give birth to the world and then offer it to men."

Sarai held his gaze, not sure she understood what he was trying to say by telling her this story.

Abram gave a gentle smile. "A god who loves humans enough not to force his priestesses to dance between the horns of bulls. A god who allows his priestess to take a husband."

Fire went through Sarai's stomach like a wave, and her neck and her shoulders felt stiff. "I've never been able to forget your face, Abram," she said, lowering her head, "or the night we spent by the river. You've been in my thoughts and in my dreams, although I never imagined that I'd see you again. All I knew of you was your name, Abram. But since our night on the riverbank, I've wanted your lips to touch mine and protect me for the rest of my life. None of that has changed. I don't know the will of the gods. Unlike you, I haven't thought about their injustices or their powers. Sometimes I think I can feel their presence, sometimes not. But I know I almost died because I didn't receive your kiss."

"A *mar.Tu* can't kiss the daughter of a lord of Ur," Abram replied, in a changed voice, a voice full of sorrow. "My younger brother, Haran, found a wife in Adad. They have a son. It's rare among us for a younger child to be a husband and a father before his elder brother. Hardly a day goes by that my father doesn't worry about my solitary state."

Sarai managed to smile. "I'm not the daughter of Ichbi Sum-Usur. He told me so himself. I'm no longer my brother's sister. I'm only a handmaid of Ishtar."

"A *mar.Tu* can't kiss a handmaid of Ishtar whom no man has the right to marry."

"In three moons, during the great seed-time festival," Sarai said, in a trembling voice, "our king Shu-Sin will open my thighs, up there in the Sublime Bedchamber. He'll lie with me like a husband, as the Lady of the Moon did with almighty Dumuzi. I still need your kiss to protect me."

Abram first froze in astonishment, then rose to his feet, shaking with anger. "You're mad!" he cried. "You Lords of the Cities are all mad!" He seized the petrified Sarai by the shoulders. "How could you do such a thing?"

She did not have time to reply.

"Sarai, Sarai!" Sililli was calling.

She appeared in the doorway, and looked at them in astonishment. Abram let go of Sarai and took a step back.

"Quick, quick," Sililli said, catching him

by the sleeve of his tunic. "You mustn't stay here. Kiddin is in the big reception courtyard, asking to be received by the Sacred Handmaid of the Blood. He's talking to the priests right now."

Abram pulled himself free of Sililli's grip. "It was time for me to go anyway."

"No, wait!" Sarai protested. "There's no question of my receiving my brother. He has no business here."

"The young handmaids are looking for you everywhere!" Sililli cried. "If they don't find you, they'll suspect something. You have to show yourself."

"I, too, have no business here," Abram said.

"Abram . . ."

"I thank the Sacred Handmaid for her hospitality. Long may she reign in this temple."

His salute was as curt and cruel as his tone. He turned his back on her and was in the corridor before Sarai could react.

"I told you," Sililli muttered, her face a picture of distress. "You shouldn't have done it. The gods don't want it."

The Shawl of Life

This was the man she loved.

A hotheaded, rebellious man, his mind bursting with ideas! A brave, combative, handsome man. A man who loved her without saying it in words, but who showed it through his jealousy and rage.

And now all hope had gone.

In the days that followed, Sarai thought about Abram constantly. Sleep was impossible. While reports flooded in that the mountain barbarians were getting ever closer to the city and the temple, cloudy with the smoke of scents and crammed with offerings, hummed with invocations and chants, she continued to perform her duties as Sacred Handmaid without emotion. Pleading the excuse that she needed a special purification to please Ishtar, she spent as much time alone as she could. She ordered Sililli to stop her endless moaning and

185

her old wives' tales.

"The *mar.Tu* has gone back to his tent. We won't be seeing each other again. Just keep quiet now, and tomorrow I won't even remember his name."

Sililli may or may not have believed her, but she did not need to be told twice. Saying these words, though, had opened Sarai's heart to despair. It was true: Abram had refused to give her the kiss she had been waiting for, and she could expect nothing more from him. At one and the same time, he had condemned the laws of Ur, the gods, and any happiness they might give each other, even in secret. The best thing to do was to forget him. That should be easy: There was so little to forget. A long-ago encounter on the riverbank, a few words, his presence for a short while in a small room.

All that was left for her was to serve Ishtar according to the rules she had been taught, if not with devotion. All that was left for her was to wait for almighty Shu-Sin to put his erect penis between her thighs in the Sublime Bedchamber. Without the thought of Abram to protect her. Without the memory of his kiss to ward off fear and disgust.

Abram was right to condemn her for accepting the will of men, men who claimed she was no longer a wife, a daughter, or a sister, merely a sacred womb with no other fate but submission.

But Abram had no idea what made her a handmaid of the Lady of War: the fact that her womb was barren. And Sililli had spoken the truth: Even a *mar.Tu* would want a wife with a fertile womb!

If the gods had the power to punish humans, Sarai's punishment had been decided long ago.

In the dead of night, unable to sleep, as if at any moment she might fall, for the second time in her life, into the pit of the underworld, Sarai lay with her eyes wide open.

It was on the third night of this torture that she heard a slight shuffling sound. It came again, and a faint light passed her door, moved along the corridor, and vanished.

Without a noise, taking care not to wake Sililli, Sarai wrapped herself in a woolen toga and slipped into the corridor, just in time to see the light disappear on the right, toward the great courtyard.

She knew this part of the *giparù* well enough to find her way in the dark. Holding her hands out in front of her, feeling the brick walls, it took her only a moment to reach the great courtyard, where the entrance to the kitchens and the door leading to the Sublime Esplanade were permanently lit by torches. Above the temple, as they did every night, the naphtha fires illuminated the staircases and terraces of the ziggurat.

At first she saw and heard nothing.

Then she made out two shadows moving in the corner of the courtyard opposite the kitchens. Sarai thought of calling the guards. Could the *Gutis* be so close to Ur that they were already sending their spies into the temple?

One of the shadows rose to its full height. She hesitated. If it was the barbarians, they would have time to kill her before the guards arrived. The small of her back tingled with fear.

The two shadows also hesitated, ready to flee. Sarai heard a whisper. "Sarai!" They had spoken her name!

She advanced cautiously. The shadow waved his hand. Another whisper. Her heart beat faster: She recognized his voice.

"Abram? Abram, is that you?"

One of the two shadows took a pottery lantern from behind his back and raised it to his companion's face.

"Abram, what are you doing here?" Sarai breathed in astonishment.

He took her by the hands. At this simple contact, a shiver ran down the back of Sarai's neck, like a fever.

"This is my brother, Haran," he said. "I've come for you, if you want me."

"Come for me?"

"The *Gutis* aren't going to arrive where the lords of Ur are expecting them. They're cleverer than that. They've made an alliance with the Huhnurs, and are using their boats. They'll be on the river by tomorrow, and land in the lower city."

"Almighty Ea!" she cried.

The exclamation drew a smile from Haran. He was a little shorter than Abram, rounder in face and body, with laughing eyes.

"You're right to invoke him, Sacred Handmaid. The lords of Ur are going to need his help."

Abram frowned to silence his brother. He clasped Sarai's hands tighter and, speaking low and quickly, told her that their father and all the tribe had struck camp two days before and headed north, anxious to get their flocks and herds out of reach of the *Gutis*.

"Haran agreed to come back here with me . . ."

"Because Abram assured me he knew

189

how to get into your temple and how to find his way around," Haran said, smiling broadly. "Well, we got in all right. But finding our way in this labyrinth is another matter! If you hadn't come to us . . ."

"Haran!" Abram protested. "We don't have time to listen to your mockery. Will you follow me, Sarai?"

"Follow you? But . . ."

"Will you be my wife? Live with me in the tents of the *mar.Tu?* Abandon the luxury of the temple, your gods, and your power?"

"And face our father's bad temper," Haran could not help adding. "He's terrified at the idea of his eldest son marrying the daughter of a lord."

Abram nodded, nervously. "Haran is telling the truth. You may not be welcome among us at first."

"But when they see how beautiful you are," Haran said, giving a kind of bow, "then they'll be like me. They'll know why Abram is so stubborn, and they'll envy him his happiness."

Sarai was barely listening, bombarded as she was by all the contradictory thoughts that had been tormenting her for these past few days. Everything came together: her fear of committing a sacrilege, her pure joy at hearing Abram's proposal, her torment at being unable to reveal her secret she could not reveal.

"Abram . . ."

"Quiet, someone's coming!" Haran breathed.

A man was advancing quickly across the courtyard, with a spear in one hand, a torch in the other, a leather cape flapping against his legs and a helmet shining on his forehead.

"He saw us!" Abram growled.

"You two hide," Sarai whispered. "It's only a guard. I'll order him out of the courtyard."

But no sooner had she approached than Sarai saw the gold leaves on the helmet. The officer lowered the torch slightly, lighting his face.

"Kiddin!"

"Yes, Sacred Handmaid. I'm the one who's been guarding the doors of the *giparù* for the past three nights. I knew when you looked at the *mar.Tu* the other day that wouldn't be the end of it. How could I ever have believed that you'd changed? Does a single day go by that demons don't stir in your heart?"

"I don't have to listen to your insults, son of Ichbi Sum-Usur. You're no longer my brother, remember. And you have no business here."

Kiddin laughed arrogantly. "What are you going to do, Sacred Handmaid? Call the guards to help you? The priests? Do you want to show them who you've introduced into the temple, even into the sacred courtyard of the high priestess?"

"Calm down, officer," Haran said, behind Sarai's back. "We're leaving. In a moment, we'll vanish into the night and nobody will know we were here. There's no point disturbing all these good people's sleep."

As if by magic, a long stick had appeared in his hand. As for Abram, he was clasping a long leather whip to his thigh. Calmly, he approached Sarai, ignoring Kiddin as if he did not exist.

"Have you decided, Sarai?" he asked.

She smiled. "Yes. I was only waiting for you to give the word. I'll follow you as far as you want me."

"Oh, so that's it!" Kiddin said. "While the enemies of Ur approach the city, the Sacred Handmaid of the Blood betrays Ishtar! How dare you?" Eyes bulging with rage, Kiddin lifted his spear. "I'm going to kill the three of you. Your blood will purify this courtyard you've tarnished —"

He raised his right arm, aiming the spear at Abram's chest. Haran leaped forward and brought his stick down on the shaft of the spear. Abram pulled Sarai out of the way. With his left hand, Kiddin threw his torch at Haran's chest. Haran parried the blow with his stick.

With a growl of joy, Kiddin twirled his spear. The heavy shaft hit Haran in the ribs, forcing him down on one knee. At that very moment, Sarai saw Abram lift his right arm and the tongue of leather unfurl in the darkness. It all seemed to happen at once. As the glittering bronze spear tore Haran's flesh, the whip whistled and cracked, and Kiddin lifted his hands to his face. Haran and Kiddin cried out simultaneously. Haran's tunic was red, and blood ran down between Kiddin's fingers.

Abram rushed to lift his brother. The wound on his chest was black and as big as a hand.

"It isn't deep," Haran groaned. "I'll be all right."

Kiddin was on his knees, breathing harshly. With his right hand, he was trying to reach his spear. Sarai kicked it away. The whip had torn Kiddin's face from top to bottom, taking away both eye and eyelid. Sarai felt neither compassion nor satisfaction.

"There's no point in dying for me, son of

Ichbi Sum-Usur," she said, in a hard voice. "Die for your gods, your city, and your lineage. I haven't been one of you for a long time."

Behind her, Abram was tearing the top of his tunic to make a bandage for Haran's wound. Kiddin got to his feet, his beard red with blood, his good eye wide with hatred. Sarai thought fleetingly of the eyes of the bulls before which she had danced.

"Listen to me," she said, raising her hand. "I'm going to give you a more important gift than my death and those of the *mar.Tu*. The *Gutis* are setting a trap for you. They aren't going to arrive from the east, where Shu-Sin's troops are stationed, but on Huhnur boats that will reach the lower city tomorrow. Go and warn the lords. You can show your wound with pride: It was the price you paid to bring them the news. You'll be a hero. And if you're brave enough, you'll save the city."

Without stopping to listen to Kiddin's curses, Sarai led Abram and Haran to the entrance of the narrow corridor that went around the inside of the *giparù*.

"Let's hurry. We've made enough noise to wake the temple."

The light of a lamp suddenly pierced the darkness.

"Sarai!" Sililli whispered. "What are you doing? And who are —"

She broke off, mouth open wide, when she saw Abram and Haran, his chest wrapped in a red cloth. "Great Ea!" she exclaimed.

Sarai gently put her fingers on her mouth. "I'm leaving, Sililli. I'm leaving with Abram. I'm leaving the temple and the city. I'm marrying Abram the *mar.Tu.*"

Sililli pushed away Sarai's hand. Her mouth was quivering. For once, she was speechless.

"Quick," Abram said. "We must get through the south gate before the guards stop us."

"And before I can't run anymore," Haran breathed.

"You leave, you get married . . ." Sililli said, in an almost childlike voice. "But what about me? What's to become of me? Have you even thought about that? Their anger will fall on me!"

Sarai stroked Sililli's cheek tenderly. "Come with me."

"But make up your mind quickly," Abram said.

Sililli hesitated, looking at him as if she had never seen him before. Then her gaze rested on Haran's chest, where the blood was now oozing through the material.

"To live in a *mar. Tu* camp!" she sighed. "O Almighty Ea, protect me!"

"Be careful," Haran said, with a grin. "It's quite likely Ea won't be able to do anything for you in a *mar. Tu* camp."

"Oh, I'm sure of that!" Sililli replied. "But you, my boy, would do better to save your breath and your blood if you want to get out of here." She turned to Sarai and Abram. "Run to the small door. I'll go and get some linen and some herbs to make a better bandage once we're out of the temple."

They left Ur, hidden among the cargo on a boat. Abram had paid the oarsmen handsomely. After going upstream for about ten *ùs,* they were let off on the opposite bank. There, a light wagon with slatted sides of bulrushes and matting, drawn by two mules, was waiting for them.

As soon as possible, Abram left the Nippur road, to avoid the royal checkpoints. Harnessed in turn, the mules followed the tracks of the herds, which they knew well. They did not stop to rest. Occasionally, Abram and Sarai got down off the wagon to lighten the load, and walked together hand in hand, without a word.

It seemed to Sarai that her nuptials were beginning. They had not yet kissed, but she did not dare do anything to provoke a kiss. It would come in good time.

She recalled their encounter on the banks of the Euphrates, when Abram had taken her hand, led her to the shelter of the dune, and lit a fire. She remembered his mocking words.

"It isn't every day that the daughters of the lords of Ur get lost in the bulrushes by the river. I could take you to my father's tent. But he'd think I was bringing him a bride, and my brothers would be jealous."

Now it was finally happening: Abram was taking her to his father's tent. Tomorrow he would be her husband. The interrupted night of their encounter could finally resume.

It was the middle of the following day when they arrived at the encampment.

Terah's tribe had grown so large that the array of tents was like a small city.

At first, they paid less attention to Sarai than to Haran. Sililli's herbs and care had limited his fever, though not his pain. When his wound had been anointed, and he had drunk some spiced wine to help him sleep, he pointed at Sarai, who had been standing in the background.

"This is my brother Abram's wife," he said, with a wan smile. "Let us rejoice at his stubbornness. We, the shepherds without a city, should feel honored, not because she was born among the lords of Ur, but because of her beauty and her courage. Believe me, her presence here among us is a promise of better things to come."

Sarai bowed her head at the compliment. Abram's eyes misted over with gratitude to his brother.

She only fully realized how fine Haran's words had been when Abram took her to see Terah. Up close, he looked older than he had in the courtyard of Ichbi Sum-Usur's house. His eyes were bright and cold, and his thin lips accentuated the hardness of his expression. Despite his wrinkles and his graying hair and beard, he exuded a sense of power, before which even Abram bowed his head.

He looked at Sarai without any tenderness. It was quite obvious that the beauty and courage of the woman chosen by his son had little effect on him. He let the silence linger longer than necessary.

"My son has decided it would be you," he finally said. "It isn't customary for the daughter of a lord to mix her blood with ours, but I shall respect Abram's wishes. Among us, everyone is free to make his own choices just as he is responsible for the consequences of his mistakes. Accept our welcome."

Without any further effort to be friendly, he entered his tent.

Sarai bit her lips.

"Don't be angry at my father," Abram said in a low voice. "He likes only what he knows. He'll change his mind when he gets to know you better."

Abram was wrong. It wasn't Terah's bad humor that had suddenly brought a chill to Sarai's happiness, but the thought of the blood that the old *mar.Tu* feared to see mixed with his own. In truth, her womb contained not the least drop of the life-giving substance. She felt less able now than ever to reveal her secret. Could Abram's love possibly have the power to take away the barrenness within her?

Abram led her to the women's tent, accompanied by laughing children. The young women inspected Sarai, unable to hide their curiosity or, in some cases, their jealousy. But the older ones welcomed her with open arms. One of them, a tiny woman with fine, smooth skin despite her age, dragged Sarai to the great mothers' tent.

The others followed.

For the first time, Sarai discovered the warm light filtering through the canvas, the sweet smell of skins and rugs that covered the ground, the painted wooden chests, the jewels hanging from the tent posts.

The old woman opened one of the chests and took out a length of fine linen fabric with openwork stitching, embroidered with colored wools and encrusted with slivers of silver. Approaching Sarai, she held out the cloth with a smile.

"Welcome, Sarai, Abram's betrothed. My name is Tsilla. Abram's mother died a long time ago and when necessary I've taken her place. Among us, bride and bridegroom wed with less ceremony than where you come from. We eat lamb outside the bridegroom's tent, we drink beer and wine and listen to flute music and sometimes a few songs of good omen. The bride wears a simple robe and this shawl, which covers her whole body. It's an old shawl, and a precious one: It has covered more than a hundred women. It has heard their sighs and their fears, their joys and their disappointments. We women call it the Shawl of Life."

She fell silent. All around, the women were observing Sarai with a mixture of friendliness and severity that reminded her of the faces of the young handmaids as she prepared to confront the bull. She smiled, and her eyes shone with happiness. Tsilla nodded her head and smiled back at her.

"That's good," she said, approvingly. "You must wear the Shawl of Life with those eyes! When you are in the tent, alone with your bridegroom, before he lifts the Shawl, you have only one thing to do. You must turn around him, at arm's length, three times in one direction and three times in the other. For the rest, Abram will teach you . . ."

The women chuckled, and the chuckles grew until everyone in the tent was laughing loudly, including Sarai.

It happened just as Tsilla had said.

Sarai entered the tent covered with the Shawl of Life. Her heart was in her mouth. Through the loose stitches, in the light of the lamps, she could see Abram's face, full of desire.

Her thighs and belly painful with her own desire, she turned around him, three times in one direction and three times in the other. Then she stopped. In spite of the laughter and the flute music outside, she could hear Abram's breathing.

He approached and spoke her name.

"Sarai, my beloved."

He came closer still and placed a kiss on her lips, through the shawl. Sarai began to tremble.

Abram took the hem of the shawl and lifted it. She did not move. They looked at each other while his hand rose to Sarai's temple and his fingers slid down her cheek to the back of her neck. She stopped trembling. He smiled.

He slid her dress off her, and she was naked. He moved back as though he were afraid to touch her. A moan came from his mouth. His tunic fell all at once, and he, too, was naked, his penis erect.

Sarai raised her hand to place his fingers on the smooth skin at the base of the neck. The blood was throbbing so rapidly there that her fingers trembled. Abram was panting, shivering under her caress. Sarai felt her own sexual organs beating lightly against her womb. Then her knees gave way. Abram lay down with her on the rugs, his lips on hers, sharing the same breath, the same moan of happiness. And sharing the kiss that would at last protect her to the end of her days.

Part Three

HARRAN

Sarai's Tears

Terah's tribe followed the Euphrates down-
stream along the route used for trade with the
northern barbarians. They advanced slowly
so that the herds could graze regularly
without becoming exhausted. Every night,
Sarai and Abram shared a joy as bright as
starlight. Sarai submitted to the privations
and obligations of *mar.Tu* life with an ease
that astonished even Terah. In less than one
season, the girl who had been the daughter of
a lord of Ur and the Sacred Handmaid of
Ishtar, surrounded by slaves and servants
ready to pander to her slightest whim, eating
only what other hands had prepared for her,
had abandoned her golden-hemmed togas,
sumptuous jewels, and makeup, and opulent
hairstyles without slightest regret. As naturally as if she had been born in a camp, she
wore a modest tunic, plaited a braid of red-
and-blue wool in her hair, and slept in a tent.

She learned to grind cereals, cook meat, bake bread, and make beer. The only thing she carried over from her former life was the skill she had acquired from her aunts for carding, spinning, and dyeing wool, which won her the admiration of the other women in the encampment.

They left the kingdom of Akkad and Sumer, with its rich, powerful cities where the *mar.Tu* were despised. As they approached the mountains to the north, they passed merchants coming from Ur. Sarai learned that Kiddin had died defending the walls of the city from the *Gutis*. She spared hardly a thought for her father, Ichbi Sum-Usur, who had dreamed of his son's glory, though she did think about the streets of Ur and the house where she had spent her childhood, now perhaps overrun by the barbarians. But her sadness did not last. Her childhood seemed distant, and Abram was watching over her now, protecting her.

She saw snow for the first time, discovered how real cold felt and what it was like to spend whole days under sheepskins, forgetting the ice outside by making love with Abram until she was bathed in sweat. Abram did not seem surprised that his seed had not made his wife's belly round, nor did he show any impatience to have a child. There was nothing to mar the happiness they felt on waking each dawn lying side by side.

The misfortune happened suddenly, one gray, icy afternoon. Despite his father's warnings, Haran had decided to take a shortcut by fording a river at a hazardous spot. His wife, Havila, and their son Lot were on a wagon laden with heavy baskets of grain. The cold was so intense that the stones protruding from the water were covered with ice. As they crossed, the wheels slipped on a rock and became trapped in a hole. The wagon was sturdy, but it could not withstand the strength of the current and began to come apart. The terrified mules struggled in vain to free themselves from the backbreaking weight. Lot and his mother screamed with terror. Haran and Abram dived into the water.

Abram, his face blue with cold, managed to grab hold of Lot's hand. A human chain was formed to pull them out of the water. But a splinter from one of the broken wheels reopened the wound Haran had received from Kiddin during their fight in the great temple. Trying but failing to pull Havila out from under the overturned wagon, Haran was swept away by the raging current, his blood draining from him as he went.

They had to walk for two days along the river before they recovered his body. That evening, the funeral rites were observed for Haran and Havila. When the weeping and chanting finally stopped, Terah and Abram asked Sarai to take care of Lot as if he was her son.

It was after this tragedy that Tsilla started to worry about the fact that Sarai's belly was not getting any bigger, and that Sarai was never seen washing linen soiled with her menstrual blood. In order to allay suspicion, Sililli stole the blood of animals during slaughter and stained Sarai's sheets with it. She made heaps of offerings to her gods in secret, fetched herbs, and suggested various remedies to Sarai: circling trees on the nights when there was a full moon, anointing her thighs with pollen, eating snake, sleeping with a purse full of bull's sperm. Not a moon went by without Sililli coming up with some new solution. But Sarai soon refused to have anything more to do with such pointless magic, as much through revulsion as through fear of being discovered by Tsilla or one of the other women.

Meanwhile, even though Abram's desire for her showed no sign of lessening, and even though they slept in the same bed more often than many couples, Sarai, like everyone, became aware of her husband's increasing hard-heartedness.

When they reached Harran, Terah wisely decided to stop their march and let the herds graze their fill. It was a rich city, constantly crossed by convoys transporting wood from the north toward the powerful cities of the kingdom of Ur. The wealthy local traders soon began to take an interest in Terah's statuettes. With his agile fingers, he fashioned a thousand idols, satisfying every one of his customers' whims. No two statues were alike.

The orders came flooding in so fast that it was decided that Abram would work with his father. But the following moon, Abram refused to place offerings on the altar of Terah's god or any other, and they quarreled violently. From that day on, relations between father and son grew increasingly sour. Terah avoided talking to his daughter-in-law. The mood of the whole tribe changed. Sarai felt she was being subjected to more and more speculative looks, to which she would respond with downcast eyes, for the truth was that she, too, thought it was her flat stomach that was causing Abram's ill humor.

Sometimes she would sit up in the middle of the night, listening to Abram's breathing beside her. What would happen if she woke him and told him the truth? Would he understand her childish terror? Would he understand how much she had loved him, even then, to resort to a *kassaptu*'s spells? Could her words ever make up for the barrenness of her womb?

She doubted it, and instead of waking him, she would merely stroke the back of his neck and lie down next to him again with her eyes wide open, the silence gripping her chest like ice.

The ball of wool rose into the air, wrapped in a piece of linen, and the children shrieked with joy. When it fell back to the ground, they threw themselves on it in a furious scrum. As usual, Lot was the first to extricate himself from the heap of legs and arms, the ball in his hands. Sarai, who had been watching with furrowed brow, relaxed. She resumed her work, spreading the newly woven and washed pieces of wool on the sun-warmed rocks.

The boys ran, shouting, through the fields of thick grass that bordered the encampment. Then their game took them farther, toward the river, the workshop, and Terah's kiln. They disappeared behind the brick wall, from which smoke rose constantly. Sarai thought to call them back, but they were out of earshot by now and she had no desire to run after them.

She glanced at the women who were busy around her, washing the newly woven wool or pressing it with stones to wring it and soften it. One of them smiled at her and waved her hand toward the river.

"Let them be, Sarai. If they disturb Terah, he'll know how to get rid of them!"

"He'll put their ball in his kiln," another said, "and then we'll have to make them another one!"

They resumed their work, beating the cloths and rugs in time to the songs they hummed. Suddenly, the children's cries grew more shrill, and were followed by a suspicious silence. All the women looked up.

"They've been fighting again!" one of them sighed, rubbing the small of her back.

Lot came around the corner of Terah's workshop. He was alone and was holding his face in his hands. Swaying like a drunk, he began to climb the slope. Sarai lifted the bottom of her tunic and ran to meet him. Halfway up the slope, just before he reached her, Lot fell to his knees in the grass. Blood was gushing between his fingers and down his neck. Sarai parted his hands: There was a nasty cut, full of brick dust, running from his temple into the thick mass of his hair. It wasn't really a deep or serious wound, but it was bleeding profusely.

"You almost split your head open!" Sarai exclaimed. "Does it hurt a lot?"

"Not that much," replied Lot in a blank voice. He was making an effort not to cry, but was shaking like a leaf. "They pushed me down on the piles of broken pottery behind grandfather's workshop."

By now, his cheeks were bathed in blood, and it was running down inside his tunic. Sarai quickly untied her belt and wrapped it around his head.

"Do you need any help?" a woman asked, above them.

"No," Sarai shouted back. "It isn't serious. Just a cut. Sililli must have some herbs."

She wiped Lot's face as best she could with the bottom of her tunic. He was finding it hard to hold back his tears.

"They were all against me!" he said, his mouth quivering with pride and anger. "Not one of them was on my side!"

"That's because you're the strongest," Sarai whispered, kissing him on the cheek.

"If they didn't get together to fight you, they'd never win."

Lot looked at her with dark, serious eyes, and sniffed. The red stain was spreading on the bandage, making him look like a little warrior back from the wars.

"I'm proud of you," Sarai said.

Lot forced a smile. He slipped his arms under her lifted tunic and hugged her bare thighs with all his strength.

"Let's go into the tent," she said, gently freeing herself.

Sililli, of course, cried out when they appeared. But in next to no time Lot had been washed and given new clothes and a big bandage over a plaster of crushed clay and grass.

"No more fighting, my boy!" Sililli ordered, stabbing his chest with an authoritative finger. "The bandage has to stay in place until tomorrow. If not, I'll let you bleed like the little pig you are!"

Lot shrugged. "It isn't serious," he said, confidently. "Sarai will take care of me." He hugged Sarai, while Sililli pretended to be offended. "I like it when you look after me. You're as sweet to me as you are to my uncle Abram."

Sarai laughed softly, gave Lot several little

pecks on the cheek, and pushed him away.

"Listen to that, the greedy little man!" Sililli said, slapping him on the buttocks.

Lot skipped to the opening of the tent. On the threshold, he turned to Sarai. "It's when you take care of me that I know you're really like my mother."

Sarai, her eyes abruptly misting over, gestured to him to go. Nervously, she began putting away the bags of herbs and pots of plaster, aware of Sililli's eyes on her back. As she picked up Lot's bloodstained linen, Sililli decided to speak.

"Tsilla asked me again this morning: 'Still nothing in Sarai's womb?' I answered no, as usual. She asked me if Abram and you often slept in the same tent. I said, 'Too often for my taste. Three nights never go by without them waking me with the noise of their love-making!' That made her laugh — her and the rest of the gossips who were listening so hard."

Sarai shook her head, wiping her cheeks with the back of her hand. Sililli approached, and took the bloodstained linen from her hands.

"Tsilla laughed to make the others laugh," she went on, lowering her voice. "Because she likes you. She's liked you since the first day, when she gave you the bridal veil. She laughed because she loves Abram as much as I love you. But she's no fool. She's understood. She knows."

Dry-eyed again, Sarai tried hard to stop her voice from trembling. "How can you be so sure? Did she say something?"

"Oh, no! She didn't need to. Old women like Tsilla and me don't need to tell each other everything, we understand each other perfectly well. She's been asking me the same question every month since we arrived in Harran. I'm sure she even knows about the blood on the sheets."

Sarai turned away. "I have to get back to the others. I haven't finished my work."

Sililli held her back by the arm, determined to spare her nothing. "Tsilla knows, but she's a good woman, and she knows how difficult life is. The others, the ones you work with, aren't so forgiving. I can read it in their eyes like a scribe reading a clay tablet. They're thinking: Sarai's beautiful, the most beautiful of us all. There isn't a man here — husband or son — who doesn't dream of having the girl from Ur in his bed and sharing some of Abram's happiness. Yes, their eyes are full of jealousy and their hearts full of poison. But time is passing, and the girl from Ur, the girl Abram chose as a wife against his father's wishes, the girl who drove all the virgins in the tribe to despair, has a belly that's still flat. And I see the smiles coming back to their faces. Because they're starting to realize that Sarai isn't going to have a child. Beautiful she may be, but she's as sterile as desert sand."

"I know all that," Sarai said, angrily. "Keep your moaning to yourself. I don't need anyone to see and hear for me."

"In that case," Sililli went on, undaunted, "perhaps you've realized that Abram's character has changed? Almighty Ea, your husband has become as dark and closed as a cellar! He doesn't play with Lot anymore, even though he loves him as if he were his real father. He's as stubborn as a mule. Not a moon goes by that he doesn't quarrel with someone or other, beginning with his father, Terah. Those two have been as daggers drawn since the start of spring — and over nothing."

Sarai pushed Sililli's hand away and went out of the tent and into the sun. Sililli followed her, the soiled linen still clasped to her ample chest.

"Sarai, listen to me. You know I live only for your happiness. Do I still need to prove it to you?"

Sarai did not move. Mealtime was approaching, and the camp was full of activity. She thought of the loaves stuffed with meat and herbs that she had baked for Abram without the help of any handmaid. She had invented the recipe herself, as a surprise for him. Instead of listening to Sililli's whining, which was breaking her heart, she ought to be doing her duty as a wife: She ought to get the loaves, find Abram, and give him his meal. But Sililli could not stop talking.

"This is the truth, Sarai, my child: Everyone's afraid for the tribe. Everyone thinks Abram made the wrong choice of wife. Everyone thinks, 'Terah's eldest child, Haran, is dead, and soon Abram will become chief of the tribe.' But what is a chief if his wife can't give him sons and daughters? They'll start to argue about the family's behavior, and they'll all turn against you."

Sarai remained silent for another moment, then shook her head. "I'm going to see Abram and tell him everything. I don't care what the others think. It isn't right for me to hide the truth from him any longer."

"Think of the consequences. He'll reject you. Or take a concubine. You'll be reduced to nothing. Even if he chooses a handmaid, once she has his child in her womb, she'll be the mother, and you'll be nothing. That's how it happens. The best thing would be to undo what you've done. I can find herbs, and we'll try to bring your blood back."

"Haven't you given me enough herbs already? All they ever made me do was run into the bushes!"

"We can try again. I've heard of a very good *kassaptu* who lives on the edge of town —"

"No. I don't want any more magic. And you're wrong. Abram isn't like other men. He loves the truth. I'll tell him why my womb is barren. I'll tell him I did it because I loved him from the first moment I saw him. He'll understand."

"That would certainly be the first time a man understood a woman's sorrow! May Inanna, our almighty Mother Moon, hear you."

With a heavy heart, Sarai put her loaves, a gourd of cool water, another of beer, and some grapes and peaches in a basket, and covered it with a fine cloth she herself had woven. Since she had started living with the *mar.Tu,* she had learned to love these simple gestures. At that moment, though, the mere fact of carrying a basket brought a lump to her throat.

Aware that she was being watched, she

stood up, and left the encampment with a confident step, responding to the smiles and greetings as she usually did.

In the distance, she saw a group of children gathered around Lot, whose turbaned head stood out above the others. Despite her distress, she could not help smiling fondly. She was sure Lot had succeeded in using his wound to compel respect from the other boys. She was sure, too, that the tenderness and pride she felt for Abram's nephew was the same as a mother feels for her beloved son.

She walked toward the river as far as Terah's workshop, where Abram had been working with his father since their arrival in Harran. The fire roared in the cylindrical kiln, which was twice the height of a man. Terah's assistants were throwing big logs in through an opening, behind which flames could be seen dancing. Although they wore only loincloths, the heat was so intense that their torsos streamed with sweat.

Sarai hung back: Terah did not really like women to enter the lean-to where the statues of the gods were kept for polishing and painting before being taken to the customers. She called one of the assistants over and asked for Abram. The assistant told her that Abram wasn't there. He had left the workshop early in the morning and nobody had seen him since.

Sarai's first thought was that he had had another quarrel with his father.

"Do you know where he went?"

The assistant asked his workmates. They pointed to a path that led across the river and up a slope to a high plateau where the herds grazed. She thanked them and, without hesitating, set off along the path.

Tree trunks had been thrown across the river as a bridge. As she crossed, Sarai was sure that Terah was following her with his eyes from the door of the lean-to. She hurried on, anxious to join her husband.

As she climbed the path to the plateau, she tried to formulate the words she would say to Abram. She had been his wife for nearly twenty moons. Twenty moons since she had fled the great temple of Ur. Twenty moons filled with joy and sorrow. Yet she had never found the courage to tell Abram the truth. Now she had to. There was no turning back.

She walked quickly. By the time she reached the top of the slope, she was out of breath, and her heart beat so loudly that her ears hummed. As far as her eyes could see, the plateau was empty. No herds, and no people.

She went up to the great sycamore, older than many generations of men, which sat in solitary splendor on the edge of the plateau. Its shade was vast and cool. Abram often came here to rest and think, sometimes even to sleep when the nights were too hot.

But there was nobody resting against the grooved trunk now. Abram was nowhere to be seen.

Sarai stopped into the shade of the sycamore and put down her basket. The grass was bending in the breeze. In the far distance, to the north and the east, the mountains seemed as transparent as petals in the blue sky. From here, everything seemed immense and infinite.

She sat down and rested her shoulders and head against the rough bark. All at once, she felt terribly weary, and as helpless as an abandoned child. If only she could curl up in Abram's powerful arms, hear his warm voice, feel his soft lips, then she could tell him what was so important!

But Abram was not here.

At that moment, his absence seemed absolute. As if, wherever Abram was, he was an infinitely long way from her.

The tears she had held back for so long gushed from her eyes like an overflowing spring. They streamed down her cheeks, into her mouth, and over her neck. There was nobody to see her, and Sarai wept all the tears that were in her.

Then, when her eyes were dry again and her heart calmer, her trust in Abram returned. Sooner or later he would appear. She would wait here and rest, regaining her strength so that, when she spoke, her words would be strong and right.

Despite herself, a very old prayer to Inanna rose to her lips:

> *Inanna, holy Moon, holy Mother,*
> *Queen of Heaven,*
> *Open my heart, open my womb, open*
> *my mouth.*
> *Take my thoughts for offerings.*

Abram's God

Noises rose from the village of tents. Fragrant smoke spread from Terah's kiln as far as the eye could see, mingling the scents of oak, cedar, sycamore, and terebinth. The path out of the encampment led past the workshop, wound between the opulent hills, and joined the main road to Harran. From the edge of the plateau, Sarai could see the fine houses of the city. The shadows were lengthening. Abram still had not reappeared. The coolness of the shade and the immense tranquility of the plateau was making Sarai drowsy.

Feeling hungry and thirsty, she ate one of the loaves she had made for Abram and drank the water — the gourd had kept it cold.

She continued waiting, struggling against her anxiety. It was unusual for Abram to be absent like this without a word to her or Lot.

223

By now, they must have noticed his absence in the camp, too.

What if Abram didn't come back before nightfall? What if she had to go back to the tent alone?

Suddenly, she felt something. His presence.

Perhaps even his footsteps.

She got to her feet, searching the plateau from one side to the other. And then she saw him. She was surprised at herself: How had she known he was coming?

He was still such a long way away. Nothing but a silhouette, advancing through the tall grass!

But she recognized him. She did not need to see his face to know it was him.

He was walking quickly, with long strides. A rush of joy swept away all Sarai's doubts and fears. She wanted to call to him but only raised her arms to signal to him.

Abram responded. She began running.

When they were quite close, she realized he was laughing. His face was radiant with joy. It was many moons since she had last seen him looking like that!

He stopped, and opened his arms wide. "Sarai, my beloved!" he said.

They embraced like lovers separated by a long journey.

Beneath her cheek and in her hair, Sarai could still hear Abram's laughter. Then his words came, rapid and breathless:

"He spoke to me! He called me: 'Abram! Abram!' I replied: 'Here I am!' Then there was silence. So I walked, far away, beyond the plateau. I didn't think I would hear Him again. But He did call me: 'Abram!' And I said: 'Yes, I'm here!' " Abram laughed again.

Sarai stepped back, frowning with incomprehension, a question on her lips. Abram took her face in his hands, in a gesture identical to the one he had made that very first time, on the riverbank in Ur, the night they met. This time, he placed his lips on hers. A long kiss, full of spirit, power, and desire. A kiss of pure happiness.

When at last they separated, Sarai laughed. "Who? Who called you? What are you talking about?"

"Him!" Abram said, lifting his hand and pointing to the horizon, the mountains and valleys, the earth and the sky.

"Him?" Sarai insisted, uncomprehending.

"Him, the One God! My God!"

Sarai wanted to ask him so much, to understand. Who exactly had spoken to him? What did this god look like? What was his name? But Abram's hands were shaking. His whole body was shaking. He, Abram, the strongest man in Terah's tribe, was shaking! Sarai squeezed his hands in hers.

"He said: 'Go! Go, leave this country . . . ' We're going to leave, Sarai. Tomorrow."

"Leave? For where? Abram . . ."

"No, not now! No questions now. Come, I must speak to my father. I must speak to everyone."

He took her hand and pulled her toward the path that led back to the river and Terah's workshop.

Sarai realized that she couldn't tell Abram the truth now. Not today. And not tomorrow. There was no point. And they had all been wrong — Terah, Tsilla, Sililli, and she herself. Abram's angry, bitter mood lately had had nothing to do with her flat stomach.

Abram took up position outside the workshop. From the way he looked, everyone could tell he had something important to say. An assistant went to fetch Terah, who was making his evening offerings to his ancestors. Other men and women appeared with him, coming down to the banks of the river. Even the children stopped playing and came close.

Lot, his brow still turbaned, came to Sarai, who was standing back, and took her hand. He looked up at her, and she read in his eyes the same anxiety she could see on everyone's face. They were all thinking that Abram had decided to confront his father and take over the leadership of the tribe. That was why they were so surprised when he started speaking.

"Father, today God Most High called to me. I was here, with all of you, preparing the kiln, when I heard a cry in the air. But with all the noise of breaking wood, I couldn't hear. I climbed up to the plateau and walked. Suddenly I heard: *'Abram!'* My name was being called. It was in the air all around me, spoken by a powerful voice I didn't know. *'Abram!'* My name again. I said: 'Here I am! I'm Abram.' There was no reply. So I walked. I went down into the valley that leads to Harran in the north, and suddenly the voice was everywhere. In the air, the clouds, the grass, the trees, even in the depths of the earth. On the skin of my face. It was calling my name: *'Abram!'* I knew who was speaking. 'Here I am!' I cried again. 'I'm Abram!' The voice asked: *'Do you know who I am?'* I replied: 'I think so.' He said: *'Abram. Leave this land, leave your father's house, and walk to the land I will*

227

reveal to you. I will make of you a great nation, I will make your name great. I will bless those who bless you, and those who insult you, I will curse. Through you, all the families of the earth will be blessed.' Those were His words, Father. I've come back to tell you what He said, because I want you to know why I'm leaving."

When Abram stopped speaking, there was a heavy silence. After the initial surprise, anxiety returned to everyone's face. So the son wanted to leave the father and deny his ancestors? They all waited for Terah's reaction. He seemed tired, but anger glinted in his eyes. He passed his hand through his thick beard.

"You say, 'Those were his words.' Whose words, my son?"

"The One God, who created heaven and earth, the God of Abram."

"What's his name?" Terah asked.

Abram could not hold back a laugh, a genuinely amused laugh, without pride. He shook his head. "He didn't tell me His name, Father."

"Why not?"

"He doesn't need a name to speak to me or for me to recognize Him. He has nothing in common with these gods with their ridiculous faces that we make and sell to the

Lords of one city or the merchants of another."

A murmur of disapproval ran through the crowd. Terah raised his hand. "So this god of yours has no face?"

"No face," Abram replied, "and no body."

"How can you see him, then?"

"I can't see Him. No human being or animal on this earth can see Him. He doesn't shine, he doesn't wear a toga or a diadem. He has no claws, no wings. He doesn't have the head of a lion or a bull. He possesses neither the flesh of a man nor the forms of a woman. He has no body. He can't be seen."

"How do you know all that if you can't see him?"

"He spoke to me."

"How can he speak to you if he has no face or mouth?"

"Because He doesn't need a face to speak. Because He is who He is."

There was a burst of mocking laughter behind Terah. Lot huddled closer to Sarai. The women no longer hesitated to draw near and listen.

Terah also laughed. "So this is what's happened," he said, raising his voice. "My son Abram saw his god today, but his god has no flesh, no body! He's invisible."

"That is how the One God is," Abram retorted, ignoring the mockery. "He is the source of all that lives, all that dies, and all that is eternal."

An old man stepped forward to stand beside Terah. "Either it was all a dream, or else a demon was having his sport with you."

"Demons don't exist," Abram replied patiently. "There is good and evil, justice and injustice. It is we who make good and evil. It is you and I who are just or unjust."

This time, angry protests broke out in the crowd, everyone shouting at the same time.

"A god you can't see doesn't exist!"

"A god who doesn't shine is powerless!"

"What's the use of your god if he can't prevent evil or injustice?"

"And if he doesn't give us rain or protect us from thunder?"

"Who makes the barley grow?"

"Who makes us die? Who makes us ill?"

"Without Nintu, how would women give birth?"

"You're talking nonsense, Abram. You're insulting your ancestors."

"You're insulting our gods, too!"

"They can hear you and I can hear them. Already they're getting angrier, I can feel it."

"They're going to punish us for your words."

"May they forgive us! May they forgive us for being here listening to you!"

"You're putting your father's whole tribe at risk, Abram."

"Terah, ask your son to purify himself!"

"Condemn your son, Terah, or misfortune will fall on us all . . ."

"Listen to me!" Abram cried, holding out his arms.

Sarai thought at first that he, too, had lost his temper. But then she saw his lips and eyes, and she knew he was still calm and self-assured. He stepped forward and, more than his cry, it was his calm and the expression on his face that caused them to stop talking.

"Do you want proof that the One God exists? That He spoke to me and called me by my name? I am that proof, I, Abram, whom He called today. Tomorrow at dawn, as he asked of me, I will set off with my wife Sarai, my brother Haran's son Lot, my herd, and my servants. I will go westward, toward the country He will reveal to me."

For a moment there was silence, as if everyone was trying to fathom the mystery of these words. Then, from here and there in the crowd, came bursts of derisive laughter.

"That's a fine proof!" a woman exclaimed. "The man who isn't even a father is going away. Much good may it do him!"

Sarai saw Abram purse his lips. Lot's hand in hers felt hot and shivery. Abram took a few steps forward, and the crowd drew back, as if afraid to be too close to him.

"All right," he muttered. "I'm going to give you more proof."

To everyone's astonishment, he ran into Terah's workshop and came out again carrying two big statues, perfect in every detail of form, color, and dress. Sarai knew immediately what he was going to do. She felt a shudder down her spine, and her mouth went dry. To a general cry of horror, Abram threw the statues into the air. They fell at Terah's feet. There was a dry sound, like the crack of a whip or the noise of rain on hard soil. The idols lay on the ground, no more than shattered fragments now.

"Are your gods mighty?" Abram cried. "Then let them kill me, here and now! Let them strike me with lightning! Let the sky fall on me and crush me! I've just broken the faces and bodies of those you call Inanna and Ea!"

Sarai, like the others, was unable to hold back a groan.

"You worship them," Abram went on,

pointing to the sky. "You bow to them morning and night. There's nothing you do that they don't see. The figures my father makes are their flesh, their body, their sublime presence."

The crowd's lamentations grew in intensity. It was as if an enemy army had cut a swath through them.

"I've just broken what is sacred to you," Abram's voice rang out above the cries. "I should be punished! Let Inanna and Ea strike me down!"

He began to turn in a circle, his arm still held high, his face raised to heaven. Clasping Lot's thin body to her, Sarai heard herself murmuring, "Abram! Abram!"

But Abram was still whirling. "Where are they," he asked, "those you fear so much? I can't see them. I can't hear them. All I see is broken pottery. All I see is dust. All I see is the clay I took from the river with my own hands!"

He bent and picked up the head of the god Ea, whose nose was broken, and threw it against a stone, where it smashed.

"Why doesn't Ea extinguish the sun? Why doesn't he open the earth beneath my feet? I break his face and nothing happens . . ."

Men had fallen to their knees, holding their hands over their bowed heads, screaming as if their stomachs had been cut open. Others stared wide-eyed and recited prayers without pausing to catch their breath. Women wept and ran away, pulling their children by the arm, tearing their tunics on the undergrowth. Some stood openmouthed, searching the sky. Terah's old body was shaking like a branch in a storm. Lot was staring at Sarai, but she could not take her eyes off Abram. He was horribly calm. He turned and smiled at her, so tenderly, so serenely, that it melted her heart.

And nothing happened.

A strange silence returned.

In the warm sky of twilight the birds still flew. Small, high clouds still hung in the air. The river still flowed.

Abram strode to the kiln and seized a long wooden log. "Perhaps it isn't enough? Perhaps I must destroy all these statues, leave not a single one standing, before your almighty gods manifest themselves?"

He was already walking toward the entrance of the workshop, his arm raised.

"Abram!" Terah cried.

Abram turned.

"Don't destroy my work, my son."

Abram put down his stick. Father and son confronted each other, face-to-face. For the first time in many moons, they again seemed of one flesh.

Old Terah bent down and picked up a shard of pottery: the mouth, the nose, and one eye of Inanna. He rubbed his fingers over the terra-cotta lips, then pressed the shard to his chest.

"Perhaps the gods will punish you tomorrow, or in a few moons," he said, in a low, unsteady voice that obliged everyone to be silent. "Perhaps soon, perhaps never. Who can know what they decide?"

Abram smiled and threw the log on the ground. Terah walked right up to him, as if he wanted to touch him.

"Your god says, 'Go.' He says, 'Leave, you owe nothing to your father, Terah the potter.' He tells you that henceforth you must place in him the trust a son usually grants his father. Well, if that is what you also want, go. Obey your god. Take your share of the animals and get away from our tents. All will be well. But as for me, I no longer have a son named Abram."

There was so much to do, and the night seemed short. The chests had to be made ready, the tents taken down, the herds, mules, and wagons gathered by torchlight. With the servants who were leaving with

Abram and Sarai bustling about, the whole camp seethed with activity. There was a constant movement of lamps and dark figures. From time to time there came the weeping of children, or the braying of animals disturbed in their sleep.

Just before dawn, Sarai moved away from the loaded wagons and sat down on a stone, rubbing the small of her back to relax herself. The crescent moon lay between little clouds and, here and there, the stars glittered, as cool as spring water.

Sarai smiled: The sky had not collapsed, fire had not ravaged everything, water had not engulfed the world, as everyone had feared after Abram had broken the holy idols.

Someone's hands touched her shoulders, and she immediately recognized their weight and pressure. She leaned back until she was resting her back and shoulders on Abram's stomach.

"You didn't hear Him as I heard Him?" he asked, softly.

"No. Your god didn't speak to me."

"But you were on the plateau. You could have heard him, too."

"No. I was waiting for you."

"Are you only coming with me because it's your duty as a wife?"

"I'm going with you because you are Abram and I am Sarai."

"Yet not long ago you were still the Sacred Handmaid of Ishtar."

"Ishtar should have struck me down for abandoning her. It's been many moons since I last placed offerings on her altar. Inanna hasn't struck me down, any more than Ea has killed you."

Abram laughed, startling Sarai. He stroked her cheek. "Do you believe that He who spoke to me exists?"

"I don't know. But I trust you. I, too, know that the day will come when you lead a great people."

Abram fell silent as if pondering her words. Sarai was suddenly afraid that he would ask "How could I create a great people with your barren womb?" But he bent and kissed her on the temple.

"I'm proud of you," he whispered. "I wouldn't want any other wife than Sarai, the girl from Ur."

By the time the sky turned white, they were exhausted but ready to depart. Sililli was in a tetchy mood, complaining that it would bring them bad luck if they left without chanting and without saying farewell to those who were staying behind. This was the way you left when you had committed a sin or a crime. Even Terah had not come to bid farewell to his son. According to Tsilla and the other old women, such a thing was unheard of, and sure to bring misfortune!

Irritated by her words, Sarai told her that she was under no obligation to follow her. "I'll understand if you want to stay."

"Oh, yes!" Sililli retorted, offended. "And what would you do without me and my wisdom, my poor girl? You who always does the opposite of what you ought to! Who would you tell the things you can't confide in anyone else? Of course I have to go with you. Even though they say there's only barbarians and desert where your husband is taking us, and that it's the end of the land of men and beyond it there's only sea."

Sarai could not help laughing.

"There's one advantage in being as old as I am," Sililli went on. "I'll die before I see these horrors. But you can tell your husband this: I'm not walking. I'll sit in a wagon."

"In a wagon," Sarai said. "All right."

By the time Abram was ready to give the order for departure, Lot was nowhere to be seen. They were about to go and look for him when he came running.

"Abram! Sarai!" he shouted at the top of his voice. "Come and see, come and see."

He took them by the hand and dragged them through the camp, which seemed very quiet, as if everyone had finally decided to sleep. But when they came to the path overlooking Terah's workshop, they discovered a long column of wagons. The slopes of the hills on either side of the road were white with the herds gathered there. A hundred faces, perhaps two hundred, turned toward Abram. Men, women, children; young and old. More than a quarter of Terah's tribe.

They were all waiting patiently for him.

A man by the name of Arpakashad came forward. He was the same height as Abram but a little older, and known for his skills as a shepherd.

"Abram," he said, "we've been thinking about your words during the night. We've seen that neither Ea, nor Inanna, nor any of the gods we feared until today have punished you. We trust you. If you agree, we shall follow you."

Abram was moved. "My father says his gods may punish me later. Don't you fear them?"

Arpakashad smiled. "We're always fearing one thing or another. It would be good to stop being afraid."

"So you believe the God who spoke to me exists?" Abram insisted.

"We trust you," Arpakashad repeated.

Abram glanced at Sarai. Her eyes shone with pride.

"Then come with Sarai and Abram. And you will be the beginning of the nation the One God promised me."

Part Four

CANAAN

Abram's Words

At first they walked every day, from dawn to dusk. They left the mountains of Harran and followed the Euphrates southward, as if they were returning to the kingdom of Akkad and Sumer.

And so they walked, for three or four moons. The lambs, the women, and the children took turns in the wagons. They learned to make larger goatskins, longer tunics, and sandals with thicker soles to protect them from the heat of the day and the fierce cold of the night. Whenever they came in sight of a town or another tribe's camp, people would come to meet them. They became known as the "men from across the river" — the Hebrews.

Nobody complained about these long, tiring days. Nobody asked Abram why he was taking this route rather than another. Only Sarai saw the disquiet that sometimes seized her husband in the early hours, before they resumed their march.

One morning, with the sun not yet completely risen in the east, Abram was searching the horizon, a frown on his face, his mouth tense with anxiety, when he felt Sarai's eyes on him. He turned and smiled at her, but the frown remained. She came to him, stroked his brow with her fingers, and placed her cool palm on the back of his neck.

"He doesn't speak to me anymore," Abram said. "Not a word, not a command, since we left Harran. I don't hear His voice anymore."

Sarai gently continued her caress.

"I'm going where I think I have to go," Abram went on, "toward the land he promised me. But what if I'm wrong? What if we've come all this way for nothing?"

Sarai added a kiss to her caress. "I trust you," she said. "We all trust you. Why shouldn't your god also trust you?"

They never spoke of it again. But a few days later, Abram decided to change route and head westward. They left behind them the rich pastures beside the Euphrates and entered a country of sand and rough, sparse grass. Arpakashad came to see Abram and asked him to let the herds rest.

"Soon we'll be going into the desert, and nobody knows when we'll see grassland again. Better to let the animals grow fat and gather their strength. A little rest will do us good, too."

"Are you worried?" Abram asked.

Arpakashad smiled. "No. Nobody's worried, Abram. Or impatient. You're the only one who's anxious. We'll follow you. Your road is our road. And as it's likely to be a long road, what's the point in hurrying?"

Abram laughed and declared that Arpakashad was right. It was time to pitch camp for a moon or two.

From that day, their march again became what it had been when Terah was leading the tribe. It took them more than four seasons to cross the desert of Tadmor from one oasis to another, and reach the country of Damascus, where they discovered strange trees and fruit, but cautiously avoided the cities, settling only in the poorest pastures in order not to attract the anger of the inhabitants.

They grew so accustomed to this wandering life that some almost forgot that it would end one day. Sometimes, during a halt, a member of the tribe would form a relationship with a man or woman they had met around the wells or while trading.

Abram would give him or her permission to marry. More and more children were born. The only woman whose womb remained stubbornly empty was Sarai. But there were no more insistent looks. Even Sililli refrained from pestering her with advice and had stopped reporting the women's gossip. It seemed to be generally agreed that if Abram himself was prepared to wait for Sarai's womb to become fertile, then they, too, had to be patient. Abram's nephew Lot would take the place of their son. It was only Sarai herself who could no longer bear the emptiness of her womb.

One day, she entered the women's communal tent as a young married woman was giving birth to her first child. The woman's name was Lehklai, and she was younger than Sarai, with very pale skin, big dark eyes, and opulent breasts. For moons, Sarai had watched as her belly had become rounder, then her whole body: her hips, her buttocks, her breasts, her shoulders, even her cheeks and her lips. Every day, she had watched her with envy. There were quite a few other pregnant women in Abram's tribe, but, for Sarai, Lehklai was by far the most beautiful. Although she did not show it openly, she envied her, loved her, and hated her with an intensity that gave her more than a few sleepless nights. So, although she usually avoided the communal tent when women were giving birth, she had come in now to be present at Lehklai's confinement.

From the start, it was clear that things were not going according to plan. Lehklai was moaning. Sweat plastered her hair to her face, her mouth gaped open, her lips were dry, and her eyes wide and staring. It seemed as though her whole body were wracked with pain. The rest of the day passed in this way. The midwives spoke encouragingly to Lehklai and anointed her belly and thighs with sweet mentholated oil. Their words and gestures were the usual ones in this situation, but Sarai could see that they were growing increasingly worried. Lehklai would moan, become short of breath, then moan again. Her eyes still stared, as if turned inward.

By the afternoon, she was no longer answering when they talked to her. Finally, the midwives asked Sarai and Sililli to help them to massage Lehklai, for it seemed that the blood was refusing to circulate normally within her. Yet when Sarai stroked Lekhlai's body she found that it was burning hot.

The midwives decided they could wait no

longer. They placed the bricks of childbearing on the ground of the tent and, supporting Lehklai, tried to draw the baby into life. A long and terrible struggle followed. The midwives plunged their hands into Lekhlai's womb and managed to pull out a tiny baby girl, her mouth already formed for weeping and laughing. In the last light of day, Sarai and Sililli emerged from the tent, both shaking, their heads and chests still resounding from Lehklai's screams, which only death had stopped.

Sililli and Sarai looked at each other in silence. On the handmaid's aged face, Sarai read the words her mouth would not speak: "At least you won't die like that."

Sarai stood watching the sun as it vanished below the edge of the world like a drop of blood. A glittering full moon loomed over the approaching night. It was very hot, with a dense heat the evening breeze did nothing to allay.

Sarai shook her head. "You're wrong," she said in a low voice, just loud enough for Sililli to hear. "Lehklai doesn't frighten me. I envied Lehklai when she was full of life, so beautiful and so big with child. And I still envy her."

That night, Sarai decided to do some-

248

thing she had not done since Abram had become her husband. She opened one of the chests in her tent and took out a bag containing a handful of cedarwood shavings and a painted wooden statuette of Nintu. In spite of Sarai's scorn, Sililli had insisted on keeping it.

She slipped a few brands into an openwork pot with a leather lid. Then she left the encampment as stealthily as she could and walked in the moonlight to the other side of a hill. When she was certain she could not be seen, she lit a small fire between some stones.

Kneeling, her mind empty, Sarai waited until the fire was an ember, then threw in the cedarwood shavings. When the smoke was thick enough, she took from her belt a thin ivory knife Abram had given her, and slashed first her left palm, then her right. She then took the wooden statuette, rolled it between her hands until it was smeared with her blood, and murmured:

Nintu, mistress of the menstrual blood,
Nintu, you who decide on life in the
wombs of women,
Nintu, beloved patroness of child-
bearing, hear the lament of your daughter
Sarai,

Nintu, patroness of childbirth, you who received the sacred brick of childbearing from the hands of almighty Enki, you who hold the scissors to cut the birth cord,

Nintu, listen to me, listen to your daughter's pain,

Do not leave her in the void.

She fell silent, her throat rough and her eyes stinging from the cedarwood smoke. Then she stood up, and turned her face to the moon. The statuette against her belly, she resumed her lament. She repeated her prayer seven times, until the blood stopped flowing from the cuts. Then she crushed the embers with a big stone and returned to the encampment.

Cautiously, she walked to Abram's tent. The lamps were out. Abram liked to spend all night in conversation with Arpakashad and some of the old men of the tribe, but tonight, luckily, he had chosen to go to sleep early.

The cloth over the entrance to the tent had been folded back to let the air circulate. Sarai let it drop noiselessly. In the milky half-light that filtered through the material, she picked her way between the tent posts and the chests. Abram lay naked on the heap of rugs and skins that served as his bed.

250

His breathing was slow and regular, like that of a man in a deep, dreamless sleep.

Delicately, Sarai slipped the statuette of Nintu between the layers beneath Abram's feet. She took off her tunic, knelt beside her husband, took his penis between her palms, and gently stroked it. Abram's chest and stomach began to tremble. Sarai let her long curly hair slide over her husband's torso, grazed his chest with her nipples, kissed his neck and his temple, found his mouth. Abram opened his eyes like a man who does not know if he is still dreaming.

"Sarai?" he whispered.

Her only response was more caresses. She offered the small of her back to his hands and her breasts to his mouth. He was a mere shadowy figure to her, and she to him. Abram whispered her name again and again, "Sarai, Sarai," as if she were about to escape him, as if she might dissolve in his arms at the very moment she took him into her, wrapping him deep inside her womb. They grasped at each other like starving people, their whole bodies offered up to their voracious desire. They were both aware that their lovemaking was different tonight, fierce and unrestrained. The waves of pleasure that shook Abram's body swept through Sarai, too. She felt as though she had suddenly become as vast as an entire country, as light and as liquid as the horizon between sea and sky. Then the waves of her own pleasure took her breath away and Abram turned her over on the bed. Clasping his neck as if she was hanging from an enormous bird that was taking flight, Sarai offered her mouth and chest to Abram's breath, and let the final rush of his desire flood her.

"I'm a sterile woman, Abram," Sarai whispered: it was later, and her chest and hips were still painful with pleasure. "The blood hasn't flowed between my thighs for years. Putting your seed into my womb is like abandoning it in the dust."

"I know," Abram replied, just as gently. "We all know. We've known for a long time."

"I deceived you," Sarai insisted. "When you came to find me in the temple of Ur, I was already barren, already incapable of giving birth to a child. I didn't dare tell you. The joy of being carried off by you was too great; nothing else mattered."

"I knew that, too. A Sacred Handmaid of Ishtar is a woman who can't menstruate. Everyone in Ur knows that."

Sarai lifted herself on one elbow and

stared at her husband. In the pale moonlight, Abram's face was as clear and smooth as a silver mask. He was more beautiful than ever, with a beauty so calm and tender that it brought a lump to her throat. With trembling fingers, she stroked his eyebrows and lightly touched his cheekbones above his beard.

"But why? If you knew, why take me as a wife? A wife with a barren womb!"

"You are Sarai. I want no other wife than Sarai."

She shook her head, full of questions, uncomprehending. "Your god promised you a people, a nation. How can you become a people and a nation if your wife can't even give you a son?"

Abram smiled. "The One God didn't say to me: 'You chose a bad wife.' Abram is a happy husband."

Sarai sat down on the bed and observed him in silence. These words should have calmed her fears, but she could not be satisfied with them. The memory of her pleasure had now entirely vanished from her body, leaving only sadness.

Why couldn't she be delighted at Abram's words? Didn't they express all the love, all the kindness, she could ever wish for?

No, it seemed to her that Abram did not

fully grasp how heavy was the burden of sin that she carried, a burden not only on the two of them but also on those who accompanied them.

"I fell in love with you that first night," she said, in an almost inaudible voice. "That night I fell over you on the riverbank while I was fleeing the bridegroom my father had chosen. I wanted you to kiss me."

At last, she told him why she had bought herbs of infertility in the *kassaptu*'s lair. How she had almost died because of them and how, although he had left the city of Ur with his father, she had never stopped waiting for his kiss.

"I was barely a woman. My sin was due as much to the ignorance of youth as to my desire for you. The desire is still there, but I've become useless to you. You need a mother for your children, a fertile wife who will allow you to accomplish what your god expects of you."

Abram shook his head. He seized her hands and pressed them to his chest. "You're wrong: I need Sarai. Your stubbornness is my happiness. He who speaks to me, He who calls me and guides me, knows who you are. Just as I do. He wants you to be by my side. You, too, are blessed by Him, I know you are."

He kissed her palms ardently. And then, abruptly, he looked up. His lips had touched the new gashes she had inflicted on herself out of devotion to Nintu. Sarai saw his neck stiffen with anger.

"What have you done?" he cried.

She left the bed and took the statuette of Ninta from under the sheepskins. She stood naked before him, bold but fearful, the statuette in her hands.

"A sterile woman," she said, "would swallow earth, mud, and even monsters or demons if that could bring life back into her womb. Young Lehklai died today giving birth to a daughter. In spite of all my love for you, Abram, I wish no other death for myself."

Abram got to his feet before her. In the opalescent half-light of the moon, his features were indistinct, as if his face had disappeared. He was breathing rapidly, his chest rising and falling.

"This evening, I caressed Nintu with my blood," Sarai stammered, showing him the statuette. "Your seed is in my womb. The greater the pleasure the man and woman have had, they say, the more powerful the seed, the more agile . . ."

She fell silent, thinking that Abram was going to cry out, perhaps even hit her.

He held out his hand. "Give me that doll," he said, in a calm voice.

With a trembling hand, Sarai held out the statuette. Abram grabbed it by the head. From one of the tent posts, he unhooked a short bronze sword with a curved blade, a heavy, solid weapon with which Sarai had seen him cut the head off a ram. Not even taking the trouble to put on a loincloth, he walked naked out of the tent. He placed the idol on the ground and, with a few blows, smashed it to pieces, then threw the fragments as far as he could.

By the time he came back inside the tent, Sarai had put on her tunic. She stood there, her body stiff with humiliation and sorrow. Her eyes were dry and her mouth closed. In spite of the heavy heat, she was shivering.

Abram approached, seized her hands, and raised them to his mouth. He stopped the trembling of her fingers by pressing them to his lips. Then he kissed her palms, licking them with the gentleness of a mother kissing a graze on her child's skin to take away the pain. He drew Sarai to him.

"In Ur," he whispered, "they wanted you to confront the bull until it disemboweled you, on the pretext that no blood flowed between your thighs. My father, Terah, and all those who stayed with him thought badly of you, because we made love for nothing but our own pleasure. I know the questions Tsilla asked, moon after moon. I know the withering looks they all gave you. And I left you alone with the shame and the questions. I had no words to soothe your pain. How was I to tell them all that there was no shadow over the happiness I felt in having Sarai as my wife? That my wife's love was growing as much as any sons or daughters she could have given me? They all invoked their gods, talked of sin and resentment. They saw nothing in your womb but evil spells. And I, who saw nothing but their credulity and submissiveness, I left you alone with the burden of your sorrow."

He fell silent. Sarai held her breath. Abram's words, the words for which she had been waiting for so long, were coming at last, pouring into her, as warm and as sweet as winter honey.

"Don't keep taking upon yourself their fears and their superstitions. Trust my patience, as I trust you. You think that Abram's god isn't yet yours. You're sure you haven't heard or felt Him. Yet who knows if the herbs of infertility weren't a message from Him to you, Sarai, daughter of a lord of Ur, in order to turn you away from their vain worship? Who knows if it wasn't the road He showed you so that we could become husband and wife? In Harran, He said, 'Leave your father's house.' He didn't say, 'Leave your wife, Sarai, who can't transform your seed into a child.' He always says what He wants and what He doesn't want. He says to me, 'You are a blessing. I bless those who bless you.' Who blesses me more, day after day, night after night, than my wife, Sarai? He promised me a people, and He will give me one. Just as He will give us the land He promised me. Sarai, my love, stop wounding yourself with the knife of shame, for you are in no way at fault and your pain is mine."

Abram slid Sarai's tunic off her, and let it fall to the ground. He kissed her shoulder.

"Come and sleep beside me. Tonight and every night, until the One God shows us the land where we will settle."

Salem

It happened less than one moon later.

For some days now, the hills they had been crossing had seemed rounder and greener. There was no dust on the meadows or on the leaves of the trees. No need to search for wells, or to be content with stagnant water for the animals. Streams flowed from one valley to another, some of them so deep you could plunge your whole body in them. There were insects in abundance, such as are found only in fertile country. One morning, it started raining. Abram decided that they wouldn't walk that day, to let the rain clean the fleece of the sheep and the canvas of the tents. When it stopped, just before evening, the sun peeped out again from between the clouds, and they were all stunned by the beauty of the scene that confronted them.

Alas, although they had seen nobody for

days, it was clear to everyone that this land was not deserted. The pastures were bounded by walls; the paths bore traces of herds. That evening, they sat silently around the fires, dreaming of how happy they would be when Abram's god led them to a country like this.

The next day, in the pale light of dawn, Sarai woke with a start. Abram's place beside her was damp but empty. The tent flap was still swinging.

She rose in silence and was outside in time to see her husband walking quickly away. Without a moment's thought, she followed him.

Abram broke into a run. He dashed across a stream, sending up a spray of water around him, up the side of a small hillock, and into a large copse. Sarai followed him into the trees. She could not see him, but ahead of her she could hear the dead branches crackling under his hurrying feet. As she was about to leave the copse, she stopped dead and hid behind the trunk of a green oak, recovering her breath. A hundred paces ahead of her, on the summit of the hillock, Abram stood motionless in the tall grass. He had his back to her, his face lifted slightly and his arms half raised as if he were about to grasp something in his hands.

But there was nothing before him but the morning air, ruffled by a slight breeze.

Sarai stayed where she was, as motionless as Abram, watching for a movement, a sound.

But there was nothing: no noise, no gesture.

She could feel the breeze on her face. The grass swayed. Tiny yellow and blue butterflies whirled above the grass and the flowers. Birds chattered in the foliage. Some took flight and came to rest on other branches. The sun rose above the horizon and tinged the big puffy clouds with gold. There was nothing to see. Just the ordinary activity of a morning.

Yet she was sure of it: Abram was meeting his god.

Abram was listening to the voice of his invisible god.

How could a god give so little sign of himself? No face, no glow? Sarai could not understand it.

And if Abram was speaking with his god, she could not hear him.

All she saw was a man standing in the grass, surrounded by the indifferent birds and insects, his face lifted to the sky as if he had lost his reason.

It seemed to her that a long time had

passed, but perhaps it had not. Then, all at once, Abram raised his arms, and a cry rang out.

The birds ceased their din.

But the insects continued to whirl and the grass to sway.

Abram cried out again.

Sarai made out two syllables. An unknown word.

She took fright and ran away, as silently as possible. Her face was on fire, as if she had seen something she should not have seen.

"There was really nothing to see," Sarai said. "Nothing was moving, I swear it. Abram wasn't moving, either. If he was speaking, his voice was inaudible. And what he was seeing was invisible to my eyes."

Sililli was grinding corn, while Lot listened openmouthed. When Sarai had finished, Sililli shook her head, silent and unconvinced.

"But Abram spoke the name of his god," Lot said, enraptured, ready to hear the story again.

"I didn't realize it was a name," Sarai said. "When he cried out, I heard only two sounds. Like the sounds Arpakashad makes with his ram's horn to gather the herds. It was Abram, later, who said, 'The One God spoke to me. He told me his name. It's Yhwh.' "

"Yhwh!" Lot laughed. "Yhwh! Easy, no chance of forgetting it. And it *is* like the sound of a horn: Yhwh!"

"A god who can't be seen," Sililli grumbled, "who doesn't speak, and who only gives his name to one man! And then only when he feels like it. What's the point of a god like that, I wonder?"

"To find us a beautiful, fertile country full of water!" Lot replied, peremptorily. "You aren't listening to what Sarai is saying. Abram's god didn't only give his name: He said this land was now ours. The most beautiful land we've seen since we left Harran. But you, Sililli, you're too old to appreciate fields of thick grass. Nobody wants to roll in the grass with you anymore —"

"Now, now, boy!" Sililli scolded, landing a vigorous blow on Lot's buttocks with her wooden pestle. "You just hold your tongue, you. I may be too old for what you're thinking about, but you're still too wet behind the ears to think about it either!"

"That's just what I was saying," Lot laughed, unconcerned. "Too old to see the beauty of a country and too old to see the beauty of a boy who's becoming a real man!"

"Just listen to him!" Sililli guffawed, astounded at Lot's boldness.

Lot had taken up a pose before the two women, his hands on his hips, a thin, provocative smile on his lips and in his eyes, playing at being a man. But although Sarai and Sililli concealed their surprise, they both had to admit that he was right. These last few moons, they had paid too little attention to Lot; for them, he was still a boy, energetic, proud, and sensitive. In a short period of time, though, as often happened with adolescents, the boy had become a man. He was a full head taller than either of them. His shoulders were growing broader, more supple, with firmer muscles. There was a silky down on his cheeks and around his mouth, and the gleam in his eye was no longer as innocent as it had once been. The smile he now gave Sarai brought a blush to her cheeks.

"Seeing my aunt's beauty every day," he murmured, in his slightly husky voice, "is enough to make anyone impatient to be a man."

Sililli squealed, pretending to be offended, and shooed Lot away. Lot went and sat down some distance from them, muttering under his breath. It was only when he turned his back on them that Sarai and

Sililli exchanged an amused look.

"He isn't the only one to think that way," Sililli said in a low voice. "Your beauty is starting to excite all these idle young rams. It's time Abram decided to make a real halt and build our city. Then these youngsters would finally have something to spend their energy on."

Sarai remained silent for a moment. She threw grain into the mortar, watched as Sililli's pestle crushed it. "What if we've already reached the end of our journey? Abram is sure that his god has given us this land. To all of us, now and in the future, even to those who are not yet born."

Sililli shook her head, skeptically. But as Sarai fell silent again, she looked up. There was no need of words: They were both thinking the same thing.

"Who knows?" Sililli said, tenderly. "Perhaps he's right."

"Abram was trembling with joy when he came back to the tent. He threw himself on me and covered me with kisses. He kissed my belly and repeated the words of his God: 'I give this land to your seed!' When I reminded him that the hills and valleys of my country were not very fertile, he almost lost his temper. 'You don't understand! If Yhwh says that, it means He's thinking of you, my wife! Be patient, the One God will soon show you how powerful He is.' "

Sililli shook her flour-whitened fingers. "Hmm. Who knows?" she repeated.

"But Abram isn't exactly patient," Sarai said, amused. "I tell you, there isn't a single night or morning that he doesn't make sure his god will be able to make his seed bear fruit!"

Eyes sparkling, they both burst into a great laugh full of joy and lightness.

Lot had stood up. "Why are you laughing?" he asked. "Why are you laughing?"

The following day, they came to the entrance of a vast valley that stretched beside a chain of mountains. The mingled greens and yellows of the fields of flowers, cereals, and pasture were like a woven cloth. Animals grazed in the pastures, and men were working in the meadows.

Their awe was marred by frustration. Why had Abram's god marked out this country for them?

Sarai turned to Abram and summed up what everyone was thinking. "This land is magnificent, but it doesn't seem to be clear of people. How can we possibly put up our tents here or build a city?"

Abram looked for a long time at the landscape before his eyes. Clearly, Yhwh had wanted to show him how beautiful this country was before he entered it. Yes, this land could support them. To the west and the south there was no sign of sheep or cattle.

"There is enough here for us," he said.

"It's quite possible," Arpakashad replied, somberly. "But Sarai is right: As soon as our herds drink from the rivers, and our buckets lift water from the wells, there'll be disputes."

Abram smiled, without taking offense. It was a long time since they had seen him look so joyful and so serene. Nothing seemed to mar his good humor. He shook his head.

"Parts of this country are empty. Look: There's a city on top of the mountain. Come."

He asked for three of the best wagons to be brought forward, drawn by the finest mules, and had their interiors covered with clean sheets.

"Fill these wagons with all the loaves baked yesterday and this morning," he declared. "Add all the good food we have: newly killed lambs, fruit picked in the last few days. And let's go and offer it all to the inhabitants of this city."

"You're stripping us completely bare," a woman cried out, in a shrill voice. "What will we have left to eat in the next few days?"

"I don't know," Abram replied. "We shall see. Perhaps the inhabitants of the city will give us something to eat in return . . ."

Abram was so sure of himself that as presumptuous as his words seemed, they knew they had no other choice than to follow him in his obstinacy.

In the heat of the afternoon, they took the path leading to the city.

They formed a long procession: more than a thousand men, women, and children, at least double that in small livestock, not counting the wagons carrying the tents and the chests, and the herds of mules and asses. The cloud of dust raised by their sandals and clogs could be seen from a long way away. Then there was the noise of bleating animals, creaking axles, and even the pebbles dislodged by their steps.

It was no surprise that they had hardly come within sight of the city when trumpets and drums sounded the alarm. His long stick in one hand, the other resting on his mule's saddle girth, Abram took care to advance slowly. He wanted the people of the city to be able to examine them at leisure from the walls and see that they were approaching peacefully, unarmed and not in any warlike spirit.

But when they arrived an arrow's length from the dazzling white walls, the huge blue-painted gate that constituted the only opening remained resolutely shut.

Above the crenellated walls, helmets and spears could be seen moving, and in the vertical openings of the narrow towers shadowy figures were visible.

Abram raised his stick, and the column came to a halt. He placed his hands around his mouth.

"My name is Abram!" he cried. "I come in peace with my people to salute those who have beautified this land and built this city!"

Abandoning his stick, he held out his right hand and took Sarai's hand, then with his left took Lot's. He asked all of them to do the same. Families joined hands, forming clusters, and came together with Abram and Sarai, until all were united in a crescent shape. It was obvious now to those watching them that they were not concealing any weapons.

They remained like this for a while, in the sun.

Then suddenly the door creaked, rumbled, half opened, then gaped wide open.

Soldiers appeared. Dressed in harsh-colored tunics, with shields and spears in their hands, they advanced with a firm stride in two parallel columns toward Abram and his people. Some could not help taking a few steps backward in fear. But when they saw that Abram had not moved an inch, they resumed their places.

When they were some twenty paces away, the warriors came to a halt. Everyone noticed that they were not pointing their spears at the newcomers' chests but toward the sky, and resting the shafts on the ground. They also noticed that their faces were similar to theirs. Their eyebrows, beards, and hair were jet black. Unlike the warriors of Akkad and Sumer, they wore neither wigs nor helmets, but strange-colored hats. Their eyes, as black as their skin, glittered with kohl.

A trumpet sounded at the gate of the city. A gentle, solemn sound.

An excitable, colorfully dressed crowd of people came out. At their head were ten old men with round bellies and long beards, dressed in capes of intense red and blue, their heads wrapped in wide yellow turbans, and necklaces of silver and jasper hanging from their necks. Young boys walked beside them, carrying palms to give them shade.

The surprising thing about the old men was that they were smiling a smile they all recognized, and Sarai first of all: It was the same smile her husband had had since morning.

The wise men of the city came to a halt. Abram let go of Sarai's and Lot's hands and took two big loaves from the nearest wagon. He bowed respectfully to the oldest, most richly dressed, and most noble-looking of the men, and offered him the loaves.

"My name is Abram. I come in peace with my people. They call us the Hebrews, the men from across the river, for we have come a long way. These are the loaves we baked yesterday and today. I am happy to offer them to the inhabitants of this city, although it is a rich city and well able, I'm sure, to bake a hundred times as many."

The old man took the loaves between his ringed fingers and passed them to those beside him. Behind them, the soldiers could no longer hold back the crowd, who thronged around the newcomers, curious and excited. Children cried and gesticulated to attract the attention of the travelers' children.

The old man Abram had addressed raised his hand. The trumpet rang out, and silence returned.

"My name is Melchizedek. I am king of

the city of Salem, of this people, and of this land, which we call Canaan. From the river in the east to the shores of the sea in the west, other peoples share this land with us."

He spoke slowly and calmly, in the Amorite language, though with an accent that Sarai had never heard before.

"I, Melchizedek, welcome you, Abram, and those who are with you. Salem and Canaan welcome you. We open our arms to you. In the name of God Most High, who created heaven and earth, I bless your coming."

A heavy silence fell.

Abram turned to Sarai, his face jubilant. "Did you hear?" he cried, in a voice loud enough to be heard by everyone. "Lord Melchizedek, King of Salem, blesses us in the name of the One God. These people are our brothers."

Sarai's Beauty

Their happiness lasted ten years.

That first day, there was a great feast, at which both food from Salem and the new-comers' food was served. They all became drunk on beer and stories. It was an occasion for mutual admiration and discovery. It was decided that Abram would pay a tithe for each animal from his flocks that grazed on the lands of Canaan. It was also decided that he would not build a city, in order not to compete with the beautiful city of Salem, and that, as their fathers had done in the past, he and his people would put up and take down their tents according to where they found pastures.

King Melchizedek and his wise men questioned Abram about the land from which he had come and the lands they had crossed in the course of their long march to Salem. They were astonished that Abram's people had found their way to Canaan across a thousand mountains and valleys, rivers and deserts. They knew nothing of the kingdom of Akkad and Sumer and asked Sarai to show them, on a tablet of fresh clay, the writing that was used there. They found it remarkable that things, animals, men, colors, and even feelings could be depicted by signs.

Finally, they asked Abram what he knew of the One God. They themselves venerated Him: He was the God of their fathers, and He had always assured them peace and prosperity on their land. However, the invisible God had never yet spoken to them. He had not told His name to any of them.

Yhwh.

King Melchizedek declared that Abram, although he looked like a shepherd leading an ill-assorted group of people, some not even related to him, was undoubtedly a king as noble as himself. He announced, in his youthful voice, that he would bow to him, despite the difference in age, and with all the respect he would have granted an equal.

Following his words, all the wise men and all the inhabitants of Salem did the same. Then Melchizedek turned to Sarai, who had been standing there in silence.

"Abram," he said, "allow me also to bow

to your wife, Sarai. Perhaps her beauty seems quite normal to all of you, and she doesn't sear your eyes with rapture. But she is the most beautiful woman the One God has ever set across my path. And I have no doubt that he placed her by your side as a sign of all the beautiful things he intends to offer your nation."

And Melchizedek bowed to Sarai, seized a tail of her tunic, and brought it to his lips. When he stood up again, his mouth was quivering.

"I am old," he whispered so that only she could hear, "but that's fortunate, because if I were young and knew you existed but could never be mine, I wouldn't be able to go on living."

Sarai had hoped that once they had reached the land promised by his god, Abram would order a city to be built. A real city, with brick houses, alleyways, courtyards, doors, and cool roofs. Yes, all the grandeur of a city. The truth was, she was missing the beauty of Ur. She was missing the solid, immutable splendor of the ziggurat. And the shade of her bedchamber in Ichbi Sum-Usur's house, the scents of the garden, the noise of the goat-skins being filled, the murmur of water in the basins at night.

She was not the only one who was weary of putting up and taking down the tents and following where the animals' hunger led them. But it did not take many moons for everyone to see how miraculous a country Canaan was.

It was possible to stay on the same piece of land for two or three seasons. Milk and honey seemed to ooze from the hills and valleys. Rain alternated with dryness and coolness with heat without one ever exceeding the other. Abundance made both the herds and the children fat. Sons grew taller than their fathers. As the days went by, they all forgot their dream of a city, even Sarai.

The tents grew bigger, until they consisted of several rooms divided by curtains. Abram had a huge tent made, with black and white stripes, as a meeting place for the heads of the different families. The women of Salem taught the newcomers to dye wool and linen in bright, cheerful colors, and showed them new patterns into which they could be woven. They put away their old white-and-gray tunics and began to dress in reds, ochers, blues, and yellows.

Within two years, word of the peace and prosperity of Canaan and Abram's and Melchizedek's wisdom had spread far and wide, carried by shepherds and caravans of merchants.

Strangers began to arrive from the north and the east with their meager herds — only a few at first, then in greater numbers. They would bow to Abram with the same words and the same expectations.

"We have heard about you, Abram, and your invisible god who protects you and leads you. Where we come from, there is only poverty, dust, and war. If you accept us among you, we shall obey you and follow you in all things. We shall serve your god, and make offerings to Him as you instruct us. You will be our father and we will be your sons."

Some arrived from the south after crossing the three deserts on Canaan's borders. They seemed richer, less like peasants, than those from the north and the east, but were just as eager to belong to Abram's people.

"We come from a land of great richness, irrigated by a huge river whose source nobody knows," they recounted. "The king who reigns there is called Pharaoh. He is a living god, and has unlimited power. He sits beside other gods who are half men and half birds, cats, or rams. His cities and palaces are magnificent, the tombs of his fathers even more beautiful than his palaces. But his power intoxicates those who serve him. In Pharaoh's land, they kill men as easily as others squash flies. It isn't hunger that we fear, but servitude and humiliation."

Abram never refused the pastures of Canaan to any of the newcomers. He blessed their arrival with as much pleasure as Melchizedek had blessed him at the foot of Salem. With a tolerance that surprised everyone, he never forced anyone to believe in his god, even though his own devotion to the One God was absolute. He built altars to Him all over Canaan, and never let a day go by without making offerings to Him and calling His name: Yhwh! Yhwh! His only sorrow was the silence that answered him. Not a day passed that he did not hope for a new call from God Most High, as he had started calling Him, a new command to perform a new task.

But Yhwh was silent. What was there for him to say? As promised, Abram was becoming a people, a nation, and a great name. And without Sarai giving him a son or a daughter! Since they had settled in the land of Canaan, they had stopped being surprised by Sarai's sterility.

Everyone — men and women, new arrivals, and those who had walked from

Harran — was captivated by Sarai's beauty.

Hers was a beauty that seemed in itself such a perfect expression of abundance that they were obliged to suppress their feelings of jealousy or lust. Similarly, it was understood that Abram, taking advantage of this beauty like a newlywed, seemed to feel no sadness at having no heir. All was well. Peace and happiness were numbing their hearts and minds. Well-being had become their daily bread. It was an intoxication from which no sorrow roused them. Sarai's beauty, her flat stomach, her smooth cheeks and neck, her young girl's breasts and hips, had become a sign of the happiness that Abram's god, Yhwh, had granted them.

For a long time they did not realize the true miracle they had before their eyes: Sarai's beauty was untouched by time. The moons, the seasons, the years went by, but Sarai's youth seemed immutable.

The weight of this silent miracle, though at first it delighted her, was beginning to terrify Sarai herself.

One summer's day, Sarai was bathing in the hollow of a river, as she liked to do when the sun was at its hottest. It was a spot where dense trees formed a chamber of greenery, where the current had hollowed a deep basin in the rock, and where the greenish-blue water was deep enough to dive in. Sarai would often come there to bathe naked. Then she would emerge, shivering, while the hot sun sizzled on the foliage above her, and lie down on the bank, where the rocks, polished by the winter floods and as soft as skin, were still cool. More often than not, she would fall asleep.

That afternoon, a noise startled her out of her drowsiness. She half sat up, thinking it was some animal, or a dead branch that had fallen from a tree. She saw nothing, and the noise was not repeated.

She was resting her chest and cheek against the rock when she heard a laugh above her. A body leaped out from between the trees, seized her tunic, and disappeared with a splash into the water. Sarai had recognized him.

"Lot!"

Lot's head emerged from the water. With a great burst of laughter, he waved Sarai's streaming wet tunic above his head. Sarai huddled on the ground and covered her nakedness as best she could.

"Lot! Don't be stupid. Give me back my tunic and get out of here!"

With two strong bounds, Lot was at her feet. Before she could make a move, he threw her tunic away and embraced her calves. He kissed her knees and thighs fiercely, trying to put his arms around her waist. With a cry of rage, Sarai gripped a handful of his hair. Twisting her hips and pulling on his head, she freed her legs. No longer mindful of her modesty, she managed to place one foot on Lot's shoulder and push him away. But Lot had become a strong young man. He loosened his embrace, although he did not let go completely. Laughing, and drunk with excitement, he struggled, gripped Sarai's neck from the back, and placed a hand on her chest. Sarai, her muscles hardened by anger, moved to the side, kicked Lot in the crotch, and at the same time slapped him across the face with all her strength.

In shock and pain, Lot rolled off the rock and fell into the water. Sarai got to her feet, found her tunic, and quickly put it on, soaked as it was. With a childlike moan, Lot hoisted himself out of the river. He lay for a moment on his side, his features distorted with pain and embarrassment. Sarai stared at him, her rage still not abated.

"Shame on you! Shame on you, nephew of Abram!"

Lot stood up, his face pale, his chin quivering. "Forgive me," he stammered.

"You're so beautiful."

"That's no reason. I'm Abram's wife. Have you forgotten that? I can't forgive you."

"Yes, it's a good reason, and a true one!"

He had almost shouted. He looked away, and sat down on the rock, with his back to Sarai.

"You don't notice anything," he went on. "I see you every day. At night, you're in my dreams. I think of you as soon as I open my eyes in the morning."

"You mustn't."

"It isn't my choice. You don't choose the woman you fall in love with."

"You shouldn't even dare to say such words. If Abram's god heard you —"

"Abram's god can hear me if He wants!" Lot interrupted, fiercely. "You're the one who doesn't hear me! You don't even see that I'm near you more often than Abram. You don't see that I pay you more attention than he does. There's nothing you ask of me that I don't do gladly. But you don't see me. And when you speak my name, it's as if I'm still the child you used to scold. I'm no longer that child, Sarai. My body has grown and my thoughts, too."

Sarai suddenly felt confused and embarrassed. Lot's voice was throbbing with pain.

282

Why hadn't she seen his suffering? He was right. She didn't see him. Or rather, while she saw the handsome young man he had become, thinner and more delicate than Abram, with something feminine in his suppleness, she continued to think of the child he had been, always laughing and playful. Meanwhile, everywhere in Canaan young women must be going to sleep with his image in their minds, dreaming of having him as a husband one day.

Sarai's anger ebbed. She tried to find some wise and tender words with which to calm Lot. But he faced her, his eyes as bright as if they were coated with kohl.

"I know what you're thinking. I know all the words you have in your mouth, all the words you could use to condemn me or calm me down. You're thinking of Abram who's like my father. You're going to tell me you're like my mother."

"Isn't that the truth? Is there any greater sin than to covet your mother — your father's wife?"

Lot's laughter was terrible to hear. "Abram isn't my father! He doesn't even want to be my father; he didn't adopt me. And you say you're like my mother. But what mother ever looked like you?"

"Lot!"

"You are the woman I loved for years like a mother, yes. But who could think you as a mother now? Nobody — not even me."

"What do you mean?"

Lot plunged his hand in the river and sprinkled water on his face and chest, as if he were burning hot despite the shade of the trees. "They're like blind people," he said. "But you can't be blind. Not you."

Lot seized Sarai's hands. When she tried to break away, he held them tighter, kissed them, and lifted them gently and respectfully to his brow.

"I've always loved you, Sarai. With all my heart, with all the love I'm capable of. I love you so much I was even happy when you had to become my mother. Fortunately for me — or unfortunately — apart from Abram, I'm the only man who knows how soft your skin is, how firm and warm your body. You used to hug me. A long time ago — though I remember it as if it were only yesterday — we even slept in the same bed for a few nights. I woke up with the smell of your breasts in my nostrils."

"Lot!"

"Every day since I was a child I've been looking at your face. And every day it's the same perfect face."

Sarai abruptly took her hands away from

284

Lot's hands. Now it was she who avoided his gaze.

"How can they not see it?" Lot went on. "I was a child, then a boy. Now I'm a man. Time has done its work on me. It's molded my body. But on you, Sarai, it hasn't put a single wrinkle. The women who were young when I was a child now have heavy hips, and their bellies are soft from bearing children. They have wrinkles around their eyes and mouths, their brows and necks are lined. I look at you and see none of that. Your skin is more beautiful than the skin of the girls who want me to caress them behind the bushes. Time has no effect on you, and that's the truth."

"Be quiet," Sarai implored.

"You can ask me anything," Lot said in a low voice, looking down, "except not to love you as a man loves a woman."

One night soon after, when Abram had joined her in her bed and they were lying side by side in the darkness, still numb from their caresses, Sarai told Abram how Lot had surprised her on the riverbank.

"If Lot's passion surprises you," Abram laughed, "you must be the only one. When Lord Melchizedek asked him why he didn't seem very eager to make offerings on the altar of God Most High, he replied that he'd only be certain that Yhwh existed if He appeared to him looking like you!"

They both laughed.

"When Lot was still a young boy," Sarai said, "and we were walking from Harran, he was enthusiastic about your god. He wanted me to keep telling him over and over what you said about Him. Now he's a man, and he says he can't love me as a mother or an aunt because time has no effect on me. Is that what you think, too? That time no longer has any effect on me?"

For a moment, Abram remained silent and still. Then, in a warm, joyful voice, he agreed.

"But isn't that a curse?" Sarai asked under her breath. "A punishment sent by your god?"

Abram sat up, letting the cover slide off their bodies. In a long kiss, he ran his lips from Sarai's neck to the hollow between her thighs.

"My flesh, my fingers, my heart, and my mouth drink their fill of happiness at your beauty, night after night. It's true: The seasons pass and Sarai's beauty doesn't fade. On the contrary. The days move us closer to death as the donkey moves the wheel to raise water from the well. But my wife,

Sarai, is as fresh tonight as she was the first time I undressed her."

"And doesn't that frighten you?"

"Why should it frighten me?"

"Aren't you afraid that others are as aroused by it as Lot is, but with less affection and less reason? Aren't you afraid that your wife may become a source of envy, resentment, and hatred?"

Abram laughed confidently. "There isn't a man in Canaan who isn't mad with desire for you. How could I not be aware of it? There isn't a man or a woman who doesn't envy Abram and Sarai. But not one of them will dare to do what my nephew Lot dared. Because they know. They know what Melchizedek saw in you as soon as we arrived in Salem: Yhwh wants you to be beautiful, and not just for me. Your beauty is a beacon for Canaan, an offering from Him to the people of Abram. You may not be able to give birth, but Yhwh makes your beauty the seed of our eternal happiness. God Most High is holding back the effects of time on you because you are a messenger of all the beautiful things he will accomplish. Who among Abram's people would dare to sully this messenger?"

Sarai would have liked to protest. To say that she did not feel that way at all, that all she felt was the weight of the time that never passed and the endless desire to have children. She would have liked to say that such thoughts were merely a man's imagination, that Abram's god had not announced or promised anything of the sort, only a people and a fertile seed. But Abram covered her in caresses, reducing her to silence and once again drawing from her the pleasure that was his fulfillment.

Later, in the darkness, Abram's breath against her shoulder as he slept, Sarai was overcome with sadness. She bit her lips and pressed her eyelids to stop her tears. How she would have preferred her belly to grow round and her face to crease with wrinkles! What could she do with this beauty, which was as dry as grassland cracked by heat? How could a sterile beauty be preferable to the cry of life and the laughter of a child?

Filled with anger and fear, plagued by questions she could not answer, she found it impossible to get to sleep. For the first time since they had left Harran, Sarai was seized with intense doubt.

What if Abram was wrong? What if he was misled by his wish to love his god and achieve great things? What if, in thinking he could hear an invisible and intangible god, he was the victim of his own imagination or a demon's scheming? In all honesty, what use was the power of a god who could not even make the bridal blood flow between her thighs?

A Child of Drought

Soon after that night, the happiness they had
known in Canaan began to disintegrate. The
number of people coming to swell Abram's
tribe suddenly increased. Most were from the
north, some even from the cities, artisans
rather than shepherds.

"Where we come from, the harvests have
been bad," they all said. "The rains haven't
fallen, the fields are barren, the rivers have
run dry."

Abram would welcome them without hesitation. Soon, there was not a single patch of
land in the whole of Canaan that was not
being used for livestock. In the autumn, the
tents were not taken down. The grass in the
pastures was short and hard. When they
gathered in the big black-and-white tent,
there was the first sign of unease from those
who had been with Abram from the beginning.

"Aren't you afraid?" they asked Abram.

"Afraid of what?"

"That there are too many of us in the land of Canaan now?"

"God Most High gave me this land and no other," Abram replied, "and He did not put any limits on my people."

Abram might not want any limits, the others thought, but a bad season might well set them. But they said nothing. Just as Sarai said nothing. Abram had become so sure of himself, so confident, that he repelled doubts and questions as easily as a bronze shield repels arrows. He also began to share Sarai's bed less often.

"Even the greatest of beauties can tire a husband," Sarai told Sililli, bitterly. "He doesn't need to make love with me anymore; he's quite happy now just thinking about it."

"Men never get tired of those things!" Sililli joked. "They may not be able anymore, but as long as they can get their shaft up, they're always ready and willing!"

Sarai shook her head, unsmiling. "Abram knows my face and my body will be the same tomorrow as they are today. There's nothing he can get from me that he hasn't already had. Why should he be in any hurry?"

She did not say what she was really thinking. There was no need: Sililli was thinking the same thing.

Lot could also see her distress. Since his declaration of love, he had avoided doing anything that might provoke Sarai's anger. But he stayed beside her, affectionate and silent. They often spent whole evenings together, listening to singing and music in the encampment, or to tales and legends recounted by passing merchants or the old men of a newly arrived clan.

Sarai would sometimes let her gaze linger on Lot's handsome face. She would give a start whenever he burst out laughing at a joke told by one of the storytellers. His loyalty, his attentiveness, his constant presence made her feel a curious mixture of joy, tenderness, and remorse.

"There are lots of girls who'd like to see you," she would say to him. "Why don't you go to them? That's where you belong."

She did not dare add, "You'll have to take a wife sooner or later."

Lot would look at her, with an expression at once serious and calm, and shake his head. "This is where I belong," he would reply. "This is all I want."

Sometimes, then, Sarai would open her arms to him. She would clasp him to her, kiss his neck, and let him kiss her, as if he were still a child.

"You're going to drive him mad," Sililli would say, whenever she caught them.

"If we can't be mother and son," Sarai would reply, blushing, "we can at least be sister and brother!"

"Sister and brother!" Sililli would retort, seriously angry. "When the cows come home! I love Lot as much as you do, and I tell you that what the two of you are doing to him, you with your beauty and Abram with his indifference, is really cruel. You ought to force him to take a wife and a herd and go and make children in the Negev Desert!"

Sililli was right. Sarai would feel a coldness in her chest, and her back would tighten with fear: The sins committed by her and Abram were accumulating.

One night, she had a bad dream she did not dare tell anyone about, least of all Sililli. She saw herself emerging from the river where Lot had surprised her. Lot was not there. She was surrounded by a large number of children, both boys and girls. Strange children with round bellies, as if they were pregnant, and empty faces. Completely empty: no mouths, no noses, no eyes or eyebrows. And all exactly alike, despite the absence of features. But Sarai was not afraid. She walked across the pastures, accompanied by this swarm of children. Everything in Canaan seemed as beautiful as ever. Extravagant flowers had grown in the freshly plowed fields. Flowers on big stems, with vast yellow corollas. Sarai and the children ran toward them, shouting with joy, eager to pick them. But as they drew nearer, they noticed that the stems were covered in hard thorns that made it impossible to take hold of them. The flowers themselves turned out to be balls of fire, like incandescent suns. They burned everyone's eyes, they burned the fields, they dried up the trees. Sarai began to cry out in terror. She wanted to warn Abram, Melchizedek, and all the elders of the tribe: "Careful, the flowers are going to destroy you, they're going to transform Canaan into a desert!" But the children calmed her tenderly, happily showing their big bellies and saying, "It isn't serious, it isn't serious! Look how big our bellies are. We're going to give birth to all your sins, and you can eat them when the fields are empty."

"Abram is playing at being a father," Lot said, with a scornful laugh.

It was a few days later, and Sarai had resolved that she would try to persuade Lot to leave her and take a wife.

"What do you mean?" she asked.

"Among the newcomers from Damascus, there's a young boy who never leaves him, who's always dogging his steps. Or else it's Abram who never leaves him, whichever you prefer."

"How old is he?"

"Eleven or twelve. The same age I was when you became my mother." Lot smiled, and his face creased like a peach that had fallen in the sand. He shrugged his shoulders. "A good-looking boy with very curly hair, a big mouth, and a long nose the women will like. He's crafty, too, and cheats at games. I've been watching him. He knows just how to win Abram over. He's more affectionate than I ever was."

"Why does he hang around Abram?" Sililli asked. "Doesn't he have a father or a mother?"

"He has everything he needs. And now he has all Abram's attention."

"Point him out to me," Sarai said.

The boy's name was Eliezer, and he was exactly as Lot had described him: handsome, lively, affectionate, and endearing. And yet, from the moment she set eyes on him, Sarai disliked him. She really did not understand why. Was it the way he tilted his head to one side when he smiled? Was it his rather heavy lids that made his eyes into slits?

"Could it be you're jealous?" Sililli asked, with her usual frankness. "You have every reason to be. All the same, the boy is good news. Abram has finally noticed how tired he was of not being a father. He's discovering the joys of fatherhood with this Eliezer. Who could blame him? Wanting to be king of a great people without knowing what it is to be a father, your husband was starting to worry me."

"Well, I can't see anything in this boy to delight me!" Sarai replied, dryly.

She took the first opportunity to ask Abram about him. "Who is this boy who's never out of your sight?"

Abram's smile was radiant. "Eliezer? The son of a muleteer from Damascus."

"Why do you like him so much?"

"He's the most adorable child in Canaan. He's not only pleasant-looking. He's intelligent, brave, and obedient. And he's a quick learner."

"But he already has a father, Abram. Does he need two?"

Abram's smile faded. For the first time in all their married life, Sarai had the feeling that he was forgetting his love for her.

They stood looking at each other in silence, both dreading the wounding words that might emerge from their mouths. Sarai knew that for several moons now, she had been right. Her beauty was no longer enough. Was the sin of it weighing more heavily on her than on Abram?

"I've known for a long time that it was bound to happen," she said, as gently as she could. "Nobody could have been better than you, having a sterile wife."

Abram remained silent. He waited, a severe expression in his eyes, sure she was about to add something.

"We've both always thought of Lot as our son," she went on. "Not only in our hearts, but in reality, he has been our son for years. Why prefer an unknown boy who has his own father and mother, when you could adopt Lot and make him the heir I can't give you?"

"Lot is my brother's son," Abram replied, coldly. "He already has a place beside me, now and in the future." He turned and left the tent.

Night had only just fallen. Once more, he spent it far from Sarai's arms.

The following winter, the wind blew but

the rain did not fall. The earth became so hard that it was almost impossible to dig furrows. In the spring, the rain still did not fall, and the seeds dried in the soil without germinating. At the first shimmer of warm air above the pastures in summer, the thought on everyone's mind was drought.

Sarai, like many, spent each day dreading the next. She recalled her bad dream. Sometimes, it seemed to her that the land of Canaan was becoming like her: beautiful and barren.

She would have liked to be able to confide in Abram, question him again. "Aren't you wrong about the meaning of this beauty that clings to me? By forcing this beauty on me, isn't your god trying to tell you that my sin is greater than you think? Must I go away before the barrenness of my womb spreads to the pastures of Canaan?"

But whenever she spoke of these torments, Sililli would give a cry of horror and urge her to keep silent.

"What pride, my child, to think that the rain falls or doesn't fall because of you! Even in Ur, where you lords were quite capable of thinking you were the cat's whiskers, it took more than one sin for the gods to stop the rain! And I'll tell you something: This nonsense isn't going to get your husband back between your thighs!"

During all this time, Abram seemed the most heedless of them all. Not a day went by that he did not set off across the pastures with Eliezer. They would sleep in the open air, or cast nets on the seashore. He would teach the boy to weave baskets or mats out of bulrushes, to carve horn and train mules.

Seeing them, Sarai would feel a lump in her throat, and her saliva would turn acid, as if she were chewing green lemons. She would try to see reason, to listen to Sililli's advice: "It's all right. It's as it should be. Love this child as Abram loves him, and you'll be happy again. What else can you expect?" But however hard she tried, she still did not like Eliezer.

Then a day arrived when Melchizedek came to the black-and-white tent.

"Abram, the seeds are no longer germinating, the grass in the pastures is drying up, there's less water in the rivers and wells. Our reserves are not large. Nobody can remember a drought here in the land of milk and honey in living memory. But the soil of Canaan has so many people on it now, it can no longer feed us all."

"God Most High gave us this land. Why would He cause a drought?"

"Who could know the answer better than you, since He speaks only to you?"

Abram frowned and said nothing.

Melchizedek placed a hand on his arm. "Abram," he said, affectionately, "I need your help. We don't have your confidence. We need to be reassured and to know the will of Yhwh. Remember, I greeted you before the walls of Salem with the words 'Abram is my dearest friend.' "

Abram clasped him in his arms. "If Yhwh has a wish in this trial, He will tell me."

He ordered young heifers, rams, and lambs to be offered up, and went off with Eliezer to call on Yhwh in all the places where he had built altars in Canaan. But after one moon had passed, he had to admit the truth.

"God Most High is not speaking to me. We must wait; nothing happens without a reason."

"What's the use of a god who doesn't help when we make him offerings?" someone dared to say.

Abram's mouth quivered with anger, but he contained himself. "You have all known ten years of happiness," he said. "A happiness and a prosperity so perfect that they have aroused the envy of all the people around Canaan. Now at the first drought you forget all that. You're free to think what you like. But I say: We have known happiness, now we must know hardship. Yhwh wants to make sure that we trust Him, even when times are hard."

The drought lasted another year. The wells dried up, the pastures yellowed, then became dust. Long crevasses opened in the fields of cereals and became the lairs of snakes, which lay in wait for any prey they could find. The grasshoppers began to die, then the birds. The animals went mad, tearing off at a gallop until they fell to the ground dead. Sometimes they would simply drop dead in the heat of the sun or the cold of the night.

King Melchizedek opened the jars of grain kept in reserve in the cellars of Salem, but it was far too little. Hunger was a constant companion. Everyone was ashen-faced and hollow-cheeked. Sarai no longer dared show herself. Like everyone else, she was growing thinner, but her beauty was unchanged.

"I'm ashamed of my appearance," she said to Sililli one night when neither could get to sleep. "How can I exhibit this horrible beauty that never leaves me, when the women don't have enough milk in their breasts to feed their children?"

The only response was Sililli's harsh breathing.

"Sililli?"

Sililli was gasping for breath. She was shivering, her eyes large with fever, her body hunched in order not to collapse.

"What's the matter?" Sarai asked, anxiously.

"It started this afternoon . . . ," Sililli breathed, with great effort. "There's a lot like me . . . It's the water . . . The dirty water . . ."

Sarai sent for Lot and a midwife. They wrapped Sililli in covers and skins. She began to sweat and gnash her teeth. From time to time, her lips drew back to reveal unnaturally pale gums.

"The fever is taking her," the midwife observed.

"She knows about herbs," Lot cried. "She'll know what she needs."

"She isn't in any fit state to tell us how to save her," Sarai said, with a lump in her throat. "She can't even speak."

By the middle of the night, Sililli was no longer conscious. The fever seemed to have turned her eyes inward. The midwife was called to other tents, where the same horror was being repeated. Lot stubbornly tried to pour beer down Sililli's throat. She choked and vomited, but for a time she seemed to settle down.

The next morning, in the cold dawn, she opened her eyes. Apparently quite conscious, she gripped Sarai and Lot by the wrists. They asked her where they could find herbs and how they should treat her. She batted her eyelids.

"My hour has come," she murmured, in an almost inaudible voice. "I'm slipping into the underworld. All the better — it'll be one less mouth to feed."

"Sililli!"

"Leave it, my girl. We're all born and we all die. That's as it should be. You've been the great joy of my life, my goddess. Don't change, stay as you are. Even Abram's god will bend his knee before you, I know it."

"He has no body, remember," Sarai tried to joke, her face flooded with tears.

Sililli half smiled. "We'll see . . ."

Sarai bent, in a gesture familiar from her childhood, and placed her forehead between Sililli's breasts. Her body was almost cold, but still throbbing with fever. Gently, Sililli's hand came to rest on the back of Sarai's neck.

"Lot, Lot," Sililli breathed in a last effort. "Forget Sarai and find a wife."

She died before the sun had cleared the horizon.

For a long time that morning, Sarai stood outside her tent, overcome with anger. She did not weep, though she could hear weeping all around her. The sorrow of loss and the pain of living were feeding the only abundant streams left in Canaan: streams of tears.

All at once, Sarai set off in the direction of Abram's great tent. She found him with the other men, having one of their usual endless discussions. Eliezer was sitting a few steps away.

Abram's face had a closed, severe, weary look. Like a rock abraded by sand. But as soon as he looked at Sarai, he understood. He asked everyone to go out and leave them alone. Eliezer remained seated on his cushion.

"That means you too, boy," Sarai said.

Eliezer looked her up and down, fire in his eyes. He looked to Abram for support, but Abram gestured to him to obey.

"Don't be too hard on Eliezer," Abram said, as soon as they were alone. "The drought isn't his fault, and his father and mother died yesterday."

Sarai took a deep breath to calm her rage.

"And dozens will die today. Sililli died this morning."

Without a word, his eyes dimming, Abram lowered his head.

In the silence, Sarai's voice was like the crack of a whip. "Who is this god, Abram, who can neither feed your people nor make your wife's womb fertile?"

"Sarai!"

"He's your god, Abram, not mine."

Abram's hands were shaking, his chest heaved as he breathed, and the blood throbbed in his temples. Thinking of Sililli's fever, Sarai took fright. What if the sickness had struck him, too? She rushed to him, seized his hands in hers, and lifted them to her lips.

"Are you sick?" she asked, anxiously.

Abram shook his head, gasping, unable to speak. Suddenly, he gripped Sarai's shoulders and clasped her to him, burying his face in her hair. "He doesn't talk to me anymore, Sarai. Yhwh is silent!"

Gently, Sarai pushed him away. "Is that a reason for you, too, to become powerless, Abram?"

Abram turned away.

"Your god is silent," Sarai went on, "but this silence must remain between you and him. Abram, my husband, Abram, the

305

equal of Melchizedek, the man who led us from Harran, who opened up the land of Canaan to the newcomers: That man is not reduced to silence! We are here, outside your tent, waiting for your words. They are here, those who came running to you, trembling with hunger and fever. They're waiting for Abram to give the order to strike camp."

"Strike camp and go where? Do you think I haven't been dreaming of that for moons? Canaan is surrounded by drought and deserts: to the north, the east, and the south. To the west, there's the sea!"

"To the south, after the desert, there's the land of Pharaoh."

Abram stared at her in amazement. "You know as well as I do what they say about Pharaoh, how cruel he is, how he loves to enslave men and make them sweat blood for him."

"Yes. But I've also heard how fertile his land is, with its huge river, and how rich his cities are."

"Pharaoh believes he's a god!"

"Why should that worry a man whose name has been uttered by God Most High?"

Abram looked sharply at Sarai. Was she mocking him?

"Abram," she continued, more gently,

"don't you understand that you have to decide without waiting for help? The worst thing we can do at the moment is stay in Canaan. We'll die here. And the people of Salem who welcomed us will die with us. What do we risk by going and asking for Pharaoh's protection? What death can he add to the death that already awaits us?"

Abram made no reply.

"Your god is silent," Sarai went on, "and you're like a child who's angry because his father's ignoring him. I, Sarai, who abandoned forever the protection of Inanna and Ea for yours, want to hear your word."

That evening, Abram told Melchizedek that they would set out for the land of Pharaoh the very next day. Moved, Melchizedek kissed him and promised him that the land of Canaan would always be his. When the barren times were over, Abram could return and would be welcomed with the greatest of joy.

Abram asked another favor of Melchizedek.

"Speak, and you shall have it."

"The parents of young Eliezer of Damascus are dead. Before you, I declare that I consider him my adopted son. The favor I ask is that you keep Eliezer with you while

I'm in the land of Pharaoh. Nobody knows what awaits us there. If I were to be killed, Eliezer will be able to stay in the land of Canaan and represent my name."

Melchizedek thought the decision a wise one. But when Lot heard about it, he gave a cold laugh.

"So, Abram's found himself a child of drought," he said to Sarai.

Part Five

PHARAOH

Sarai, My Sister

They moved slowly, walking for short periods, and only in the morning and the evening, when it was cooler. It was Abram's intention not to exhaust those, human or animal, whose muscles had been weakened by the famine in Canaan.

The sea was resplendent with light. It dazzled the eyes, intoxicated the gaze, with its immensity. Most of Abram's people were not accustomed to it. At night, the noise of it kept them awake. But it gave them food. Abram showed them how to weave nets and then cast them, either standing on rocks or on the vast golden beaches with the water at their feet. He also showed them how to collect shells from beneath the sand and catch crayfish in baskets. The children, rediscovering laughter, were the quickest learners.

Sarai would watch him, and her heart would fill with tenderness as she recalled the words he had said to her on the banks of the Euphrates: "I was fishing. It's the best time for frogs and crayfish. If nobody steps on you and screams!"

They reached villages where the houses were nothing but huts. The wind from the sea blew through the bulrushes. They could be seen from afar: a motley crew moving slowly in a long line with their sparse flocks whose fleece had turned gray with dust. They were greeted with both suspicion and curiosity. Despite the fact that many of his animals had perished, Abram was always prepared to give up a sheep in exchange for dried fish, dates, fragrant herbs, figs — and information.

"We're going to the land of Pharaoh," he would say, "because in the north, where we come from, there's drought everywhere."

"Take care" would come the reply. "Pharaoh has waged many wars. He doesn't like foreigners. He takes the women and the livestock, and kills the men and the children. He has soldiers every-where, vast numbers of them, armed to the teeth. He says he's a god, and he's so pow-erful everyone believes him. They say he can transform things, bring rain or drought. They say he surrounds himself with gold. His palaces are covered in gold

— even his wives' bodies are made of gold."

Abram would raise a skeptical eyebrow. "Wives made of gold?"

The old fishermen would laugh, and point at Sarai. "Not as beautiful as yours, of course. But that's what they say, yes. Wives made of gold. Pharaoh wants only beautiful things around him. That's his power."

Abram would shake his head, incredulous but worried. From time to time, he would put up the tent with the black-and-white stripes, and listen to the complaints and suggestions of his people.

"What are we going to say to Pharaoh when he sends his soldiers to meet us?" many would ask.

"That all we need is some grass in order to let our flocks graze and grow."

"But what if he wants to steal our women, like the fishermen say?"

"These fishermen are so scared of Pharaoh," Abram would reply, with an angry, ironic snort, and a glance at Sarai, "that they're ready to grant him all sorts of imaginary powers. Anybody would think we were back in the kingdom of Akkad and Sumer."

But as they went from village to village, the same warnings were repeated. Pharaoh had an invincible army. Pharaoh was a god.

Pharaoh sometimes changed heads and became a falcon, a bull, or a ram. Pharaoh was insatiable in his taste for beauty, both in cities and in women.

Sarai could sense the growing fear around her. The word *Pharaoh* passed surreptitiously from mouth to mouth, casting a shadow over everyone.

Abram spent whole days away from the camp. Sarai guessed that he was off calling the name of Yhwh, hoping for His advice. But, when he returned, he said nothing, and his features were set hard with disappointment. He threw Sarai a look that seemed to say, "You insisted I lead my people to the land of Pharaoh. You see the danger we're running because of that decision."

Lot caught this look and understood it. That very evening, he brought Abram the last pitcher of beer that remained from Canaan.

"Look how many of us there are, Abram," he said, after drinking two goblets. "Thousands of us. A whole people. Without counting the animals, even if our flocks have become thin. It's like an invasion of locusts! Who wouldn't be scared to see us arrive on his land?"

"What do you mean?"

"Every day we're getting closer to the

land of Pharaoh. We have to be careful."

Abram laughed, sourly. "I don't know anyone here who isn't thinking the same thing."

"But I have an idea: Let me go on ahead with a few companions to locate Pharaoh's soldiers."

"To do what?"

"To find out how many of them there are, which roads they're using, whether or not they're expecting us."

"Do you plan to fight them?" Abram cried. "As soon as you lift an arm, they'll cut it off! Besides, we're going to be asking Pharaoh for help. You don't fight someone you're holding out your hand to."

"Who said anything about fighting?" Lot protested. "All I want is to meet Pharaoh's soldiers. There'll be only a few of us. They certainly won't think we're locusts come to ravage their pastures. We'll ask them for permission to enter the land of Egypt. They may accept; they may refuse. Either way, we'll know where we stand."

"There's nothing to stop them slaughtering you."

Now it was Lot who gave a mocking smile. "Well, at least I'll have shown that even if I'm not Abram's son, I'm worthy of his name."

Abram ignored the sarcasm. He consulted the elders, who all came to the conclusion that the idea was a good one. Some twenty young men agreed to accompany Lot.

They left the very next day, taking with them nothing but a mule, some food and water, and their staffs. Sarai clasped Lot to her, kissed his eyes and neck, and in a tender whisper begged him to be careful. She watched, full of apprehension, as the little group moved away over the slope of a sandy hill and disappeared.

In the days that followed, on Abram's orders, the column progressed even more slowly than usual. Everyone was waiting for Lot and his companions to return, and at the same time dreading to see Pharaoh's soldiers appear from around a dune or a grove of palm trees.

Finally, one afternoon, at the hour when the sun seemed to melt like silver over the sea and everyone was seeking shade, they were back.

After much laughing and hugging, they told their story. Less than four days of walking across the dunes and cliffs along the coast had brought them to Egypt.

"It's the greenest place you've ever seen.

Greener even than Canaan before the drought. And huge. Wherever you look, you see only lush green fields."

"But what about Pharaoh's soldiers?" Abram asked impatiently.

"We didn't see any!" Lot exclaimed. "None at all! Livestock, roads, brick buildings, villages, storehouses, yes — but no soldiers."

"What did people say when they saw you?" someone asked.

Lot smiled. "Nothing. Or nothing we understood. They don't speak our language. And they don't have any hair on their faces. The men's chins are as smooth as the women's. And their character seems as gentle and calm as their cheeks are hairless. Several times, to welcome us, they gave us barley beer. The sweetest I've ever drunk. I still have the taste of it on my tongue. It's called *bouza*."

There was laughter.

"So what those fishermen told us is wrong?"

"As far as we could tell," Lot's companions asserted, "the land of Pharaoh is the most peaceful, most welcoming place there is. We didn't see anyone who looked like a slave, and we didn't see anyone lording it over anyone else with a whip in his hand."

Joy and hope did not, however, completely dispel everyone's anxiety. Could they really settle on the land of Pharaoh like that, without fear of the consequences?

The noisy talk continued unabated until twilight, when it was time to attend to the animals. Through it all, Abram remained in the background, pensive. Toward evening, he withdrew to make offerings to Yhwh. When night had fallen, he joined Sarai, who was laying out a meal for Lot, now washed and cleanly dressed.

He sat down beside them in the dim lamplight. Sarai handed him a loaf of bread. As he took it, he kissed her fingers. Sarai and Lot looked at him more closely, guessing that he had made his decision.

He broke the loaf into three pieces. "I think the fishermen told the truth. Pharaoh's soldiers will come to us. I have no doubt about it."

Lot opened his mouth to protest.

Abram raised his hand to silence him. "You didn't see the soldiers, Lot, but the people who saw you will tell them. That's how things happen."

"How do you know?" Sarai asked.

"In Salem, the merchants who came from the land of Pharaoh all told the same story. Their caravans advanced into Egypt without incident. One day, two days, without anyone questioning them, without anyone asking, 'What are you doing here, where are you going, what do you have in your bags and your baskets?' Then, suddenly, Pharaoh's soldiers appeared."

Lot lost his temper. "So why let me go if you knew all that?"

"It was what you wanted. It was what everyone wanted. And it's a good thing that you went. Now we all know that the land of Pharaoh is as rich as they say, and that'll give us the courage to face his soldiers. And I know that the merchants in Salem were telling the truth."

Abram smiled. Sarai echoed his smile, amused at his ruse.

"They will come on Pharaoh's orders," Abram resumed, his eyes fixed on Sarai. "They'll examine our flocks, discover whether we're rich or poor. And they'll see how beautiful my wife is. If they don't already know it. They'll turn to me and ask: 'Is this your wife?' 'Yes,' I'll reply, 'this is Sarai, my wife.' Then they'll slaughter us and carry Sarai off to Pharaoh's palace. That's what will happen."

There was a stunned silence.

Lot was the first to react. "How can you be so sure?" he asked, in a shrill voice.

Abram did not reply, still staring at Sarai.

She nodded. "Abram is right. If what they say is true, things could happen like that."

"Then we must hide you!" Lot cried. "We could . . . dress you as a man. Or put soot on your face. Wrap one of your legs in rags, as if you'd had an accident. Or else —"

"The soldiers will be fooled the first day, perhaps the second," Abram interrupted him, calmly. "But eventually someone will tell them that Abram's wife is the most beautiful woman anyone has ever set eyes on. Then they really will be angry, knowing they've been tricked, and fearing Pharaoh's wrath."

Once again they fell silent.

"What to do, then?" Sarai asked.

"Nothing like that will happen if I say you're my sister."

Sarai and Lot both gasped.

"If I say you're my sister," Abram went on, "Pharaoh may invite you to his palace. In fact, I'm sure he will. He'll want to see you. But he'll leave me alone. And the rest of us."

Lot stood up. "You want to give Sarai to Pharaoh?" he cried, his mouth twisted with rage. "To save your life? Is that what the great Abram's courage amounts to?"

"No," Abram retorted. "I don't want to give Sarai to Pharaoh. And it's not about

320

how courageous or afraid I am."

"I understand," Sarai murmured, pale-faced, holding Lot back by the wrist.

"It's about my people's lives, not mine," Abram insisted. "That's what we have to think about."

"No!" Lot cried. "I don't want to think about it. You don't have the right to think about it."

Sarai placed her hand on Lot's cheek. "Abram's right." There was a sad, resigned gleam in her eyes.

Abram stood up in his turn, pushed Lot aside, and took Sarai in his arms. "It's up to you to save us all," he said.

"If your god wishes it."

Abram had guessed correctly.

They reached the outskirts of Midgol, a town of low white houses, without incident. It was clear to everyone that Lot had not lied. The inhabitants smiled when they saw them. Men with smooth cheeks greeted them with incomprehensible words in a slippery, sinuous language that sounded like flowing water.

There was water everywhere. Midgol stood very close to one of the branches of the Nile. The gardens, the pastures, and the groves of palms and orange trees were surrounded by well-maintained canals. They were allowed to water their animals there. Abram thanked them and presented them with a pair of turtledoves. Everyone laughed. They talked to one another with signs, grunts, and handclaps.

"Now let's go to the river," Abram declared, once the flocks had been watered. "We may find fallow land there where the animals can graze."

The road leading into the land of Pharaoh was broad and shaded by tall palm trees. Abram walked in front, vigilant. Behind him, Lot and his young companions preceded the main part of the column. As Abram had ordered, the wives and children were standing in the wagons, surrounded by the animals, which had been brought together into a single flock.

Men and women working in the fields gathered at the side of the road to watch them pass. At the sight of all these bearded men, the children rubbed their cheeks and laughed.

Suddenly, the road opened out onto the river, which was straddled by a big wooden bridge. The bridge itself and both banks were covered with Pharaoh's soldiers.

Two or three hundred of them. Perhaps more.

They stood in serried ranks, shield touching shield, so close together that a rat could not have squeezed between them.

Young, clean-shaven men in loincloths, their shoulders covered with very short capes. They wore no helmets, and their hair was thick, black, and shiny. Some carried spears and round shields, others bows, with brass daggers or stone maces at the belts of their loincloths.

Abram stopped and raised his staff. Lot and the others surrounded him. Farther back, men gave the call to halt the flock and the mules. The noise of the big wagon wheels ceased.

The soldiers moved forward in two columns, their spears raised, and surrounded Abram and the head of the flock. Those who had been on the other bank now occupied the bridge.

Three men holding gilded staffs approached Abram. There were bronze leaves sewn on their leather capes, and their forearms were covered with thick brass bracelets. They, too, were clean-shaven, but their cheeks were creased with age. Of the three, only one wore anything on his head: a kind of tall leather helmet, like a folded veil, with a little bronze ram's head fixed above the forehead. His eyes came to rest without hesitation on Abram.

"My name is Tsout-Phenath. I serve the living god Merikarê, Pharaoh of the Double Kingdom."

Surprisingly, they understood him perfectly. He spoke the Amorite language almost without an accent. His light-brown, expressionless eyes moved from Abram to Lot and the others, then returned to Abram.

"Do you know you have entered the lands of Pharaoh?" he asked.

"I know. I've come to ask for his help. My name is Abram. Drought has chased me from the land of Canaan, where I was living with my people. There is famine there. The earth is dry and cracked and everything is dying. All I ask of Pharaoh is some grassland so that our flocks can be replenished and my people no longer have to weep over the deaths of their children."

Pharaoh's officer remained still for a moment, his eyes narrowed, his lips curled with doubt. Perhaps he was taking his time in order to instill even more fear into them. Or perhaps he was simply trying to understand Abram's words. In the silence, the anxious bleating of the animals could be heard, and the scraping of clogs, but not a word was spoken.

Then, all at once, without moving, the officer gave orders in his own language. Soldiers advanced along the column until they reached the wagons. They pushed the animals aside, causing the whole flock to became agitated. Lot made as if to stop them.

"No!" Abram said. "Don't move."

The second of the three officers, who had been silent until now, shouted something. Another group of soldiers pushed back Lot and his companions. A dagger prodding his ribs, Abram was forced to the side of the road. At the rear of the column, the soldiers made the women get down from the wagons. It took a long time. The man named Tsout-Phenath gave another order, and the third officer joined the soldiers.

Time passed. Tsout-Phenath stood impassively, waiting.

"What are you doing?" Lot asked, unable to stand it any longer.

Tsout-Phenath did not even deign to glance at him.

"They're only following Pharaoh's orders," Abram said. "Stay calm. There's nothing to fear."

This time, Tsout-Phenath turned to Abram, looked at him closely, then nodded and half smiled.

Now the soldiers were returning, pushing

a group of women — the youngest and pretties — in front of them.

When they came to a halt, Tsout-Phenath gestured the soldiers to move aside. He stepped forward, and examined each woman's face in turn, sometimes lifting their veils with his gilded staff. When he reached Sarai, he stopped. She stood there with downcast eyes. He spent so long contemplating her that she finally looked up, confronting his gaze with a severe expression.

Tsout-Phenath nodded. "What's your name?" he asked.

"Sarai."

He gave a sign of approval, as if the name pleased him, and said a few words in his own language. The other officers came forward and surrounded Sarai, separating her from the other women.

"Pharaoh wants to see you," Tsout-Phenath said, turning to Abram. "You and this wife of yours, whose name is Sarai."

"She isn't my wife," Abram replied, without batting an eyelid. "She's my sister."

Tsout-Phenath stopped dead, surprised. "Your sister? We were told you were coming with your wife, the most beautiful woman ever seen among you in the land beyond the desert, near the city of Salem.

Looking at this woman whose name is Sarai, I don't see how you could have a wife more beautiful than this."

"How do you know we've come from Salem?" Lot cried, unable to contain his anger.

Tsout-Phenath gave an arrogant laugh. "Pharaoh knows everything." He approached Sarai. "Is this true? Are you the sister of the man named Abram?"

"Yes," she said, without hesitation.

Tsout-Phenath considered her a moment longer. His look was so sharp, so insistent, that Sarai had the impression that her tunic no longer covered her. He finally turned back to Abram.

"We're going to take one of your mule carts. Pharaoh wants to see that, too. So your sister won't have to walk. Appoint a chief for the others while you're away. We'll take them somewhere where they can pitch their tents and your flock can graze while Pharaoh decides what to do with all of you."

Land and Grain

Draped in a green toga, a necklace of red stones hanging between her breasts, the woman advancing toward Sarai had dark skin and teeth as white as milk. Her beauty seemed to echo Sarai's own. She gave a deep bow.

"My name is Hagar. As long as you are within these walls, consider me your hand-maid."

She stood up again and clapped her hands, and ten young girls appeared, carrying linen, goblets of scents, pots of unguent, combs, and caskets.

"Your journey must have been long and tiring," Hagar said. "We've prepared a bath for you. Follow me . . ."

She was already turning her back and leaving the terrace. Sarai followed her, docile and powerless, with the young girls at her heels.

The journey had indeed been long and tiring. They had had to cross six branches of the Nile and plunge deep into the rich lands of Egypt before reaching Pharaoh's palace in Neni-Nepsou. Separated from Abram, Sarai had spent the whole journey imagining Pharaoh's ferocity and the humiliations that she — who was now Abram's sister — was going to have to endure.

Throughout the journey, in fact, her resentment toward Abram had continued to grow. She may have accepted his decision, but now, with Pharaoh's officer Tsout-Phenath never letting her out of his sight, she felt alone, abandoned, and under threat.

But her anger and fear faded as soon as she saw the walls of Neni-Nepsou. Everything here was splendor, opulence, and sweetness. The palace was vast but elegant. Purple flowers cascaded from the top of its dazzling white walls. There were many gorgeous terraces and colonnades, some of stone, some of painted and gilded wood, linked by countless staircases.

The great halls were calm and shady, their walls painted with extraordinary images, their alcoves overflowing with sculptures, fabrics, and pieces of furniture inlaid with gold and silver. From the terraces, as far as the eye could see, the view was of gardens and canals and ornamental lakes so vast that boats sailed on them. High fences surrounded enclosures of the strangest animals: elephants, lions, monkeys, tigers, gazelles, giraffes, and some especially ugly beasts called camels.

Sarai had really never seen anything to equal it. Not even the most splendid palaces in Ur, whose memory she cherished, could compare with such richness. She had felt as if she were dreaming when she was welcomed and taken into the very heart of the palace.

The handmaid Hagar approached a door with bronze fittings, guarded by two soldiers in loincloths and capes with silver leaves. Hagar waved her hand, and the soldiers glided to the side and opened the door. Sarai followed the handmaid into a high, light-filled hall.

The first thing that struck her was the strange scent, sickly sweet and pungent. Then she saw the long pool, surrounded by columns — a pool containing not water, but ass's milk.

Hagar, seeing Sarai's surprise, smiled. "It's wonderful for the skin. Ass's milk with added honey washes away fatigue and bad memories. It preserves beauty better than any other unguent — not that you need it! Pharaoh himself ordered this bath to be prepared for you."

Sarai wanted to ask a question but she did not have time. The young girls who had followed her had already taken hold of her tunic and were undressing her. The handmaid Hagar also undressed. Her hips and breasts were heavier than those of Sarai, and her body would have been perfect but for a long scar, pink at the edges, which stood out between her shoulders.

She took Sarai's hand gently and walked her to the steps that led down into the pool. The milk was tepid. Sarai sank into it slowly, letting herself be enveloped up to her waist by its soft caress.

"There's a stone bed in the middle of the pool," Hagar said, pointing.

She showed Sarai how to lie on it, flat on her stomach, her head held out of the milk by a cushion filled with sage placed on a wooden stool.

"Breathe deeply," Hagar said. "The sage will clear the dust of the roads from your nostrils."

She asked the young girls kneeling by the pool for oils and unguents and, with expert hands, began to massage Sarai's shoulders and back, stirring the surface of the milk in fragrant little waves.

Sarai closed her eyes, abandoning herself to this unexpected pleasure. For a brief moment, she thought of Abram, wondering if Pharaoh was granting him such gentle treatment. She also wondered why they had been so afraid of the king of Egypt. Could a mighty king who gave such a welcome to foreigners asking for his help be as cruel as they said? Hadn't they allowed themselves to be misled by gossip? Alas, if that was the case, Abram and she had had no reason to lie. And wasn't this lie, far from protecting them, going to bring about their ruin? Would she be in this milk bath if Pharaoh knew the truth, knew she was Abram's wife?

"Did they tell you who I was?" she asked Hagar.

"Sarai, the sister of Abram, the man who believes in an invisible god. They also say that your beauty is untouched by time. Is that true?"

"How do you know all that?"

"My mistress, Pharaoh's newest wife, told me. Besides, since you arrived yesterday, the wives and the handmaids have been talking about nothing else."

"But how does Pharaoh know who I am?"

Hagar laughed. "Pharaoh knows everything."

Sarai closed her eyes, her heart pounding. Did Pharaoh really know everything?

Hagar's massage became more insistent, more caressing. Despite her anxiety, Sarai felt her fatigue leave her. Her body, made hard by the journey and the heat, now seemed to dissolve in the milk of the pool.

As her agile fingers worked, Hagar rambled on. "My mistress said, 'Tomorrow, you'll serve the woman they say is the most beautiful woman beyond the eastern desert.' She also said, 'I've chosen you, Hagar, because you're the most beautiful of my handmaids, and we'll see if this Amorite will have as much luster in your presence.' "

"It's true," Sarai agreed, "you are very beautiful. Your hips are more beautiful than mine."

"That's because you aren't a wife and you haven't yet had children."

"You have children?"

Hagar took her time before she replied. Pushing her shoulder, she turned Sarai over onto her back. "I was born far south of here, by the sea of Suph," she said, as she massaged Sarai's thighs. "My father was rich and owned a city that did a lot of trade with the country you come from. That's why I speak your language. He gave me away as a bride when I was fifteen, and I gave birth to a little girl. When my daughter was two years old, Pharaoh made war on my father. His soldiers killed both him and my husband. They brought me here. I tried to run away, which was a stupid thing to do. An arrow tore the skin from my back. Pharaoh would have offered me as a wife to whomever he liked, but because of this scar, he couldn't. So I became a handmaid. Sometimes I regret it, sometimes not."

Surprised and moved by the sincerity of this confession, Sarai did not know what to say. She took her hands out of the milk and stroked Hagar's shoulder, lightly touching the tip of her scar. They looked at each other with eyes of friendship.

"Now I don't feel sad anymore," Hagar said. "That's how the life of women is. Men give us and take us. They kill each other, and others decide what's to become of us."

Sarai closed her eyes with a shiver. She would have liked to tell Hagar how she had run away from Sumer with Abram, and the price it had cost her. She also would have liked to tell her that she was lying, and that she now knew that even Abram could behave just like any other man!

Hagar sighed. "Perhaps, one day, I'll leave this palace. But perhaps by the time that day comes, I won't want to anymore.

Life here can be very sweet. You'll see that eventually."

"Eventually?"

"My mistress is a jealous wife, and she's already afraid of you. She doesn't know how right she is. When Pharaoh sees you, he'll be dazzled."

Sarai sat up. "What do you mean? What's going to happen?"

A look of surprise came over the handmaid's face. With a knowing, suggestive smile, she placed her soft palms around Sarai's breasts. "What do you suppose is going to happen? What do men usually do when a woman dazzles them? Pharaoh's no different. We're going to dress you, perfume you, make you up, adorn you with jewels, and send you to Merikarê, the god of the Double Kingdom."

Sarai gripped Hagar's wrists, as much embarrassed by her caresses as she was alarmed by her words. "And then?"

"Then, you are neither a handmaid nor a slave. If he thinks you're really the most beautiful of women, which he's sure to do, and if you give him as much pleasure in his bed as he imagines you will, he'll take you as his wife."

Sarai advanced along the terrace, which

was crowded with men and women in the balmy light of evening. They all wore makeup, and sported jewels and ornaments, and their wrists and necks glittered with gold.

The terrace led into a huge hall. Between the columns separating the inside from the outside, young men played solemn but constantly changing music on instruments that consisted of two lengths of wood curved like a bull's horns, with strings stretched between them.

All faces turned toward her. A gong sounded, and the music ceased. And nothing happened as Sarai had been expecting.

With each step she took, the folds of her toga danced against her hips and thighs. The diadem of bronze and calcite holding her hair in place weighed on the back of her neck. A long necklace of lapis lazuli swayed on her chest, hollowing the cloth between her breasts and revealing their form. Her makeup emphasized the incredible charm of her face. Earlier, she had caught Hagar's look of surprise and admiration when she had traced a line of kohl around her eyes. She knew she was beautiful. And she knew how powerful that beauty could be.

Powerful enough perhaps to confront

Pharaoh. To stand before him and have the courage to confess to him, before anything irreparable happened, that because of Abram's fear they had both lied to him.

The courtiers stepped aside to let her pass, looking her over greedily and making whispered comments as they did so. There, sitting on a large seat covered in lion skin and with sculpted armrests shaped like ram's heads, was Pharaoh. Merikarê, eleventh god-king of the Double Kingdom.

The first thing that surprised Sarai was that he was bare-chested — he wore only a transparent veil over his shoulders — and very thin. Although he had fine skin, his face was like a mask. A curious gold cone hung beneath his chin. His features were delicate and regular, his cheeks perfectly smooth. His lips were highlighted with a red unguent, his eyes and eyelids were coated with kohl, and the line of his eyebrows was extended by a line of night-blue makeup. On his head, putting the finishing touch to his unreal appearance, he wore a headdress made of cloth with a gold stripe, gauze, and leather. Two giants with skins as black as night stood behind his seat, wearing helmets shaped like suns.

Abram stood among the courtiers, dressed in a purple tunic she had never seen before. She tried to attract his attention, but he avoided her gaze.

As Hagar had advised her, she went right up to Pharaoh. They stared at each other, each as motionless as the other.

That was her second surprise: She detected neither emotion nor pleasure in Merikarê's masklike face. He examined every inch of her — first of her face, then of her body — without showing any sign of the astonishment or the desire she usually aroused in men.

Disconcerted, Sarai lowered her eyes, not daring to speak the words she had been ready to say. The anxious thought came to her that her beauty had somehow diminished, become tarnished, and that everyone in the hall was aware of it.

"Your sister is as beautiful as I had been told she was, Abram of Salem," Pharaoh declared, in a soft, light voice with a strong accent. "Very beautiful indeed."

Sarai looked up again, relieved, ready to express her gratitude, only to find that Pharaoh was no longer looking at her, but at Abram.

"I'm flattered and surprised, Pharaoh," Abram said, "that you know so much about us. I know so little about you and your country."

"I can tell you how I learn things that happen out of my sight. The merchants come and go, they listen and they see. And if they don't tell Pharaoh's officers what they've seen, they lose their merchandise. Simple, isn't it? So, I know you believe in one invisible god."

"That's true."

Sarai listened to this chatter, increasingly angry. Was that the extent of the impression she had made on Pharaoh?

"If your god is invisible and has no appearance," she heard him ask Abram, "how do you know he exists? How do you know if he likes you or not?"

"He speaks to me. He directs my actions and guides my steps by speaking to me. His word is his presence."

The whole court, except perhaps for some of the women, had eyes only for Merikarê and Abram, as they exchanged their learned questions and answers. Sarai tried to brush aside her annoyance. Wasn't it fortunate, after all, that her beauty did not dazzle Pharaoh? Abram had been right to pass her off as his sister after all. Despite what the handmaid Hagar had said, Pharaoh did not even desire her, let alone want to make her his wife.

The thought should have satisfied and reassured her. But it didn't.

Her cheeks burned with a resentment she could not suppress. She pursed her lips in anger. Anger with Abram, anger with Pharaoh! Anger at their insulting indifference, anger at their eagerness to cross swords and impress each other and everyone else with the brilliance of their ideas.

Pharaoh furrowed his elegant brows, breaking the masklike austerity of his face.

"No body or mouth?" he asked in astonishment, his voice both suspicious and incredulous.

"He has no need of them. His word is sufficient presence," Abram replied, in a mellow tone, calm and amiable.

Abram was sure of himself and without fear. Not even fear that Pharaoh might spurn the beauty of his wife who was now his sister! And now Pharaoh was standing up, leaving his royal seat, brushing against Sarai like a forgotten shadow, and going right up to Abram, who was a whole head taller than him.

"So your god created the world?"

"Yes."

"All worlds? The world of darkness and the world of light, the world of evil and the world of good, the world of the dead and the world of the unborn?"

"All worlds."

"Ah . . . And how?"

"By His will."

Sarai, in her humiliation, did not dare confront the eyes of the courtiers. She was about to withdraw, disappear, flee to some other part of the palace. But at that moment Pharaoh turned, and looked her up and down, with a more intrigued expression. His irises were tinged with green and bronze specks, his full lips curled mockingly. His muscles rippled, forming moving shadows on his bare chest with its dark nipples. Despite her anger, Sarai found him handsome, attractive, although strangely inhuman.

"How can a world be created by will alone? It must be engendered, given birth. How can a lone god accomplish what can only come from copulation? I think you're wrong, Abram. Our scholars have thought long and hard about these matters. According to them, Atoum came into existence by himself. Splendid, dazzling, but incomplete without a woman to give birth. So he masturbated and cast his seed into the void. From it was born Chou, the air you breathe. Atoum took his penis in his hand again, and created Tphenis, the humidity of the world. Only then, from Chou and Tphenis, were born Geb, the earth that sustains our steps, and Nout, the sky that sustains our gaze. And today I, Merikarê, use my will. But only to choose where I deposit my seed and engender life."

He smiled. All around, the courtiers laughed and clapped. Still smiling, Pharaoh raised his right hand to demand silence. He tipped his hand like the point of a spear toward Abram.

"I like you, Abram. A man whose god only reveals himself through words cannot be a barbarian. My father, Akhtoés the Third, also knew the power of words. He made a scroll for me with his teaching. On the scroll it is said, 'Be an artist in words to attain victory, the tongue is the sword of the king. The word is mightier than any weapon, and words are superior to all battles.' "

A murmur of approval went through the hall. Pharaoh went back to his seat. But this time, as he passed Sarai, he startled her by taking her hand in his thin, hard fingers and drawing her close to the royal seat before letting go of her.

Pharaoh's voice rang out, imperiously. "Music, entertainment, and food!"

There was enough food to feed an entire people. There were female singers with plaintive voices and supple, lascivious hips, and dancers who swayed and whirled, twisting their spines into the shapes of wheels or tops. There were magicians turning rods into snakes by throwing them to the floor, releasing horrible spiders into the air, pulling doves from between the breasts of the ladies of the court, lighting fires in basins of pure water, bending the blades of daggers with a mere look.

Pharaoh ate little, enjoyed himself abstractedly, and continued talking to Abram about his god, the cities of Akkad and Sumer, wars, the land of Canaan. But while he ate, enjoyed himself, and talked, he rarely took his eyes off Sarai, although he did not address her until Abram said that she knew how to write in the Sumerian manner.

He ordered fresh clay to be brought, along with some of the styli his scribes used for writing on papyrus. Carefully, Sarai inscribed several words, making little conical strokes that crossed and recrossed.

Pharaoh pointed to a star shape. "What does that mean?"

"The god-king."

"And that?"

"*Shu,* hand."

"What does your sentence say?"

" 'The god-king with strong, gentle

hands.' "

Pharaoh barely smiled. With the tips of his fingers, he touched the raised words on the tablet lightly, and printed his mark below them. Then he stroked the back of Sarai's hand with those same fingers, and she felt the damp coolness of the clay on her skin.

"Can you dance as well as you can write?" Pharaoh asked.

Sarai hesitated. She glanced at Abram, but he was turned away from her, conversing with a courtier. So, without a word, she stood up. A gong resounded, and the music came to an abupt halt. The dancers stopped and moved aside to make space for her. The courtiers ceased their hubbub to look at her. Abram, too, turned now to stare at her.

She stood facing Pharaoh, and raised her arms to shoulder height. Gently, her hips began to sway. She bent her arms, one hand below her face, the other above it. She slid forward and stamped her foot. She moved to the side and stamped again. The musicians picked up the rhythm of her steps and began plucking the strings of their harps in time to her dance. The sounds of a flute and an oboe rose, undulating like Sarai's hips.

She closed her eyes, unconsciously becoming intoxicated with her own grace, carried away by the joy of taking Pharaoh by surprise and making herself irresistible to him. She had not forgotten the dance of the bull. Her body bent and swayed, offering itself with the same entrancing suggestiveness that had once aroused the beast. Now it was Pharaoh's heart she was inflaming.

She knew she had succeeded when she clapped one last time and came to a halt, her chest panting, and nothing moved in the hall. Pharaoh rose and approached her. The pupils of his eyes had grown bigger, more vibrant. She thought he was going to touch her, but he turned to Abram.

"Abram," he said, his voice no longer as light, "I grant you land for your flock and grain for your people until the pastures of Canaan become green again. Tomorrow, Tsout-Phenath will take you back to your people. Your sister stays with me. Perhaps she will be my land and my grain."

The Truth

The predawn cold jolted Sarai awake, touching her bare chest like an icy hand. She sat up in bed.

Behind the transparent drapes, the bedchamber was lit by the weak reddish-brown light from the naphtha fires that flickered on the terrace.

She came completely to her senses.

Pharaoh stirred beside her.

He was no longer only Pharaoh. He was a naked man, with smooth cheeks and a soft body, sleeping in a huge, shadowy bed shaped like a boat. He had short, curly hair like a child's. On his powerful shoulder, Sarai could see the mark that her teeth had left there in the night, during her transports of pleasure.

She wanted to stroke the mark, to kiss it. She managed to restrain herself. Her eyes misted over.

She looked down at her own belly, her thighs, her breasts. There were no marks on them. But deep inside, her body was still feverish with the pleasure that Pharaoh had given her. An absolute pleasure that had overwhelmed her, terrifying her at first and then fulfilling her.

How could it be?

She shivered as the memory of his caresses came back to her. She pushed the memory aside, but now the thought of Abram assailed her. She dismissed it violently. At that moment, she hated Abram. She never wanted to see him or hear his name again.

Yes, if Pharaoh wanted her, felt as much pleasure with her as she felt with him, why shouldn't she remain Abram's sister for all time?

She even hated Abram's god!

Her throat tightened with shame. She hid her face in her hands, and huddled with her thighs against her chest.

But the tears did not rise to her throat, because just then Pharaoh's hand came to rest in the hollow of her back, then moved up to the back of her neck. She shuddered, and fell back against him with a moan. She touched his smooth cheeks, already hungry for his mouth, for the suppleness of his long body against her hips.

Hungry for Pharaoh's desire that burned in the gold of his irises and feasted on her body until her pleasure drove her consciousness away.

Day had barely broken. Sarai was standing behind the transparent drapes. Through the loosely woven threads, she watched the shadows fade from the gardens and lakes.

She did not want to be in bed anymore. Did not want to be near Pharaoh. Did not want Pharaoh's desire.

She was trying to think of nothing. To feel nothing.

If only her flesh, still burning from his caresses, could become as cold as stone!

She thought of the handmaid Hagar, of the scar on her back.

If she ran away, would they shoot arrows at her?

But where could she run to?

Was there a single space in Egypt where you could escape Pharaoh's eyes?

She gave a little laugh, bitter as a mouthful of bile. "Pharaoh knows everything!" she murmured.

Pharaoh woke suddenly, with a groan,

and sat up, his mouth open.

"Sarai!"

He opened his arms in the great boat of his bed.

"Sarai!" he called again, in a commanding voice.

"Here I am."

He saw her standing by the drapes, naked and cold.

"I've just had a bad dream!" he cried. "Your people's famine was becoming my famine. Snakes and crocodiles were swarming in my lakes. My wives were rotting in my arms and a voice called out to me that you weren't Abram's sister, but his wife."

Sarai approached the bed and Pharaoh. She brushed his cheek, then pulled the big sheet off the bed and wrapped herself in it. "It's true. I am Sarai, Abram's wife."

"What have you done to me?" Pharaoh screamed.

Sarai moved away from him, calm and relieved. Watching Pharaoh's hands, to protect herself from his blows.

"Why?" he screamed again. "Why lie to me like that?"

"Because Abram was afraid you would kill him in order to make me your wife. And I, too, was afraid you would kill him."

349

Pharaoh gave a nasty laugh, like a spit. "Afraid?"

"Yes, afraid of Pharaoh."

Pharaoh sneered. He touched the bite mark on his shoulder lightly, and stood up. He was about to approach her, but changed his mind, and shook his head. "So Abram's God Most High isn't mighty enough to protect you against fear?"

Sarai lowered her eyes without a reply.

"You were mistaken, you and your husband. Pharaoh isn't going to feed you to the crocodiles. As my father wrote, 'Do not be wicked. Feed the poor man, for a rich people does not rise in revolt. Become great and lasting through the love that you leave behind.' Repeat those words to Abram."

He fell silent. His face became impassive, already resuming Pharaoh's mask of indifference. But he crossed the space separating them and took Sarai's face in his hands.

"As for you," he breathed, his mouth against hers, "I shan't flog you or stone you. I want your perfect body to stay in my mind. And you, too, will have to live with the pain of our memory."

Part Six

HEBRON

Sarai's Veil

Her brow and chest covered with gold, Sarai was led back to the encampment, swaying in a wicker basket strapped to the back of an elephant. She was preceded by a column of soldiers, while a flock of more than a thousand small livestock, asses and mules, filled the road behind her.

This was a queen returning from Pharaoh's palace, a goddess of the Nile. But Abram greeted her without asking her any questions, almost without looking at her. Lot, on the other hand, rushed to meet her, and tried to support her foot as she dismounted from the elephant, but collapsed on the ground, drunk. While Sarai had been away, not a day had gone by that he had not emptied whole pitchers of Egyptian beer.

He burst out laughing, and got unsteadily to his feet. His eyes were red, and he stank so much that Sarai refused to embrace him.

Without so much as a word or a smile for all those who stood admiring the magnificence of her return, she disappeared into the tent that had been pitched for her. A few moments later, her handmaids came out to announce that she wanted to be alone and to rest after her long journey. Lot protested, saying that he wanted to join her. He was pushed away roughly.

Even Abram did not try to enter his wife's tent. In any case, he was too caught up in the celebrations. He was lifted to shoulder height and carried around the camp in triumph. Everyone shouted his name and the name of Yhwh. Hadn't Pharaoh bent his knee before God Most High? He hadn't killed Abram, hadn't kept him captive. Instead, he was giving him enough to make his people rich again!

They danced until late at night, to the sound of flutes. Flakes from the fires rose in the darkness, swirling like phosphorescent insects. Beer and wine flowed like water. Their joy and relief were so intense that Sarai was quite forgotten. Nobody expressed any surprise that she was not at Abram's side until Lot's cries distracted them from their merrymaking.

He was on all fours outside Sarai's tent. "Show yourself, show yourself!" he was yelling, in a voice drowning in beer and tears. "I haven't seen you in such a long time. Show yourself, Sarai."

His tunic was torn and soiled, his face a battlefield. With insane eyes and lips white with saliva, he threw himself against the tent posts, as if to break them. He collapsed, gashing his chest on the wood as he did so. But even at the height of his frenzy, he took care not to tear the tent flap, which Sarai was steadfastly refusing to open.

They got him to his feet, but he still had the strength to struggle.

"Dance!" he shouted. "Dance like fools! Just don't ask why my aunt Sarai has come back to us like a queen! Be cowards! Be like Abram, he doesn't ask! His God Most High doesn't ask, either! Only their nephew Lot asks! He doesn't give a damn about Pharaoh's asses and mules! But he wants to know! He asks: Why has Sarai come back to us like a queen?"

He gave a malicious laugh, pointing at the faces around him, looking for Abram. Not finding him, he spat in disgust.

"You don't know, do you?" he bellowed, grabbing the man nearest to him. "You don't know! Well, I'm going to tell you. What she never wanted to do with Lot, Abram's sister did with Pharaoh. Pharaoh put his cock in her and Sarai gave birth to all this gold, just for us!"

The only way they could silence him was to knock him senseless. The celebration was over. Their hearts were heavy now, and as closed as Sarai's tent.

The next day, another caravan led by Pharaoh's great officer Tsout-Phenath, arrived at the encampment, bringing neither flocks nor grain, but three chests of gold and silver loaded on an elephant, from which a veiled woman descended.

Ignoring Pharaoh's soldiers who surrounded the camp with spears raised, Abram's people gathered. Tsout-Phenath ordered the chests to be opened outside the great black-and-white tent. Everyone pressed forward to see. Unlike the previous day, there were no cries of joy, no hugs and kisses. Yet none of them had ever seen so much gold and silver in their lives.

Tsout-Phenath approached Abram. "Pharaoh is giving you one moon," he announced haughtily, "to prepare your flocks, strike camp, and leave his lands. If any of you try to come back, you will die. Pharaoh wishes you a good journey home, you and your wife. He hopes you will long remember him."

Abram gave a thin smile. "Tell Pharaoh he can rest assured that Abram's people will indeed remember him. We have long memories. May God Most High bless him for his kindness." He kicked the lids of the chests shut. "Who is that veiled woman who has come with you?"

Tsout-Phenath made a casual gesture. "The last fruit of Pharaoh's kindness to your wife."

At that very moment, inside Sarai's tent, the handmaid Hagar had removed her veil and was bowing respectfully.

"Pharaoh took me away from my mistress. He has sent me here to serve you because he does not want anything in his palace that could remind him of you."

She looked up, her happy smile undaunted by the sight of Sarai's bitter expression. She took Sarai's hands and placed them on her brow then on her chest, in the Egyptian manner.

"I know these words must be hard for you, for Pharaoh ordered me to say them as soon as I saw you. Well, I've said them, and now you can forget them. This is what my heart says: Be my mistress and you will make me the happiest of women. You will be the balm on my scar, and I will be faithful to you unto death."

Sarai pulled her to her gently. "Have no fear! I shan't ask any such sacrifice of you. I'm very happy to have you as my handmaid, but I'm afraid you won't be as well housed as you were with Pharaoh. I have no palaces to offer you, no pools, only tents and long days of walking."

"I'll learn to prepare ass's milk in gourds!" Hagar said, with a singsong laugh. "I may no longer have a palace around me, but that's because you've opened the bars of my cage."

Sarai was about to order something to eat and drink when she heard cries from outside. Half lifting the tent flap, Sarai and Hagar saw a group of young people waving their arms. Lot's head stood out above them. Abram, surrounded by the elders, came out of the tent with the black-and-white stripes.

"Lot's drunk, but his question's a good one," one of the young people cried. "Why is Pharaoh chasing us away and at the same time giving us so many riches?"

Abram's voice rang out above the cries, in a tone that silenced the crowd. "Because Yhwh came to him in a dream. A cruel dream in which He showed Pharaoh all the harm He could do to him and his people if he did not treat us well. Pharaoh was afraid of God Most High and obeyed Him. With these riches He has given us by the hand of Pharaoh, Yhwh is showing us that our trials are over. That is the truth, there is no other! Tomorrow, we shall strike camp and set off back to Canaan, the land He gave me."

Hagar put her arm tenderly around Sarai's waist. "Your husband certainly knows how to talk," she whispered. "I can see now why Pharaoh prefers to keep him at a distance."

With such a huge flock, and having to go all the way around the Shur Desert, they took more than a year to reach Canaan.

It was a year during which Sarai only spoke to Abram when she could not avoid it, and no longer received him in her tent. And she never forgave Lot for what he had said when she had returned from Pharaoh's palace. Abram's nephew groveled at her feet, making open and humiliating displays of his repentance, blaming it all on how unhappy and how drunk he had been. Each time Sarai turned her back on him.

Lot stopped his lamentations, and from then on stayed at the rear of the caravan, moving forward through the dust raised by the flocks, getting drunk when evening fell, and remaining incapacitated until dawn, and sometimes until day had fully risen. Occasionally, he had to be trussed up like a sack and carried on the back of a mule.

Not once did Abram lecture him.

For several moons, they all kept their heads down.

From her wicker basket on the elephant's back, Sarai looked down on them with eyes like stone. She never took off the gold jewelry Pharaoh had given her. In the sun, it shone so intensely on her brow, her neck, and her breasts that it would have burned the pupils of anyone who had looked up at her.

It was only in the evening, when she came down from the huge beast, that some of the women would sneak a glance at her. They hoped to see sorrow or forgiveness on her face, but all they saw was indifference and beauty. That same miraculous beauty, without even the trace of a wrinkle. Neither the sea wind nor the blazing sun had caused it to fade in the slightest.

One spring morning, however, as they were finally approaching Canaan, a murmur ran through the caravan, and heads turned toward the elephant. Up there, in her wicker gondola, Sarai had covered her head with a waist-length red veil, the mesh of it loose enough to allow her to see through it while keeping her face hidden from others.

The next day, and the day after that, she wore the same veil. And all the days that followed. From then on, Sarai never appeared outside her tent without her red veil.

Some believed that her face had changed during the night. That it had grown ugly. Perhaps she had caught leprosy in Pharaoh's palace and did not want anyone to know. Abram acted as if nothing strange had happened, never questioning Sarai, never asking her the reason for this concealment.

Little by little, the whispers and the absurd rumors stopped. Soon, everyone understood, without any words being spoken: Sarai did not want her anger or her beauty to be a burden on anyone anymore. She was weary of reminding them, through her appearance, of the source of their newfound wealth. But there was still one person against whom her wrath did not diminish, the only person who could have lifted her veil and begged her forgiveness, but did not do it: her husband Abram.

There was great relief. They all grew accustomed to Sarai's red veil. They were glad no longer to have to confront her perfect and unalterable beauty. Her handmaid

Hagar's beauty, in comparison, was infinitely more changeable and infinitely less threatening. Laughter returned to the camp. Joy was overflowing, the joy of soon being back in the land of Canaan.

They approached Salem on a day of squally rain. The fields and hills were becoming green again. The roads were muddy, and their huge flock raised no dust.

Melchizedek rushed to meet them, amid trumpets and drums and his people's joyful welcome. Everyone was astonished to see these people who had left gnawed by famine now looking so rich, well-fed, and ruddy-cheeked. They surrounded the elephants, and laughed at their trunks and their outsize ears.

But Melchizedek was surprised and saddened to be greeted by Sarai with a veil covering her face. He was about to ask a question, but his eyes met Abram's, and he fell silent, blinked, and opened wide his arms. The two men embraced, while joyous chants thanked God Most High for his kindness. Before they had even separated, a boy was tugging at them.

"Eliezer!" Abram cried.

Eliezer of Damascus had grown as tall as Abram. He had shoulder-length curly hair, and the down of his first beard was on his chin. He embraced his adoptive father with all the effusiveness of a true son. Everyone saw Abram's eyes mist over.

That night, for the first time since they had left Canaan and set off for Egypt, Abram's laughter rang out over the music of the celebration. It was loud enough to be heard by Hagar, who was in the tent helping Sarai prepare for bed. She asked her mistress the name of the handsome boy who was making Abram so happy.

Sarai waited while Hagar removed her tunic and began to massage her back with a soft ointment. "His name is Eliezer of Damascus," she at last replied with weary indifference. "Abram chose him to be the son I can't give him. He's pleasant enough; quite a charmer, in fact. But don't trust him. He's like a fruit that looks nice and juicy when you see it on a hot day and your throat is parched. As soon as you bite into it, you realize it's poison."

"Why do you say that?"

"Perhaps I'm jealous. That was what my dear Sililli thought. Or perhaps I can tell good from evil whatever mask they put on to conceal their true natures."

Their return was celebrated for seven days. Every morning, Abram and

Melchizedek would join the elders in the big black-and-white tent. Abram told them about the country of the Nile and the questions Pharaoh had asked him about God Most High. In his turn, Melchizedek recounted how the rain had returned to Canaan as suddenly as it had disappeared. Rain such as they had never seen. It had come in summer, but not as a storm; it had been abundant, but not too heavy; it had watered the thirsty earth, but not drenched it. It had filled the wells and the springs all winter long, so that when spring had come, it had been as green as in the old days.

"In autumn," Melchizedek said to Abram, with a calm smile, "when I saw the turn this rain was taking, I knew God Most High was taking care of you. I said, 'Abram and his people are well. They will soon be back. Yhwh is preparing Canaan for them as a bride is prepared for her wedding night.' "

In the middle of one of these joyous conversations, Lot suddenly appeared. "I want to speak to Abram!" he declared, roughly.

They all feared another drunken rage. But although his face was red, his eyes bulging and his clothes disheveled, he was not drunk.

Abram invited him to sit down. "Speak, I'm listening."

"What I have to say is simple. You've already brought us to the point of famine once. I don't want to have to suffer any more of your thoughtlessness. I want to take my flock and anyone who'll agree to go with me and settle in a land of my own. And don't tell me your god will stop me. I don't give a damn about your god."

Melchizedek frowned. There were murmurs of disapproval.

But Abram replied with a gentleness that surprised everyone. "I understand. I agree with you. Listen, Lot. You're more than my nephew: You're my brother, as your father was. You and your father Haran have a place in my heart. There will be no quarrel between us."

"Will you let me take some land for myself?" Lot asked, surprised.

"Yes. You've made the right decision. It makes a lot of sense. Not only am I letting you take land, but I propose that you choose whichever pastures seem to you the best for your flock and those who will be your family. If you go left, I'll go right. If you go right, I'll go left."

Lot rose, even redder than when he had come in. He sized up the faces in front of him. "All right, then," he said, defiantly. "I'll take the land in the bend of the Jordan, to the east of Salem."

"But that's the richest in all Canaan!" Melchizedek cried, offended. "It gets water all year long, and it's as beautiful as a garden!"

Abram smiled and nodded. "That means it's a good choice," he said.

Melchizedek was about to protest again, but Abram prevented him. He stood up and took Lot in his arms. "I'm happy that my brother will be able to live in such a rich land."

"But think, Abram!" someone cried. "He's taking your best lands from you, and his flock is a fifth the size of yours."

"I left the choice up to Lot," Abram said, his arm still around his nephew's shoulders. "He's chosen, and I'm happy."

In the evening, the houses of Salem and the numberless tents pitched around the city buzzed with Abram's generosity to his nephew Lot. Never before had they seen anyone give up his wealth with so much good humor. And as there was nothing to suggest that Abram was weak, his generosity had to be genuine. He became even more admirable in everyone's eyes.

The story soon reached Hagar's ears, and she immediately told her mistress. Sarai could not restrain a smile. She, too, was touched by Abram's generosity, but it was more than that. The fact that Abram had acted so impulsively, as he had once before, when he had carried her off from the temple of Ur, was something that made her feel a little less angry toward him.

The next day, Abram, Melchizedek, and many others stood by the side of the road to watch Lot leave Salem at the head of his flock and those who had decided to follow him. Sarai appeared. Lot stared at the red veil, as if his eyes might burn right through the cloth. The general feeling was that Sarai was finally going to assuage his torment and show her face to the nephew who worshiped her.

She approached him. "I've come to say good-bye."

Lot said nothing. He hesitated. With his sad mouth and his drink-ravaged features, he was a pitiful sight. Around them, everyone was hanging breathlessly on Lot's reaction. Sarai waited for him to utter a word that would allow her to take him in her arms.

It was not to be. "Who's under that veil?" he sneered, with a harsh drunken laugh. "One of Pharaoh's handmaids?"

Sarai stepped back, her chest on fire, her cheeks burning with humiliation under the veil. She was about to deliver a stinging rebuke, but just then, she caught a glimpse of young Eliezer smiling broadly at Abram's side. How happy he was, sensing the quarrel to come!

She said nothing. She turned her back on Lot and the others and disappeared into her tent.

Everyone noticed that Abram had not lifted his hand to stop her, nor opened his mouth to call her back.

In the days that followed, while his flock spread over the green pastures, Abram did again what he had done years earlier, before the drought. In the company of Eliezer, he went all over Canaan, from the hilltops to the valleys, from one altar to another, offering sacrifices and calling the name of Yhwh.

Meanwhile, Sarai asked Melchizedek for a wagon and some men to help her pitch her tent to the south of Salem. She had discovered a long valley covered with terebinth and flowering bay trees, bordered by cliffs and high ocher rocks down which cool streams cascaded.

Melchizedek told her it was a large space to be alone in, and asked her if it wouldn't be better to wait for Abram to return.

"I'm already alone," she replied. "I've been alone for a long time now, in the tiny space of my own body. Abram is busy with his god. I suppose that's a good thing. If he wants to talk to me, tell him I'm in the plain of Hebron. He'll find me."

He found her less than a moon later. He arrived one day at high noon, while Sarai was baking loaves of bread stuffed with fragrant herbs and cheese. He was alone, without Eliezer. Hagar and Sarai heard him before they saw him, for he was shouting her name all through the valley.

"Sarai! Sarai, where are you? Sarai!"

Hagar climbed a slope to get a better view. "Something serious may have happened," she said, worried.

Sarai scanned the paths, the nearest copses, the banks of the streams that meandered through the pastures, but could see nothing.

"Sarai!" Abram's voice was still calling.

"He could be hurt," Hagar said.

"Go to meet him," Sarai ordered. "Follow the sound of his voice."

As Hagar moved away, Sarai put on her red veil. She saw Abram emerge from a grove of olive trees on the road leading to the Jordan. Hagar cried out and went to him. Abram began gesticulating curiously, like an excited child. As soon as they were quite close, Sarai could see that Abram was neither wounded nor in pain. He was out of breath but smiling.

"Sarai! He spoke to me! Yhwh spoke to me!"

He burst out laughing, as joyful and exuberant as a young man. He clapped his hands, and turned full circle.

"He spoke to me! He called to me: 'Abram!' Just like he did in Harran: 'Abram!' 'I'm here, God Most High,' I said, 'I'm here!' I'd been waiting for him for so long. I'd been all over Canaan, calling his name!"

Again he was shouting, laughing, weeping, wild-eyed like Lot in his cups. He took hold of Hagar's waist and began to dance with her. She burst into a great, voluptuous laugh. Behind her veil, Sarai smiled. Drunk with his joy, Abram grew bolder. He left Hagar, took Sarai's hand, put his other hand around her waist, and whirled her around. Twice, three times, his forehead bathed in sweat, singing, pirouetting as if his dance were accompanied by flutes. Hagar was still roaring with laughter. Sarai's veil lifted, as did the bottom of her tunic. They danced until Abram tripped on a stone and fell headlong, pulling Sarai down with him.

Hagar helped her to her feet.

"That's enough," Sarai said. "Stop behaving like a child, you're exhausted."

"I haven't eaten or drunk anything since yesterday," Abram laughed, puffing and blowing like an ox.

"Come and sit down. I'll give you something to drink."

"I must tell you what He said!"

"It can wait until you've eaten and drunk. Hagar, bring cushions, water, and wine, please."

She went to fetch the loaves she had been baking, along with grapes and pomegranates picked on the hill of Hebron, and ordered Hagar to stretch a canopy above Abram, to give him shade. Then she sat down and watched him eat heartily, happy and smiling beneath her veil.

When he had eaten his fill, Hagar brought a pitcher of lemon water and a clean cloth. He wiped his hands and face.

"I'm listening," Sarai said at last.

"I wasn't very far from here. I'd even been thinking of coming to see you. And then the voice was everywhere. Like in Harran. Just like in Harran, you remember?"

"How can I remember, Abram? I didn't see your god, only you running, excited, like today."

Abram frowned with disappointment, and looked closely at the veil that prevented him from seeing the expression on Sarai's face. He shook his head to dispel his annoyance. "It all happened very quickly. Yhwh said, 'Lift your eyes, Abram! Look north and south, look east, look west to the sea. All the land you can see I give to you for the future, to you and your descendants. Your seed is like the dust of the world. Whoever can count the dust of the world will be able to count your seed. Arise, Abram! Fill this country, I give it to you!' "

Abram's eyes were shining. Then he gave a great laugh. Hagar laughed, too. But Sarai did not laugh.

She did not move.

Abram and Hagar fell silent, watching her chest swell.

" 'The dust of the world!' " she said, and her veil trembled in front of her mouth. " 'Your seed, the dust of the world!' " she said again, her voice louder this time.

Abram was already on his feet, guessing at the rage that was coming. "That's exactly what Yhwh said," he said, as if to protect himself. " 'Your seed is like the dust of the world!' "

"Lies!" Sarai screamed, getting to her feet. "Lies!"

She picked up the pitcher of water and threw it at Abram. He deflected it with his arm, and it shattered at Hagar's feet. The handmaid sprang back to avoid it.

"Lies!" Sarai cried again, with all her might.

"Yhwh said so!" Abram retorted.

"How do I know? Who else heard it apart from you?"

"Don't blaspheme!"

"Don't lie! And don't mock me. How are you going to make your seed like the dust of the world? You can't even have a son. You have to stoop to making that snake Eliezer your heir —"

Abram kicked over the platter containing the remains of the meal. "Be quiet! You don't know what you're saying. You're full of bitterness and resentment. Do you know what you look like with that ridiculous veil over your face?"

"Oh, yes, I know, Abram, I know perfectly well! I'm invisible, just like your god. I don't exist, I'm a nobody! A sterile woman who's as dry as any desert! A woman who can be given and taken over and over again, without any life ever being born in her, without any mark, any wrinkle being left on her, ever! A nobody, do you hear! A nobody!"

She had screamed so loudly that the word echoed through the valley of Hebron.

She pressed the veil against her face. "You should be grateful for this veil, Abram. Because if your wife, who's a nobody, ever took this veil off, she'd be a constant reproach to you."

"Yhwh has promised me offspring," Abram cried, raising his arms to heaven, his eyes big with rage. "God Most High promised it, and it will come to pass. Everything He promises comes to pass!"

Sarai's derisive laugh was terrible to her. She leaped at Abram, gripped his hand, and placed it on her stomach. "Oh yes? How many years have you been spouting the same nonsense? My God Most High will work the miracle! Why hasn't he already done it? Why hasn't he made my belly swell, if he's so powerful? Your seed is supposed to populate this land, is it? And whose womb is it going to come from, this people of yours? Are you going to make every woman in Canaan pregnant, Abram? They already look on you as a demigod! Well, why not? You could claim I'm your sister again. Lot was right, everyone will learn to live with it."

Abram growled, trying to pull his hand away from Sarai's.

She opened her fingers abruptly and hit him on the chest to push him away, then stood for a moment, catching her breath. "Why doesn't your god care about me?" she cried. "Can you answer me that? No . . . Yhwh has spoken to you. He has promised, and you dance and laugh. While I weep. And hide! I'm empty. Empty and sick of these beautiful promises! Stop listening only to the noise of your own folly, Abram. Stop seeing what nobody else sees and face the truth: My womb is barren. You haven't been able to fill it. Your god has no idea how to fill it, any more than you do. Even Pharaoh couldn't manage it!"

Abram's roar was so fierce that Hagar rushed forward, thinking he was going to murder Sarai. But all he did was push her, propelling her to the side of the tent. She collapsed against it, while he ran off as fast as his legs would carry him.

Solitude

Sarai had lost Sililli and Lot. And now it seemed as though she had lost Abram, too.

She had nobody left but Hagar. Hagar was sweet, attentive, and helpful, but she could not replace Sililli in Sarai's heart. Hagar knew nothing of the past. She had no memory of Ur and Sumer. She could not remind Sarai of those happy times when Abram was in her bed every night and she still hoped that Abram's god was capable of a miracle. Unlike Sililli, Hagar could not mock her or reprimand her or ply her with old wives' tales at the slightest excuse.

What made matters worse was that Hagar was bursting with youth. There was life in the graceful curve of her hips. It was obvious that she was quivering with desire, ready for a man's seed as a flower is ready to receive the honeybee. One night of love, and Hagar would be pregnant. She would suffer the beautiful pain of childbearing. Whenever she thought about it, Sarai preferred to be completely alone rather than have her handmaid constantly in front of her eyes.

And so, for moons on end, the only pleasures she had left, the only ones that still gave her a sense of well-being, were solitude and indifference.

Sometimes, at night, she was haunted by dreams in which she was still a woman, making love to Pharaoh, and about to reach a peak of pleasure. She would wake with a bitter taste in her mouth, her body aching, the desire already gone. She would press her fists to her mouth to stifle her pain and her rage. Why couldn't she weep until her body dissolved like a statue of salt and disappeared into the greedy earth? Even that was not granted to her. It was as Pharaoh had promised: "You, too, will have to live with the pain of our memory!"

Then one morning, when she woke up, Hagar had news for her.

"Abram has come to pitch his tents here. He's decided to settle in the plain of Hebron."

She was telling the truth. The plain was filling with tents. The flocks spread as far as the eye could see. The blows of sledgehammers on the tent posts echoed through the air. A city of canvas was being born. By the time the sun had reached its zenith, the big tent with the black-and-white stripes had already been erected.

"Settling near you," Hagar said, "is Abram's way of showing how much he cares about you. Would you like me to go down and welcome him on your behalf?"

Sarai made no reply. She did not even seem to have heard.

Abram could well fill the plain of Hebron with those he called his "people," just as he called Eliezer of Damascus his son. What business was that of hers? In what way did that make good his god's unkept promise? Neither her desire for solitude nor her indifference were going to be swayed by it.

When Abram sent her three young handmaids as extra help, she turned them away. "You can go back where you came from," she said, simply. "Hagar gives me all the help I need."

Abram next sent baskets of fruit, lambs for roasting, birds, rugs for the winter. Sarai refused these gifts as she had refused the handmaids. But this time, Abram ignored her refusal and ordered the gifts to be taken back and deposited outside her tent.

Unrolling the rugs at the foot of Sarai's

bed, Hagar sighed with envy. "You've taught me a lesson. This is a good way to make sure your husband treats you well!"

Sarai found this annoying. She became less open with Hagar. She got into the habit, when twilight approached, of climbing to the top of the hill of Qiryat-Arba, beneath the white cliffs that looked out over the plain.

Here, her solitude was truly complete. It was a peaceful spot where, on spring days, the streams flowed in cascades and the sun released the scents of the sage and rosemary bushes. From here, if she was curious enough to do so, Sarai could follow what was going on in the camp. Occasionally, she would make out a figure walking faster, and going farther, than anyone else. She had no doubt it was Abram.

Most often, though, she would turn away her eyes to watch the flight of birds or the slow movement of the sun's shadow across the plain.

One day Hagar had another piece of news.

"They say war is threatening the people of Sodom and Gomorrah. That's where your nephew Lot lives. They say the people of Sodom have become so rich that the kings of the surrounding areas are jealous of them and want to seize their wealth."

"How do you know?"

"I met Eliezer when I went to look for new goatskins for the milk. He's a man now. Even though he's still young, he sits at Abram's side in the black-and-white tent, and is learning to be a chief."

"Did he tell you that?"

"Yes. But the women down there assured me it's true. They say he's a fast learner, and he loves it."

"I don't doubt it," Sarai said.

"He's good-looking, too. The girls laugh behind his back and squabble so that he'll notice them. He's like a young ram all proud of his new horns." She laughed, with a pretense at mockery, but her voice betrayed her excitement. "I know you don't like him," she continued. "I don't return his glances, but I can sense that he likes me. And the less I look at him, the more he likes me."

"Of course he likes you! What man doesn't like you?"

They both laughed.

"Eliezer is a deceiver," Sarai said, in a more serious tone. "Don't be misled. Don't think he's going to lead Abram's people one day. It'll never happen."

"Why not?"

"Because he'll never be worthy."

Hagar threw her a sidelong glance, and continued with her work in silence, a sullen expression on her face.

Sarai approached her and stroked the back of her neck, then placed her head on her shoulder. "Don't think these are the words of a bitter woman. I'm not bitter. Even though I keep away from everybody and don't want to be in any man's arms, including my husband's. It's true I envy you. But my wish is to see your belly grow big with child. When that day arrives, I'll hold your hand. In the meantime, keep away from Eliezer. As soon as he's had you, he'll forget you."

But after she had said this, Sarai asked herself, "Is it true I'm not a bitter woman? If my face got older like a normal face, wouldn't I see that it had that same sad, thin-lipped look that all wives have when they've stopped expecting any pleasure or any pleasant surprises from their husbands?"

She preferred not to answer her own questions. But she noticed that Hagar was going down to the plain more and more frequently, on one pretext or another. Hardly a day went by that she did not have something to attend to in Abram's camp. When she came back, she would be unusually taciturn and would say nothing about who she had met or who she had talked to. Sarai had no doubt that, in spite of her advice, she was still seeing Eliezer.

Sarai shrugged it off. After all, Hagar was enough of a woman to choose a man to give her pleasure and share her destiny.

One afternoon, there was great agitation in Abram's camp. Sarai saw people running in all directions. It seemed to go on for so long that she became worried, fearing that something bad had happened. She had already put on her red veil and was about to go down to see for herself when Hagar arrived, out of breath.

"It's war! Abram is leaving for the war! Your nephew Lot has been taken prisoner in Sodom, and he's going to rescue him!"

"But he has no army" was Sarai's immediate response. "No weapons, either, nothing but sticks! He doesn't even know how to fight!"

At the same moment, horns echoed through the encampment, and cries of alarm rang out over the plain. A column had formed at the edge of the camp, led by Abram. Wives and children could be heard screaming.

"Are they leaving already?" Sarai exclaimed, incredulously. "Abram's gone mad."

"Your nephew has to be rescued before they kill him," Hagar replied, in a reproachful tone.

Sarai barely listened to her. She was looking at the column heading off along the road that led to the Jordan. Such a thin column! She tried to make out Abram at the head, wondering how he was dressed and armed for fighting. She supposed he had taken his short bronze sword. His companions must be even less well equipped than him. She could see they were carrying staffs over their shoulders, and the pikes they used for leading the mules and the oxen.

What madness!

She thought of running to Abram and saying: "You can't go and fight like this! You're going to your ruin. The conquerors of Sodom and Gomorrah are powerful. They'll slaughter you, you and all the people with you!"

But Abram would not listen to her. After such a long silence, what right did she have to tell him what he should and should not do?

Then she thought of Lot. Hagar was right. Lot was in danger. It was only fair that

383

Abram should go to his rescue. "Lot has been waiting for Abram's love for so long," she thought. "I mustn't stand in their way. But tomorrow, or the day after tomorrow, I'm going to hear that they're both dead."

Her chest was tight with anxiety, and the small of her back prickled with a fear she had not felt for a very long time.

Having been away from him for so long, she felt a sudden desire to see Abram's face. She would have liked to kiss his lips before he left. Pass her hand over his clothes, his eyelids, his brow. Smile at him so that he should not go off to fight with his wife's coldness in his heart.

But he was much too far away by now. The column was disappearing to the east of Hebron.

"What have I done?" Sarai cried, to Hagar's surprise.

She hurried out of the tent and ran up the steep slope to the top of the hill of Qiryat-Arba, from where the whole of the plain of Hebron could be seen, as far as the mountains and rivers of Canaan.

When she got there, what she saw amazed her. From south, west, and east, other columns were flooding in to join Abram. They were coming from everywhere. From the valleys, from the mountains, from the villages in the middle of the pastures, from the shores of the Salt Sea! They were like tributaries feeding a great river, swelling it and swelling it as it flowed northward.

Hagar joined her, out of breath. Laughing with relief, Sarai pointed at the cloud of dust raised by Abram's army. "Look! They may not be well equipped but at least there'll be a lot of them. Thousands!"

That evening, Sarai folded her tent, left the hill where she had stayed for so long alone, and descended to the plain to join the others.

She discovered that since the first day he had settled in Hebron, Abram had forbidden any tent to be erected in the space next to his. Without hesitation, she pitched her tent there. For the first time in many moons, she discarded her red veil.

Everyone was able to ascertain that time had still had no effect on Sarai's body and face. Nobody made any comment; they all behaved as if this miracle were natural.

The only person to show any surprise was Eliezer of Damascus. Having been too young to know Sarai before she was veiled, he was curious to see her face. Confronted with his stepmother's beauty, he was quite taken aback.

"You are even more beautiful than I remembered," he said, in his most wheedling voice. "I was only a child then, of course. Abram has often spoken to me of your beauty. I had no idea how true his words were. I'm happy to see you back among us. I'm sure my father would be mad with joy. If you need the least thing, call on me. Use me, consider me your loving son. It will be my greatest happiness."

Sarai did not reply, but continued to look fixedly at him.

Eliezer did not seem embarrassed. "I wanted to accompany my father, Abram, to war," he resumed, with a touch of annoyance. "My place was beside him, and not a day goes by that I don't regret not being there."

"In that case, what are you doing here?" Sarai asked, raising an eyebrow ironically.

"It was my father's wish!" Eliezer exclaimed, with all the sincerity he could muster. "He wanted me to stay while he was gone, in case I needed to take his place."

"Take his place?"

"He taught me everything that's required."

Sarai's laugh cut him dead. "Whatever Abram taught you, my boy, I doubt you could ever take his place. Stop dreaming. Do as I do, and wait quietly for his return."

The summer passed, and the only news that arrived was that Abram's army had entered Sodom. But Lot was not there: The city had been emptied of both its people and its possessions. Abram was now pursuing the pillagers to the north, perhaps beyond Damascus.

Without any other information, time passed slowly, and uncertainty grew. In the autumn, the rumor spread that Abram's army had been defeated. It was possible that Abram himself was among the dead. When Hagar reported this rumor to her, Sarai silenced her.

"Nonsense! I don't believe a word of it."

"That's what they're saying," Hagar said gently, to excuse herself. "I wanted you to hear it from me."

"Who's saying it?"

Hagar turned her head away, embarrassed. "Eliezer. And others."

Sarai cried out in anger. "Where did they get this news? Has a messenger arrived? I haven't seen one."

"It's what they're saying in Salem. And in other places."

"Foolishness. Foolishness and spite! I know Abram is alive, I can feel it!"

Sarai did not add that hardly a night

passed that she did not dream about him. About Abram, her love and her husband. The young Abram from Ur, the Abram she had married, the Abram she had known in Harran. The Abram who had brought her a cover in the night on the banks of the Euphrates, the Abram who searched high and low through Canaan because of his belief in his god. The Abram who had groaned with pleasure in her arms, who had said, "I want no other wife besides Sarai!" The Abram who didn't care that her womb was barren, who aroused her with his kisses. For now she would wake up night after night, filled with terror, knowing that she loved Abram as she had loved him the first day they met. That this love had never died, just faded perhaps. Yes, now she was full of forgiveness and desire for Abram. She was Abram's wife forever, despite her barren womb, despite Pharaoh, and despite God Most High, who sometimes took Abram's mind and heart far away from her. And so each morning she would reach dawn bathed in sweat, full of hope that she might see him again that very day, but horrified at the thought she might never again place her lips on his.

Hagar lowered her eyes in embarrassment.

Sarai took her chin and lifted her face. "I know where this rumor comes from. But Eliezer is taking his desires for reality. He ought to get used to being a nobody. They'll have to show me Abram's dead body before Eliezer becomes Abram's son and heir, and that's not going to happen tomorrow. You can tell him that from me, if you want to."

The messenger arrived when the hills around Hebron were covered in snow and ice. Abram was not only alive, but victorious.

"He's escorting Lot and his family back to Sodom, along with all the women of Sodom stolen by the kings of Shinar, Ellasar, Elam, and Goim. He's bringing food and gold back from Damascus. He's acclaimed everywhere he goes. People are saying that his invisible god has supported him like no other god. That's what's delaying him, but he'll be here within one moon."

While all the wives and daughters and sisters who had waited so long danced around the fires in the cold night, intoxicated with joy, Sarai saw Eliezer's crestfallen expression. He was still questioning the messenger, arguing with him, trying to cast doubt on the news. And when he could not gainsay the truth, he grinned, in a way that seemed to express disappointment rather than relief.

Hagar was as shocked as everyone else. "You were right about Eliezer. Forgive me for doubting your judgment. I suppose that's what happens when a woman's bed is empty for too long. We're easily misled by a smile." She gave a harsh, disappointed little laugh, and buried her face in Sarai's neck. "How I envy you," she murmured, "for having such a handsome husband as Abram, a conqueror who'll soon be in your arms, full of impatience! In a few nights, all the tents in Hebron will be aquiver with lovemaking. Poor me! I'll just have to stop my ears and drink sage tea to send me to sleep!"

Sarai returned her hug, then moved away from her, pensively. She turned to look at her with a new expression on her face, tender and almost timid.

"What is it?" Hagar said, with a laugh of surprise.

"Nothing," Sarai replied.

Sarai did not wait for Abram at the entrance of the encampment, among the other wives, but in her tent. When he pushed back the flap and discovered her not only without her veil, but completely naked, he began to tremble.

He came toward her like a shy young man, filled with wonder and barely able to breathe, and fell to his knees before her. He embraced her timidly and placed his brow and cheek against her belly.

Sarai dug her fingers into his hair. How silver it was! Gently, she touched the thick lines on his brow, his tanned shoulders. With time, his skin had become less fine, less firm, and, in the places where his tunic protected it from the sun, as white as milk.

She stood him up, undressed him, kissed the base of his neck, licked his little scars, his ribs and his muscular stomach. He smelled of grass and dust.

She, too, began to tremble when he lifted her and carried her to the bed. He opened her thighs, as if unveiling the most delicious of offerings.

They did not utter a word until pleasure swept through them like a breath and they became, once again, Abram and Sarai.

It was already night.

"I made war," Abram said. "I fought with the help of God Most High. But not a day went by that I didn't think of you. I felt your love in the strength of my arm and in my will to win."

Sarai smiled, without interrupting.

"I thought of your tempers. The farther I was from Canaan, and the more victorious, the more I could see how right you had been. So when I was on my way back and Yhwh called me, the first words I said to him were 'God Most High, I'm completely naked! The heir to my house is Eliezer of Damascus. You haven't given me a child. Someone who isn't my son is going to take everything I have!' 'No!' he replied. 'He will take nothing from you. He who will take everything is he who will come from your seed.' "

Abram paused. He was breathing hard with anxiety. Sarai huddled closer to him.

" 'He who will take everything is he who will come from your seed.' Those were the words of Yhwh. That's all I can tell you. And I don't understand how it can be."

"I understand," Sarai said gently, after a pause. "Your god will not change my womb. There's no point in waiting for that. But Eliezer is bad, even worse than you could imagine. Your death would have delighted him, everyone could see that."

"So I've been told. But that doesn't matter. And driving away Eliezer won't give me a son."

"Hagar will give you one."

"Hagar? Your handmaid?"

"She's beautiful, and she's already given birth once."

Abram stood motionless, silent, without daring to look at Sarai.

"I ask it of you," Sarai insisted. "Abram cannot remain without an heir from his seed. Your god himself keeps saying it."

"Will Hagar want it? I'm no longer a young man."

"She's pining to have a man between her thighs, young or old. What's more, she admires you as much as you admire your god!"

Abram fell silent again, and looked for Sarai's eyes in the dim light. With the tips of his fingers, he stroked her lips gently. "You'll suffer," he whispered. "It won't be your child."

"I'll be strong."

"I'll be giving pleasure to Hagar. You'll suffer."

Sarai smiled to hide the mist in her eyes. "I will know what you knew when we were in Pharaoh's palace."

Jealousy

But Sarai was not as strong as she had thought.

It began the first night that Hagar spent in Abram's tent. As Sarai went to bed, she had the misfortune to recall the helix-shaped scar between Hagar's shoulders, and that made her think of Abram's lips touching the scar and covering it with little kisses.

The pain in her stomach, neck, and lower back was so strong that she could not get to sleep until dawn. At least she had the courage to stay in bed.

The next day, she avoided both Abram and Hagar. But when twilight came, her chest began to burn as if pierced with needles of bronze. As soon as night fell, she stood behind the flap of her tent and listened. She recognized Hagar's great sensual laugh, then her moans, and even Abram's breathing.

She went outside to recover her breath. Alas, the sounds of her husband's and her handmaid's lovemaking were even more audible. Unseen by anyone, she crouched like an old woman, put her hands over her ears, and shut her eyes as tight as she could. But that only made it worse. In her blindness, she saw Abram's body, Hagar's beautiful hips, her ravenous ecstasy. She saw in detail all the things she should not have seen.

She vomited like a drunk woman.

The following day, she decided to be sensible. Carrying bread, olives, a gourd full of milk, and a sheepskin, she left the encampment and climbed the hill of Qiryat-Arba. For two nights, she slept under the stars and dreamed of children's faces. When she returned to the encampment, she was smiling.

Hagar was smiling, too. At first, neither dared to look at the other. But then Sarai laughed and drew Hagar into her arms.

"I'm happy," she whispered in her ear. "But I can't help it, I'm jealous."

"You have no need to be now," Hagar sighed. "Abram left this morning to travel through Canaan calling the name of Yhwh and making offerings on all the altars he built for him."

And the jealousy did, in fact, stop.

Sarai waited impatiently for the new moon, and was the first to congratulate Hagar when she announced that no blood had flowed between her thighs.

From that day, Sarai stopped thinking of Hagar only as her handmaid. She smothered her with tender loving care, like a mother with her daughter. Hagar started to like this treatment. Although her belly was still only a little swollen, she stopped grinding grain to make flour, left the care of the tent to other handmaids, and refrained from carrying even the smallest object. The women spent long afternoons with her, brought her honey cakes and scented unguents, and showered her with compliments, just as they would have done if Hagar had been Abram's real wife.

She was truly radiant. Sarai noticed that her lips were becoming plumper. Her cheeks grew bigger and even her eyes seemed more luminous and more tender. She moved slowly, as if dancing, and laughed in a deep voice, pushing her shoulders back and thrusting her breasts forward. She slept at all hours of the day as if she were alone in the world, and called for food when she woke. In every way, she was a woman sated with the joy of bearing a child.

Seeing her like that, her body fuller and

her joy richer with every passing day, Sarai once again became overcome with envy.

Prudently, she kept her distance, taking every opportunity to work as far as possible from her tent. At night, she slept in Abram's arms, as if that could protect her — and perhaps upset Hagar a little, too.

But one evening at the height of summer, Sarai entered her tent, the flap of which had been lifted to let the air circulate, and discovered Abram kneeling before her handmaid. Hagar's tunic was up around her neck, and Abram was tenderly feeling her bare belly with his hands.

The sight took Sarai's breath away, and she leaped back out of sight. But she could not stop herself watching as Abram leaned down and placed his cheek and ear against Hagar's belly, so taut with life, and his white hair spread over her breasts.

She heard Abram's affectionate whisper. A whisper that hit her full in the chest.

She heard Hagar's chuckles as Abram kissed her round belly, her cooing as she offered her body to Abram's rapt contemplation.

Her head bursting, Sarai fled, consumed by jealousy, knowing that it would never end. That she was no longer strong enough to bear it.

One day, when Hagar was in the seventh moon of her pregnancy, she made a disgusted face and pushed away the dish that Sarai had just brought her.

"It isn't properly cooked!" she cried. "And you haven't used the right spices. This isn't suitable for a woman in my state."

Sarai was taken aback. She looked at her for a moment, speechless, then flew into a rage. "How dare you talk to me like that?"

"All I'm saying is that the meat is badly cooked," Hagar said, in an offhand manner. "It's not your fault. These things happen."

"Just because I look after you, do you think I've become your handmaid?"

Hagar smiled. "Don't lose your temper! It's only right that you should look after me. I'm carrying Abram's child."

Sarai slapped her hard across the face. "Who do you think you are?"

Hagar squealed, and rolled her eyes in terror. One hand on her cheek, the other holding her belly, she called for help.

"You aren't Abram's wife," Sarai screamed, ignoring her cries, quite carried away with anger. "You're nothing but a womb carrying his seed. That and nothing else! A borrowed womb. You're my hand-maid, a handmaid who happens to be pregnant. What rights do you imagine that gives you? Especially over me, Sarai, Abram's wife?"

A number of women ran in and tried to grab hold of Sarai's arms, for fear she would hit Hagar again.

Sarai pulled herself free. "Don't be stupid. I'm not going to kill her!"

She immediately went to speak to Abram.

"I was the one who put Hagar in your bed, but now that she's pregnant, she thinks she's your wife. I can't stand it anymore."

Abram's face creased with sadness. He took Sarai by the shoulders and pulled her to him. "I warned you that you'd suffer."

"I'm not suffering," Sarai lied. "It's just that Hagar never shows me any respect. The two of us can't be in the same place anymore — it's impossible."

Abram took a deep breath and sat down. "What do you want me to do?"

"I want you to choose between Hagar and Sarai."

Abram smiled joylessly. "I made that choice a long time ago. You're my wife, she's your handmaid. You can do what you like with your handmaid."

"In that case, I want her away from here."

Hagar left the plain of Hebron that very

evening, in tears, a bundle of her belongings over her shoulder. Pregnant as she was, she was about to face the open road.

For three days, Sarai had to live with the shame of her own jealousy. The shame of her hardness and intransigence. And the shame of her barren womb. She thought she would die of shame.

Yet nothing could persuade her to run after Hagar and bring her back. Not even Abram's face, gray with sorrow. Not even the thought that Eliezer of Damascus, who was living outside the camp now, somewhere on the plain, must be delighted to be Abram's heir again.

On the morning of the fourth day, Sarai heard shouts of joy, especially from the women. Her mouth went dry. She had recognized Hagar's voice.

She rushed out of her tent, uncertain whether to vent her anger or bestow her forgiveness. But Abram was already running to meet her handmaid.

Halfway between laughter and tears, Hagar was the center of attention. Sarai saw her clinging to Abram's neck. "Come and lie down!" she heard Abram say, as gentle as a lamb. "You can tell us what happened, but first come and lie down and eat something."

Nobody dared look Sarai in the face. She

approached, tight-lipped, swallowing her shame, anger, and jealousy, to hear Hagar's story.

"It was the day before yesterday, in the evening," Hagar began, with a contrite expression but with joy in her eyes. "I was thirsty, and I stopped at the spring on the road to Shour. I was terrified that I would soon have to cross the desert. Suddenly, a presence approached me. I say 'a presence' because it was someone who was like a man but wasn't. He had no face, but he had a body and a voice. 'What are you doing here?' he asked. And I said, 'I'm fleeing my mistress Sarai, who drove me away! I'm going to die in the desert with a child inside me!' And he said, even closer to my ear, 'No, go back where you came from. You will bring a son into the world, and you will call him Ishmael. Yhwh has heard your lament; he knows how your mistress has humiliated you. Your son will be a wild, untamable horse; he will rise up against everyone and everyone will be against him. He will be a living challenge to his brothers.' That's what he said."

Hagar fell silent. She was radiant. Nobody dared to breathe a word, or ask a question. Abram nodded his white head as if he were sobbing.

Hagar saw Sarai's grim face behind the other women. She stopped smiling, and drew Abram's hand onto her belly. "It's the truth, you must believe me. The man who spoke in the name of your god asked me to take my place again beside you. He said, 'Do not worry if your mistress humiliates you again. You will have to bear it.' So I came back as quickly as I could so that you could welcome your son, lift him in your hands as soon as he comes out of me."

"Lies!" Sarai thought. "She's the one who humiliates me. I'm her mistress, and she treats me like a handmaid. Who would believe it? And now Abram's god speaks to her! More lies. A fable she's invented to seduce Abram. Oh, yes!"

But she kept silent. She was not going to drive Hagar away a second time. That would only make her seem even harsher and more hateful in everyone's eyes.

His eyes moist with tears, Abram stroked Hagar's belly. "I believe you, Hagar! I believe you! I know the way God Most High makes His will known. Rest, take care of yourself, and give birth to my son." He turned and looked for Sarai. "Don't forget that Sarai is your mistress. I would never have gone with you to have a son if she hadn't wanted it. Don't take advantage of your own happiness to make her feel weak and jealous."

Sarai walked away before he had even finished the sentence.

Never again did Sarai demonstrate her jealousy. But jealousy consumed her as if she were a dry stem.

When Hagar felt the first labor pains, it was Sarai who sent for the midwives, prepared the linen and the calming unguents, heated the water with herbs, and made sure that everything was going well. Then she went and hid deep inside her tent and stopped her ears in order not to hear Hagar's cries or those of the newborn.

The next day, however, she came forward and kissed Abram's son, Ishmael, on the brow. For as long as she could, she smiled at Abram's great joy as he lifted the newborn in the air and called Yhwh's name. Then she left the encampment. For hours, she walked straight ahead, lifting her tunic to let the wind on the plain cool the furnace of jealousy that was consuming her.

As for Abram, he displayed his delight throughout Canaan. Everywhere he went, he thanked his god for the son Hagar had given him. But he returned quite soon. He no longer spent hours in the black-and-white tent engaged in discussion, but would sit and watch Hagar as she offered her nipples to Ishmael's mouth, which she did endlessly. And then he would start to laugh. It was a laugh such as Sarai had never heard from him before, a laugh that soon burst forth at the slightest opportunity.

As soon as he could, Abram began to play with his son. For hours on end, while Hagar looked on tenderly, Abram and Ishmael would hug each other and roll on the rugs or in the dry grass, in a cacophony of cries and gurgles. They would imagine birds in the clouds, play with the insects, and burst into laughter at the slightest thing.

Sickened by all this laughter, exhausted by the spectacle of all this joy, Sarai stopped sleeping. She got into the habit of leaving her tent in the middle of the night and wandering like a ghost. Sometimes, in the cool, dark air, the furnace of her jealousy would subside.

Fiercely proud as ever, she did her best to conceal how much she was suffering. She would force herself to take Ishmael in her arms, to cradle him, to breathe in his sweet childish odor. Tenderly, her eyes half-closed, she would let his tiny head nestle against her neck until he fell asleep. Then she would hide away again, shaking feverishly, her cheeks not even refreshed by tears.

She held out as long as she could, almost longer than she could bear. There came to be something strange, almost transparent about her beauty. Though her skin did not crease, it became a little rougher, a little thicker. It was as if it were charred from within and horribly irritable. She could no longer stand being touched, even by Abram.

In the second winter after his birth, Ishmael began to walk, to break pots and laugh out loud, to stammer his first words. One day he bumped into Sarai's legs. She bent down, as so often, to take him in her arms. With a frown, Ishmael pushed her hands away. He stared at her as if she were a stranger. Then he cried out like a hungry, frightened little animal, and ran screaming to Hagar's arms.

Sarai turned away as if the child had hit her.

This time, jealousy set her whole body ablaze. It was completely intolerable.

At twilight, Sarai climbed the hill of Qiryat-Arba. It was cold, almost freezing. But her flesh was burning as if firebrands were being applied to it. She saw again the look Ishmael had given her, and thought of all she had endured, season after season.

She could not bear it anymore.

By the side of the road, she heard a stream gushing. Without thinking, she ran into the icy water. The stream was not very deep, but the current beat against her lower back while she splashed her belly and face with handfuls of water.

It occurred to her that she could stay here like this, in the freezing cold, until her body finally yielded. She wanted her beauty to shatter, she wanted age to carry her away like a forgotten fruit, a branch broken by winter.

Yes! That was what she should do. Remain in the stream until her flesh finally yielded! The current could wear away the hardest rocks, so why couldn't it destroy Sarai's useless beauty?

Shivering, she looked up at the night sky, which was filled with stars. Those thousands of stars that the great gods of Ur — or so they had told her when she was a child — had immobilized one by one. She remembered the poem she had learned when she was a Sacred Handmaid, ignorant and avid for life:

> *When the gods made man,*
> *They toiled and toiled:*
> *Huge was their task,*
> *Infinite their labor . . .*

It was then that the cry burst from her mouth, in a scream that made everything around her shake.

"Yhwh! Abram's God Most High, help me! I can't bear it any longer. I can't bear my barren womb, my fierce jealousy, I can't bear it any longer. The trial has lasted too long. Yhwh! You speak to Hagar! You pity her and help her, and for me, nothing! Nothing for so long. You hear my hand-maid's lament, but me, the wife of the man you singled out, me, Abram's wife, you ignore! Oh, how heavy your silence is! Oh, Yhwh, what's the point of being only Abram's god? How can you give birth to his people without putting life in my body? How can you make a beginning if Sarai is dry? How can you promise a people and a nation to my husband while my life cannot engender life? If you are as powerful as Abram says you are, then you know. You know why I did wrong in Ur, so long ago, with the *kassaptu*'s herbs. Oh, Yhwh, it was for love of Abram! If you cannot forgive a sin committed through innocence and love, what is the point of creating such hope in Abram's heart? Oh, Yhwh, help me!"

Epilogue

Yes, that was what I cried.

I remember it very well. My face turned to heaven, my arms raised, my body full of pain, I screamed like a lioness howling at the moon: "Help me, Yhwh! Help me!"

Addressing Abram's God Most High without shame. Not really believing he would hear me, needing to scream more than anything.

I was still Sarai.

Everything was still hard for me.

Today, as I wait calmly for the moment when Yhwh will take my breath from me, the memory of it makes me smile. Because it happened: Yhwh heard me!

That freezing stream is not far from here. From where I am sitting, outside the cave that will be my tomb, I can see the bushes of mint on its banks. That night, there were only stones and darkness. I stayed so long in

the water I could have died. But Yhwh
didn't want that.

In the first light of day, I went to see
Abram.

"I can't help it, husband," I said. "My
jealousy is too strong. But I don't want to
cause you shame or spoil the happiness your
son gives you. Let me pitch my tent up
there, under the terebinth trees, away from
your camp."

I didn't tell him I had called the name of
Yhwh until I was out of breath. Because
then I would also have had to tell him how I
had stayed in the frozen stream, and what
was the point? They all thought I was mad
already. Why embarrass him even more
than I already had?

Abram listened to me in silence. Now that
Ishmael could jump onto his knees, he
didn't really care whether I was near or far.
He kissed me and let me leave.

In my solitary tent, away from everyone,
without even a handmaid to keep me company, I finally slept. I slept for two or three
days on end, waking only to drink a little
milk.

That sleep was as good as a caress. It
calmed me. I could even laugh at myself.
Why keep struggling, why keep going back
endlessly over something that had been over

and done with for ages? Why so many tears, so many dramas, now that a child had been born and Abram finally had his offspring? Wasn't that what I'd wanted? True, Hagar was the child's mother, but did that really matter? Soon Ishmael would grow, and everywhere, and for all time, forever, he would be known as "Abram's son." Nobody would care whose womb he had sprung from.

Yes, I thought about all that with a smile, trying to make myself see reason. Knowing full well, alas, that I was unlikely to succeed. That was the way I was. I'd been carrying my burden for such a long time, and yet I'd never been able to get used to it.

Then, one morning, when I had gone down to the river to wash linen, I discovered some little dark blotches on my hands. Irregular, like marks on the bark of a tree. In the evening, I looked at them again. They seemed darker. The next day, as soon as I woke up, I lifted my hands in the dim light and examined them carefully. The blotches were there, quite visible. Even more visible than the day before!

In the days that followed, the muscles of my arms and thighs began to shrink. My whole body was being transformed! After careful inspection, I discovered an unusually deep crease on my stomach. The next day, there was another crease. And the day after that. Yes, my stomach was becoming crumpled! I examined my breasts, and found them less high, less round. Not flaccid like a goat's udder, nothing like that, but less firm than before. I lifted them to feel the weight and they spread over my palms. Where once they had been convex, now they were concave. I ran and filled a wide-brimmed bowl with water to examine my face in the reflection. Wrinkles! Wrinkles under my eyes, above my cheekbones, on the edges of my nostrils, dozens of tiny wrinkles around my lips! And my cheeks were less taut, my neck more lax . . .

My face was becoming the face of a woman of my age. I was getting older.

I leaped in the air and screamed with joy. I started dancing, clucking with happiness like a young girl after her first kiss. At last, at last I was getting older! It was over, that youthful beauty that had clung to my limbs and had covered me with a false veneer for so long!

For one moon at least I examined myself constantly, looking at my reflection in the water, counting my wrinkles, measuring the drooping of my breasts, the creases in my stomach. Each time, it became clearer that it really was happening. I was drunk with happiness.

If anyone down in Abram's camp had seen me, they would have thought, "Look at Sarai, all alone on her slope, consumed with jealousy — she's finally lost her mind completely!"

I didn't care if I looked like a madwoman. Time had at last returned to me. Just as a newborn baby is laid in its cradle, I was being laid in my true body. And with that body, my torment could finally cease: There was no way now that I could ever have a child. For the first time since meeting the *kassaptu* in the Lower City, it was normal and natural for the blood not to flow between my thighs.

What a relief!

"Perhaps Yhwh heard you after all," I said to myself. "He heard your lament. As he can't change your womb, he's finally shattering the miracle of your beauty and soothing you with the sweetness of old age."

That was what I thought! I went so far as to stand upright with my palms open, as I had seen Abram do when he thanked Yhwh, and for the first time pray to him and name him my God Most High. What pride!

Some time later, Abram climbed up to see me, his face solemn and anxious. I thought perhaps something was wrong with Hagar or Ishmael. Or perhaps he was going to ask me to move even farther away. I was prepared for that. Prepared, too, for his surprise when he saw me.

It didn't happen. He stopped, frowned a little more, glanced with just a touch of puzzlement at my neck and my brow, but didn't say a word. Didn't ask any questions. But then, how could a man like Abram, who already had dark shadows under his eyes, slack cheeks, and a slightly bent back, be surprised by anything?

I sat him down, made sure he was comfortable, and brought him food and drink. At last he looked directly at me.

"I'm listening, husband," I said.

"Yhwh spoke to me this morning. He said, 'I am making a covenant with you. You will be responsible for our covenant, and so will your children after you, and their children, too. The foreskins of all the males will be circumcised, and of all the male children when they are eight days old, as a sign of the covenant between you and me. My covenant will be written in your flesh.' "

Abram stopped, eyebrows raised, as if expecting me to say something. But I kept my mouth shut. On the subject of Abram's offspring, I had already said more than I should.

413

He smiled, for the first time since he had arrived. "God Most High is giving himself to us," he said, as if afraid I had not understood.

I smiled, too, thinking of my wrinkles.

Abram misunderstood my smile. He put his big hand on my knee. "Yes!" he said, his voice shaking. "More than you think. Listen to this. Yhwh also said to me: 'Your name will no longer be Abram but Abraham, and you will be the father of a multitude of nations. You will no longer call your wife Sarai, but Sarah. I shall bless her, too. And will give you a son by her. His name will be Isaac.' "

I think the sky shook as Abraham spoke these words. Unless it was my womb. My mouth shook, too. I thought of my cry in the stream, of the miracle of age that had come to me this past moon and shattered the miracle of beauty. It's quite possible I thought of all that, telling myself that what Abram was saying might be true and his god might finally be coming to my aid and supporting me.

But I revealed nothing of what I was thinking. After all this time, it was too much to hope for. Besides, one look at the two of us, old Sarai and old Abram, and anyone would have laughed at the thought of us in bed together, let alone me giving birth!

No, I didn't want to hear anything about the promise contained in Yhwh's words.

I put my hand on Abram's hand. "I don't mind changing my name to Sarah. And Abraham has a good ring to it, too. I don't mind Abraham."

He sighed like a young man. His eyes shone, amused and radiant. His lips stretched in a smile, reminding me of the lips that had so seduced me once, on the banks of the Euphrates. "You don't believe it, do you?"

"Believe what?"

"Oh, don't pretend! You know what I'm talking about!"

"Abraham, if that's your name now, haven't you noticed how old I've become?"

"You're not old. You only look as old as you ought to be, and I'm very pleased for you! Sarah, my love, Yhwh has announced it. He has blessed you. Your son will be called Isaac. What more do you want?"

"Abraham, my dear, sweet husband, do stop dreaming. From whose womb is this son — this Isaac — to come?"

"From yours. Sarah's. Who else?"

"And from whose seed?"

"Mine. What a question! Oh, I see! You don't think I'm capable anymore, is that it?"

I could not restrain my giggles. "Oh yes. You're capable of anything. But it's all over for me, after all this time. Just because my name is now Sarah doesn't mean I can give you a son. I'm wrinkled and I don't have periods, which is as it should be. A woman is a woman, Abraham. Even me."

"Stuff and nonsense! You aren't listening to the word of Yhwh. I, too, doubted. I, too, laughed. It made Yhwh angry. 'Could anything be too difficult for Yhwh?' He asked. "Sarah, all we need is to . . . Oh, stop laughing!"

But I couldn't stop giggling. I embraced my old husband. I took his head in my hands, kissed his eyes, placed his brow against my cheek. "You don't need all these words just to go to bed with me, Abraham. But don't be under any illusions. The woman I am now is a woman you don't know. She can't compare with Hagar."

With a grunt, he searched for my mouth, still in a bad humor. "You are Sarah and I am Abraham. That's all that matters and, with the help of God Most High, I'm going to prove it to you."

Which he did.

By satisfying me. By giving me a pleasure I had never known before, a calm, tender pleasure. I remembered the words of my

416

dear Sililli: "Men never get tired of those things! They may not be able anymore, but as long as they can get their shaft up, they're always ready and willing!" But a woman never tires of it either, even when her body is no more than a memory of her youth.

After that, we both fell into a deep sleep. Mine was so deep that I did not hear Abraham get up in broad daylight. I was awakened by voices.

"Masters!" Abraham was saying. "Masters, don't pass your servant by. Here is water to wash your feet. Take advantage of the shade, this terebinth has thick foliage. Rest. I'll fetch bread and pancakes. You need to gather your strength."

I heard the unknown travelers thanking him. "Do as you wish."

Abraham seated them beneath the terebinth and ran into the tent. "Quick! Prepare curds and fruit."

"But who are these travelers, Abraham?" I asked.

He looked at me as if he had not understood my question.

"Why all the rush?" I asked.

"They are envoys, angels of Yhwh."

He went out again, still in a rush. Then I heard the voice of one of the travelers. "Where is your wife, Sarah?"

I stopped dead. I was perplexed. They knew my new name, even though Abraham had only given it to me the night before!

"She's in the tent," Abraham replied.

"Next year, on this very day, your wife Sarah will have a son."

I couldn't help it. I thought of the night I had just spent in Abraham's arms and I laughed. Not a giggle this time, not a chuckle or an amused little laugh, but a laugh such as I had never had in my life. A laugh of belief in Yhwh's words and of disbelief in those same words. A laugh that shook me from head to foot, that streamed through my blood and into my heart, that flooded my chest and coiled in my womb like a tremor of life.

A laugh that upset Yhwh, for the travelers asked rather dryly: "Why all that laughter?"

Immediately, from behind the flap of the tent, I tried to lie. "No, I didn't laugh."

"Yes, you did."

Impossible to hide the laugh, impossible to lie to God.

But now I know that Yhwh granted me that laugh, because I deserved it. After so many years of being only Sarai, Abram's wife with the barren womb, here I was, an old woman called Sarah, and fertile! Sarah, who would give birth to Abraham's offspring, my son Isaac! How could I not laugh?

No, I wasn't laughing at Yhwh. Who would dare? I was only laughing at myself, at the route my life had taken. At my fears, my consolation, and my delight.

For it all came to pass.

It was my turn to know how it felt to have a big belly, and heavy hips and breasts that swell and grow hard. To break out in sweats and be subject to whims. At last I saw Abraham kneeling between my thighs, his ear pressed against my navel, trembling like a young man and exclaiming, "He's moving, he's moving!"

It was my turn to be afraid, to have sleepless nights and gloomy thoughts. I remembered Lehklai, and all the women I had seen die while giving life.

It was my turn to feel a boundless pride, and parade my swollen belly through the whole valley of Hebron. "Who would have thought it?" I would say to whoever wanted to see my belly. "Sarah and Abraham are expecting a boy born of their flesh. As old as they both are, that is the will of Yhwh."

They, too, laughed.

As the travelers had predicted, it was my turn to climb onto the bricks of childbearing, with my brow moist with sweat, pain in the small of my back and screams in my mouth. But I was lucid enough to say to the midwives: "If things go badly, don't hesitate to open my belly and take the child out alive. I've had my time."

But Yhwh was in my body. To everyone's amazement, it was a short labor, the kind you might expect of a woman who'd already had twelve children. Isaac was born, a fine, round baby, soft as honey bread. My Isaac, the most beautiful child who ever came into the world!

From birth, he had Abraham's lips, and eyes that went straight to your heart. As soon as he grew, everyone would realize how strong and farsighted he was going to be — but with some of his mother's grace and beauty, too.

People came from far and wide to see him. "Who would have thought it?" they all cried. "Sarah breast-feeding a son for Abraham's old age!"

They would leave again, impressed by the greatness of Yhwh, admiring His power and the accuracy of His promises.

Even Eliezer of Damascus came to see me. He hadn't changed. He was a handsome man, but his lids were too heavy for his eyes. Seeing him again, I thought of those pretty sulfur-yellow flowers you see on the banks of the Salt Sea. When you go to pick them, you fall into one of the cracks in the rock the flowers have been concealing.

He acknowledged grudgingly that Isaac was as handsome and as strong as they said, then changed the subject. "Your nephew Lot's behavior in Sodom leaves a lot to be desired. He shows no respect for Yhwh. He's constantly drunk, and sleeps with whoever he likes, young or old, women or boys. They say he even does it with his own daughters."

" 'They say . . .' Have you seen him doing it? Were you in his tent holding a candle?"

He laughed, venomously. "They say it, and I believe them. It doesn't matter if I've seen him or not. God Most High sees him. He's going to be angry, you can be sure of that."

"Whether you like it or not, Eliezer," I replied, "Abraham loves Lot, and won't abandon him. He'll plead for Lot's life with Yhwh, if he has to."

That's exactly what happened. Yhwh destroyed Sodom, but Abraham begged him to spare Lot. He said to Yhwh, "You can't make the just die along with the wicked!" And God Most High heard him. Eliezer wasn't happy about that. I never saw him again. Good riddance. There's someone who'll be forgotten forever.

As for Lot, after Yhwh had saved him by Abraham's good graces, he sent me a calf and some scents, telling me through his servant that my happiness was his happiness and that he was going away to live with his family in the Negev Desert.

Poor Lot! I loved him less than he wanted and more than I should. He was a victim of my miraculous beauty. He remains a shadow in my life. Like Hagar.

After Isaac was born, she came to see me with Ishmael. Once, twice, then more and more frequently. We had very little to say to each other. She would hang on Ishmael's every laugh, while I, always a little afraid for Isaac, would keep my eyes open and hope her son didn't do anything naughty.

"Look how affectionate my son is with your son," she said one day. "The two brothers are going to be really happy together!"

"I don't think so," I replied.

"What do you mean?"

"I mean it's better if you go away. You're no longer my handmaid and Isaac doesn't need a brother. Your son is big. Now you can walk and find a place that's all yours."

"But why? I loved you more than a mistress. Like a sister . . ."

I interrupted her with a gesture. "No, Hagar. My jealousy isn't dead, only put aside. My wish that Isaac should be Abraham's only heir isn't dead either. Be sensible. We don't like each other. Our sons won't like each other because they'll feel the mistrust between their mothers. I can say to you 'Go!' because it's in my power. And I do say it."

I resisted all her tears and entreaties.

Even now, there are those who blame me for what I did.

Was I wrong? How to know? I was proud of my happiness and didn't want any shadow over my laughter.

But Yhwh, to teach me humility, saw to it that my laugh was transformed into a cry.

It happened one morning when the sky was low, although there was no rain. I was looking for Isaac and couldn't find him. I went down toward Abraham's tent, and there I saw the two of them, loading the packsaddles of an ass with wood. Abraham had that solemn look of his. I even thought he looked pale: There was something milky about his complexion despite his brown skin. Isaac was his usual amiable, carefree self. But he was dressed in a new tunic that I didn't remember having given him that morning.

I was intrigued. I watched them without going any closer. Abraham sat down on the back of the ass and took Isaac in his arms. He kicked the ass, and they set off at a jog along the road to Moriah.

At first, I watched them as they moved off into the distance. Then I felt my whole body tighten.

A presentiment caught me by the throat. My heart and my fingers felt ice cold. I had no idea what was going to happen; all I knew was that I mustn't let Isaac out of my sight. So I ran after them. Ran as fast as my old legs and my breath would let me. This time, I regretted being old.

As I ran, it occurred to me that the plateau of Moriah was a place where Abraham often made offerings to Yhwh. Sacrifices of ewes, lambs, or rams. Perhaps he was only taking his son with him to teach him how to make offerings and let him share in his word with God Most High.

Then I thought again of his gray face and Isaac's new tunic. The bags that hung on the ass's sides contained the wood for the fire, but where were the ram, the lamb, the ewe?

I was having difficulty keeping up with them. I could hardly breathe, so strong was my anxiety. I reasoned with myself, tried to calm down. "But what are you thinking?" I said to myself. "It's impossible. Why even think it?"

But I did think it.

When I finally reached the top of the little slope that leads to the plateau of Moriah, I saw them, a hundred paces away.

Isaac was heaping wood on the altar. A fine pyre, carefully arranged. Abraham was standing to one side, an absent look in his eyes. I saw him take his long knife from his belt and I knew I hadn't been mistaken.

I was about to scream and rush to them.

"Isaac! Come to my arms, Isaac! What are you doing, Abraham? Have you gone mad?"

But not a sound passed my lips. My screams were silent. I couldn't run, I couldn't take a single step forward. I was behind a fissure in a rock and something, some force, was keeping me there. As I watched, Abraham called Isaac to him. He stroked his cheek, took the rope that was used for binding the wood on the altar, and tied his arms with it. I fell to my knees in the dust. I was powerless to do anything but watch.

"Oh, Isaac, my son! Don't hold out your arms! Run, get away!"

But Abraham lifted him, and carried him to the pyre.

"I hate you, Abraham, how could you, how dare you? Your son, your only son! My only life."

But Abraham did it. He laid Isaac on the altar. There was a look of surprise in Isaac's eyes, but he did not weep. Abraham stroked his brow. He kissed him, and the hand that held the knife moved away from his hip. Slowly, Abraham raised his arm, and the blade glinted in his hand.

Then I, Sarah, cried out:

"Yhwh, god of Abraham, listen to my voice. A mother's voice. You can't. No, You can't demand my son's life, Isaac's life. Not You. Not the god of justice.

"Listen to my cry. If you let Abraham bring down his knife, may the sky darken forever, may the waters engulf the earth, may Your work disappear, may it shatter like Terah's idols that Abraham destroyed in Harran.

"It took me all my life to give birth to Isaac. It took Your will, the breath of Your mouth, for him to be born. What other proof of Your power do you demand? When You allowed my old body to give birth to Isaac, You became for all of us, women and men, the god of the miracle of life. Oh, Yhwh, preserve this life! Who would believe in a god who vents his wrath on innocent children? Who would obey a god who spreads death and kills the weak?

"Oh, Yhwh! When I was young, I prayed to the gods of Ur, who loved blood. I turned my back on them and grew old at Abraham's side, and in all that time I've never seen a just man abandoned by You. You saved Lot. Is Isaac worth less than the just men of Sodom?

"When Your voice resounded in the air, Abraham said at once, 'I am here!' Not a day goes by that he doesn't show us that You are our blessing. Let Isaac die, and you will be our curse.

"What is a god who kills, Yhwh? What kind of order is he bestowing on the world? I say to You, a mother is stronger than a god in such cases. There is nothing, no order, no justice, that can take a child from his mother.

"Oh, Yhwh, stay Abraham's hand! Throw away his knife! Your glory will find a dwelling place in my heart and in the hearts of all the mothers of Canaan. Don't reject my prayer; think of us, the women. It is through us that your covenant will sow the future, from generation to generation. I cry to You, Yhwh: Keep Your promise to me, and my hope will always be in You."

In fact, I'm not certain I did cry out. But

at the very moment I sent up my supplication, the thunder rumbled, the clouds poured out their waters, and a ram came trotting toward Abraham.

"Abraham!" I cried. "Abraham! The ram, look at the ram behind you!"

This time my cry rang out, though even now, Abraham maintains that it was Yhwh's voice he heard, not mine. So it seems we cried out together.

No matter. It was over. The only thing the knife cut was the ropes on Isaac's wrists. My son saw me and ran to my arms.

I didn't laugh with joy. I wept. I wept for a long time, with a terrible sense of fear.

And here I am today, alone here outside the cave of Makhpela, watching my life come to an end. Alone, for how long is it since I last saw my son's face? He has grown, and is no longer as close to me. He's becoming a man, totally occupied with his love affairs and his duties as Abraham's right hand. But such is life, and that is how it should be.

Wait and remember, that is all I can do in the little time I have left.

There is no wind and yet, above me, the leaves of the poplar tremble, filling the air with a noise like rain. Under the cedars and acacias, the light dances in patches of molten gold that remind me of the softness of Pharaoh's skin. A memory that fades with the fragrance of lily and mint that comes to rest on my lips. Swallows play and sing above the cliff. All is well with me.

Oh, I see I was wrong. I'm not going to be alone for my last journey after all. I can see a crowd setting out from the valley. A whole nation is climbing the hill. And yes, it seems to me I can see Isaac in front. And Ishmael behind him. And Abraham by their side.

Oh, my tender husband, how slowly you walk. Like a very old man. Like the man I have loved so very much and who is coming to hold my hand before Yhwh takes my breath from me. Oh, my beloved, place me, the mother of those who believe, in the cave of Makhpela, and pray to God Most High that Sarah and Abraham be long remembered.

Acknowledgments

This book would never have seen the light of day without the advice and help of Jean-Pierre Allali, Leonello Brandolini, Clara Halter, Nicole Lattes, Susanna Lea, and Nathaly Thery.

They have my deepest thanks.

About the Author

Marek Halter was born in Poland in 1936. During World War II, he and his parents narrowly escaped the Warsaw ghetto. After a time in Russia and Uzbekistan, they emigrated to France in 1950. There Halter studied pantomime with Marcel Marceau and embarked on a career as a painter that led to several international exhibitions. In 1967, he founded the International Committee for a Negotiated Peace Agreement in the Near East and played a crucial role in the organization of the first official meetings between Palestinians and Israelis.

In the 1970s, Marek Halter turned to writing. He first published *The Madman and the Kings*, which was awarded the Prix Aujourd'hui in 1976. He is also the author of several internationally acclaimed, best-selling historical novels, including *The Messiah*, *The Mysteries of Jerusalem*, and *The*

Book of Abraham, which won the Prix du Livre Inter. Halter is currently working on the second and third volumes of the Canaan Trilogy: *Zipporah* and *Lilah*, which will be published in 2005 and 2006, respectively.